CHICAGO
MOVIE GIRLS

D. C. Reep
E. A. Allen

For Kim, Trisha, and special thanks to
Barbara J. and Janet M.—DR
For Paul--EA

1

Chicago, 1914

She had to steal a wallet today. Pa had left her no choice.

He'd been rustling in the kitchen before the sun glinted off Lake Michigan. By the time she'd padded to the open door in her cotton nightgown, he'd stuffed his shirts and pants into a dirty canvas bag along with his trunks and boxing gloves. Bare toes curled on the cracked linoleum, she'd watched him empty the sugar bowl of the few dollars she'd earned for washing dishes at Rosetti's Diner.

Then he'd turned to face her. "Gotta leave town for a bit, Rae. You girls can handle yourselves. Lily—she's older—but you're the sensible one."

"Why—"

"Got some trouble." He'd hefted the bag and snatched his coat off the hook on the back of the door. "You don't need to know about it. You and Lily—stick together—you'll be all right. Delia's married. No need to worry about her."

He was gone before she'd thought to remind him the rent was due.

That afternoon, in front of the bedroom mirror, speckled with age, she twisted her hair into long curls like the ones her favorite actress Mary Pickford wore. Her faded blue cotton dress was too tight across her chest but that helped crush her bosom. She tucked a white crocheted bib in the round neckline and arranged her curls on her shoulders. Tilting her head to one side, she practiced her innocent smile. Being small and not looking her sixteen years was an advantage. With luck she could pass for twelve or thirteen. People didn't pay attention to what was around them most of the time. If a man noticed his empty pocket before she had time to disappear into a crowd or down an alley, he probably wouldn't connect a young girl to his loss.

The August air was hot and humid, but a cool breeze off the lake ruffled the hair around her temples as she walked south toward the Chicago River. A streetcar rumbled past, stopped, doors opened, and riders spilled into the street in front of Gray's Fine Clothing. When a Model T pulled to the curb, a young woman in a light summer dress kissed the young man driving, jumped out, and ran into the store. The auto drove away, wispy black smoke spiraling out of the exhaust.

Life wasn't fair. Would she ever get to ride in an automobile?

The next block was lined with tall office buildings—the best place to find businessmen with fat wallets. She wiped a thin film of sweat from her forehead as she walked. Men wouldn't wear overcoats on a hot day, and her sweaty hands might not slip easily into pockets. Slowing, she wiped her palms along the folds of her skirt.

The wind had picked up. She drew in long breaths until her heartbeat slowed to a smooth rhythm. Her confidence rose. In a crowd when everyone staggered against the wind, no one would notice a little bump. The tall buildings created wind tunnels, and people had to bend their heads to push through the gusts. Still, too much confidence was a dangerous thing. Carelessness could get her a stay in jail. When a well-dressed man walked her way, she tested the wind, lurching sideways just as he passed her.

"Here, watch out little lady." He put his hand on her elbow to steady her. In another second, he hurried away.

Good enough. He hadn't really looked at her.

A group of men stood in front of One-Eyed Mickey's Newsstand reading the front pages of the afternoon newspapers. She glanced up and down the street to check for police. None in sight.

Lingering in front of the windows of a bank, she eyed the crowd. The men wore dark suits and shirts with stiff white collars—the look of success. They were excited about the headlines, so instead of buying their papers and hustling away, they lingered, talking and huddling together in front of the newsstand. Standing so close, they'd be too aware of each other for a stranger to slip in. She waited a few minutes until a young fellow bought a paper and stepped a few feet away from the crowd. He didn't look like a businessman, but he might have money. His straw hat with a navy silk band sat on ginger-colored hair, and his summer suit was a well-cut linen. He held the *Tribune* spread open as he read. When he tried to turn to an inside story, the wind hissed and tore at the paper, making him struggle to keep the flapping pages open. Best of all, every gust of wind flipped the edges of his jacket, revealing blue silk lining and an inside pocket with a wallet.

It took the slightest brush against his side, followed by a wobble, before he dropped half the newspaper in his eagerness to help her. Light, fast fingers slid over the flat wallet, lifted it gently, and slipped it down into the folds of her skirt. A smile. A thank you. In a short minute, she disappeared around the corner. Glancing over her shoulder, she checked again for police, walked briskly down the street, and looked for an alley so she could examine the wallet.

"Rae!"

Her muscles tensed. She'd forgotten Lev Golden sometimes hawked newspapers on this corner, and newsboys remembered everything. No way avoid him now. She waited while Lev handed a copy of the *Chicago Dispatch* to a driver who'd pulled to the curb, shoved the coin in his pocket, tucked his last two papers under his arm, and hurried toward her.

Pushing the wallet deeper into her skirt pocket, she smiled. "Hi, Lev."

Lev rubbed his nose on his sleeve. "Did you see the movie people up the street? They been there all afternoon.

I hope they come back tomorrow because they bought most of my papers. I only got two left." He held out a copy.

Germans invade Belgium! Belgian army fights at Liege!

Lev pointed a dirty fingernail at the headline. "Is this *bel-gee-um* close by, Rae? Are we gonna be in a fight?"

She glanced at the front page. The *Dispatch* always had shocking headlines. "It's nothing. It's in Europe—far away from us."

"That's good then. I'll walk with you if you're heading home."

In another block, they reached the movie crew at the entrance to an alley. Actors in rough clothes pretended to throw punches at each other while the director yelled instructions. "Stagger backward, Gil. Alf, you're the villain—hit him in the stomach."

Two men paused to watch the action and bought Lev's last papers. "Sold out fast today," he said. "Cops chased me off Michigan, but that's not the best street anyway."

"Cops?" She stiffened and looked over her shoulder.

Lev eyed her. "You snatched a wallet, Rae?"

"Let's move on," she whispered.

They walked quickly, rounded a corner, made another turn, and finally stopped in an alley behind a squat brick building. "You gonna look in it?" Lev asked.

She leaned her forehead against the rough brick and pressed the red wallet against her chest while waiting for her pulse to steady. She opened the wallet, and despair settled on her. No money. One crisp folded sheet of yellow paper tucked under a flap. It was covered with numbers and letters in columns. Meaningless.

Lev peered over her shoulder. "Not money, that's for sure."

"Pa left us this morning and took every cent we had." Rae stifled a groan and checked both sides of the paper. "It's a jumble." She ran her finger over the raised design on the wallet. "Good leather though. Maybe I could sell it, but I need money right away."

"The gambling fellow might buy it. I heard he likes fancy things."

"Who?"

"Lukas Krantz. He runs some games—poker, dice. He owns that ladies' house too—off Division." A pink flush stained his cheeks.

"The house with the red flower pots on the porch?"

Lev's flush got brighter. "That's it."

She poked his shoulder. "How would you know about that house, Lev?"

He dragged his shoe across the alley dirt. "I just know Krantz owns it."

She thought for a minute. "I don't know him, but if you think he'd buy the wallet . . ."

Lev's color faded to normal. "He runs boxing matches too, so your pa knows him all right. They ain't legal, but the cops ain't never shut him down. He makes a lot of money on the boxing—and the betting."

"Pa doesn't talk about his boxing," Rae said.

Lev drew circles in the dirt with his toe. "I never seen any boxing myself."

"Where can I find Krantz?"

"He's got an office across the street from the ladies' house. It's a motor shop with a sign, Gus's Motors, in the window, but they don't do much business with motors." He sniffed and rubbed his nose on his sleeve again. "You gonna see him?"

Rae folded the paper, slipped it into the wallet, and pushed the wallet back into her pocket. "I will unless I can think of something else real quick."

After she and Lev went in different directions, the only thought running through her mind was money and how to get it. Turning a corner, she spotted Mrs. Polsky on the front steps of the three-story apartment building. Arms folded over her bosom and a dish towel over one shoulder, the landlady turned her head from side to side watching the street.

Rae eyed her. An alley opened two houses from where she stood. If she could reach the alley without being seen, she could get to the back of the building, climb the fence into the yard, and go in through the cellar door. Her luck took an upturn in the form of Mrs. Callahan pushing her twins in her extra large baby carriage. Her three older boys walked in front of the carriage, scuffling with each other while Mrs. Callahan threatened future punishments. The family filled the sidewalk, shielding Rae as she bent low and sprinted into the alley.

When she opened the apartment door, Lily jumped from the rocking chair, her mouth in a pout. "I got fired. That witch, Clementine Frederick, made me come in the shop extra early to stock shelves, and then she fired me!"

Rae leaned against a table, her skin sticky from the heat and humidity. "What happened?"

Lily glanced at her reflection in the window and patted her hair. "The witch thought Mr. Frederick was getting too fond of me."

"Was he?"

"When he came to work, he sometimes patted me back here," Lily pointed, "unless I managed to jump out of reach." She smoothed her hair once more. "He's very old—at least fifty—but our usual customers were younger men—and rich. I could have found a rich husband, Rae."

Lily was the beauty in the family. Her silky blonde hair glinted like gold threads in the sunlight, and when she twisted it into a coil at the nape of her neck, she had a perfect profile. Dark, double lashes framed her blue eyes. Men lost their minds when they saw Lily. Rae usually humored her sister's dream about a rich husband, but not today. "No rich man is going to marry a store clerk. Maybe you could learn typewriting like Delia and get a job in an office."

"A lot of good that job did Delia. She's on an onion farm in Wisconsin now."

"Hal's a nice fellow," Rae murmured. Her fingers traced the outline of the wallet in her pocket.

"I hope his broad shoulders make up for the onions and living with his mother."

A fist pounded on the door, rattling the panels in the frame. "Raeanne Kelly, I know you're in there. Let me in."

Rae shot a warning glance at Lily and opened the door. Mrs. Polsky barreled past her. Hands on hips, she surveyed the room. "Is your pa here?"

"He had a business trip," Rae said. "He'll be back tomorrow."

The woman snorted. "*Ja, ja,* a business trip. I saw him sneak away this morning. I know the look of a man who isn't coming back—the same look my Josef had when he left me."

Rae stepped closer, forcing the woman back toward the open door. "I'll get the rent."

"The rent is too high," Lily interrupted.

"Too high!" Mrs. Polsky raised her eyes to the ceiling, waving her arms in a sweeping gesture. "These rooms are one of my best *swee-ets.*"

Rae cut off Lily. "I'll get the money tonight, Mrs. Polsky."

Lily waited for the woman's steps to fade down the hallway. "What's going on?"

"Pa left us and took all our money, but I have something I can sell."

"Everything?" Lily's mouth tightened. "I knew he'd desert us some day."

"He stuck with the three of us longer than some might have after Ma ran off."

"What do you have to sell?"

"I stole a wallet, but it was empty. Lev said a fellow he knows might buy it." She took it out to show Lily. "It's fine leather. I'll talk the fellow into paying enough so we have the rent."

"Where are you going exactly?"

"To see the fellow."

2

Sean Rogan searched his pockets for the third time as he stood on the sidewalk in front of his boss's ornate stone mansion, marked by a medieval-style tower along one wall. Swearing under his breath, he shot a nervous glance at the glass-paneled mahogany door at the top of the steps.

He couldn't stay on the street forever. He was already late. He took off his jacket and shook it, hoping the wallet would tumble out of a forgotten pocket. Nothing. He gave the jacket another violent shake and searched for rips in the lining. Nothing.

Stopping off at Madame Yvonne's to have a little visit with Sadie probably had been a mistake, but a fellow needed some feminine attention after all. His jacket had been in the room, tossed over a chair, while Sadie helped him relax. The memory of Sadie's exceptionally skilled hands and mouth momentarily distracted him from his current predicament. Deliberately, he pushed Sadie out of his mind and focused on his movements at Madame Yvonne's. He'd paid Madame before going upstairs, and he'd tipped Sadie five dollars with a joke about the boys at the Ford plant who had to work all day for five dollars. His money clip was in his inside breast pocket where he'd put it. He never taken the wallet out, and he'd kept Sadie too busy to bother with his jacket. He glanced up and down the street, hoping he'd see a spot of red lying on the sidewalk.

His chest tightened. Damn it all. He shrugged on his jacket and straightened his tie before he pushed through the wrought iron gate. He took another second to draw a deep breath before he lifted the dragon's-head door knocker and dropped it with a crash against the metal plate. When Petra the maid opened the door, he stepped into the foyer with a casual swing in his gait. No need to look as if he were in the wrong. He hadn't done anything foolish with the damn wallet. He followed Petra to the library office.

"What do you mean you haven't got it?" Breath rasping in his chest, Theodore Weston eased his bulk away from his desk and poured two inches of whiskey into a glass on the sideboard.

Sean twisted in his chair. Weston was sixty, and his muscles had melted into a sagging mound around his middle, but he was rich, politically powerful, and his formidable presence wasn't easy to ignore.

Weston swirled the liquid in the glass. "It was a simple errand. You met Gruber and got a paper with his estimates for next month's payoffs. What happened to it?"

"I got it," Sean said. He kept an offhand smile on his face although he had a sour taste in his mouth. He desperately wanted a whiskey, but he knew Weston wouldn't offer him one. "When I got here, I checked for my wallet. It was gone. It must have fallen out of my pocket."

Weston glanced at the clock on the fireplace mantel. "Why did it take you four hours to get back here?"

Sean licked his dry lips. "I had to wait. Gruber was copying the numbers from scraps of paper. Then I took the trolley, but I got off too soon and had to walk. I bought a newspaper at a stand—lot of talk there. War's come to Europe."

"I know the news," Weston said. "What next?"

Next was the visit with Sadie. "I read a couple of pages in the paper while I had coffee, and then I came straight here." He met Weston's gaze with a blank stare. He wasn't going to flinch. He'd been working for Weston since he was eighteen and shouldn't have to explain every step he made. His nerves subsided while his irritation grew.

Weston lifted his glass and tossed back the whiskey. "You'll have to go back tonight. Let's hope Gruber hasn't thrown away those scraps of paper." His gaze at Sean was unforgiving. "And let's devoutly hope if someone finds that wallet, he won't have the faintest idea what those figures mean."

3

Rae slowed her pace as a group of young men walked toward her, but they ignored her and headed straight for the house with the red flower pots on the porch. A piano playing "You Made Me Love You" sent jaunty music over the transom above the entrance. She wasn't nervous, but she didn't want to be noticed, especially by men out for a good time.

The dirty windows of Gus's Motors were dark, but a dim glow came from the back of the shop. She knocked and waited. After a long minute, she pounded on the door and kicked the bottom panel.

A light flashed inside. Three bolts slid free, and the door opened a few inches.

"We're closed, kid."

The huge man standing in the doorway had had a lot of rough years. Beefy hands—big as baseball mitts—misshapen knuckles—and a nose broken so many times it lay flat against his face. White scars streaked over drooping eyelids. He looked to be in his fifties, but the way he stood, legs slightly apart, said he could still hold his own in a fight.

"Are you Lukas Krantz?"

"No. Whadda ya want?"

"Somebody told me I'd find Lukas Krantz here. I've got something to sell him."

He frowned, rubbed his scarred chin, and looked her over. "What you got?" He held out his hand.

"Can't show it to anyone but Krantz." She'd never see any money if she let him take it and shut the door. "Is he here or not?"

"Wait a minute."

He closed the door in her face. She shrank against the doorway while two more men passed her and climbed the steps to the house across the street. The piano music grew louder.

Footsteps inside. He opened the door wide this time. "Come in, kid."

She followed him through a large room full of tires and tools. Belts and hoses hung on the walls behind a counter cluttered with half-opened boxes. A battered cash register sat on one end of the counter, the empty money drawer open. The floor was gritty under her feet as she followed him down a short hallway and through the door to an office. Two dark green leather chairs sat in front of a polished wooden desk lit by a brass banker's lamp, the green shade glowing. The light in the rest of the room came from floor lamps with stained-glass lamp shades. Electrical wiring stretched across one wall. A large framed map of Chicago streets hung on the wall behind the desk.

"Here's the kid."

"Thanks, Gus." Lukas Krantz pushed his chair away from the desk, stood, and waved her into one of the leather chairs. "Sit down. Gus said you have something to sell me."

She'd been expecting a man as old as Gus, and for a minute, she couldn't think what to say. Krantz wasn't smoothly handsome like the heroes in the movie pictures, but her sister Delia would say he was intriguing. Lily would sniff and call him rough. Tall, with dark wavy hair drooping over his forehead, and solid muscles under his tailored business suit, he looked no more than thirty. He waited for her to speak, his dark eyes curious.

She slid her hands along the soft armrests, wanting to sink back into the chair, but his gaze was vaguely impatient. "I have a wallet to sell. I found it."

He sat down and smiled. "Found it? What makes you think it's worth anything?"

Fishing the wallet out of her pocket, she put it on his desk. "It's good leather. No money inside—just some paper that doesn't mean anything." She moved to open the wallet and remove the paper, but his hand closed over it.

Holding herself still, she curled her hands into fists while he examined the leather. He had to buy it. He had to. He unfolded the yellow sheet of paper and stared at it. Her nails dug into her palms. How long did it take to decide to buy a wallet?

"Who were you standing next to when you . . . found this wallet?"

She flushed. No point in lying. "There was a crowd at the newsstand reading the papers, and a young fellow was close by."

"What did he look like?"

"Skinny, good clothes, thin mustache, and ginger hair a little long around his ears."

He tapped his fingers on the desk. "How much do you want for the wallet?"

Tricky question. She didn't want to ask for too much or too little. Mrs. Polsky came to mind. "I need rent money," she began, "and there's other—"

"How about thirty dollars?"

Her mind went blank for an instant. Her wildest hope had been to get the twelve dollars rent with maybe a bit extra. She swallowed hard. "That would be fine, Mr. Krantz."

"How old are you?" His gaze held her in place.

She looped her finger in one of her curls and spoke with complete sincerity. "Thirteen."

"Why are you in charge of getting rent money? Are you on your own?"

"My sister Lily lost her job, and my pa had to go on a trip, so we're short of cash."

He opened a drawer, plucked out some bills, and thrust them across the desk. She snatched the money, resisting an urge to count in front of him, and shoved it in her skirt pocket. "Thank you very much. A pleasure to meet you."

She half rose, but he waved her back in the chair. "I like to know who I'm doing business with. What's your name?"

"Raeanne Kelly."

"Any relation to Maxie Kelly?" His voice hardened.

This was not good. She shifted awkwardly. "He's my pa."

His sharp gaze held her in place. "Maxie Kelly cost me close to three thousand dollars a few days ago. Where'd he go?"

Automatically, she felt through the folds of her skirt and curled her fingers around the wad of money in her pocket. "I don't know," she whispered. "He didn't say. He left this morning." Her heart pounded against her chest, but she kept a half-smile on her face as if they were having a friendly chat.

They stared at each other until he shrugged. "Relax. I know you don't have it." He walked to the door and called for Gus. "Take her home, so she's not walking the streets in the dark," he said when the older man entered the office. He held up his hand as she rose from the chair. "Wait a minute."

Bending over the desk, he wrote a note, folded the paper, and handed it to her. "I have a financial interest in RidgeW Pictures. They need people—especially young girls—for the background. You take this note to Matthew Ridgewood on Monday at nine o'clock. He'll give you a job. If you're any good at standing around, you can work all week."

She stared at the note. Standing around didn't sound like much of a job.

"He pays three dollars a day," he added with a grin.

"For standing around?" She didn't really believe him, but the paper went into her pocket and nestled next to the money.

"Sometimes he tells you to walk back and forth," he said, "and, Raeanne, if your pa shows up, you tell him I'm waiting to talk to him."

She mumbled thank you twice before she followed Gus through the back exit into an alley where an automobile was parked on a cement slab. She gasped. It was no ordinary Tin Lizzie.

"Pretty swank, huh?" Gus grinned as he opened the door of a Pierce-Arrow.

At last she was getting a ride in an automobile, and it was one that cost over four thousand dollars. She stepped on the running board, sank into the seat, stretched her legs, and told Gus which way to drive.

Lukas sat at his desk and gazed at the red wallet. That ginger-haired fellow had to be Sean Rogan, and if Rogan had the paper, it must contain information important to Theodore Weston. He unfolded the yellow sheet and laid it flat on the desk. If he could figure out the numbers and letters, he'd have something on Weston—maybe enough to keep the old boy out of his affairs.

Idly, he copied some of the letters on blank paper. He continued until he'd copied every set of letters. One set suddenly made sense—a tannery. Then another—a bicycle shop. Then another—a tavern. They were all in a district where he'd recently held some boxing matches. The numbers must be the amounts these owners were paying Weston for special favors or to leave them alone. Lukas focused on the other letters until he had most of the list decoded. It covered the far north side.

He hated making payoffs to greedy politicians, and Weston was one of the worst. The city council member also took sizeable payments from businesses on the west side, including a hefty slice off what Lukas made from the boxing, the gambling, and the girls at Madame Yvonne's. His anger boiled as he contemplated the list. Aside from an occasional repair job that drifted into Gus's Motors, every business he ran was illegal, so he was at the mercy of anyone who wanted a bribe, and lots of people wanted them.

Rising, he put the paper and wallet in his safe and spun the dial. Eventually, RidgeW Pictures should bring in big money. Movies were legal, and, more important they were making money every day. Thousands of nickelodeons across the country. It'd been a lucky break when Matt Ridgewood came to him because he couldn't get a bank loan big enough to start up his movie studio. People around Chicago thought Matt was the owner, which was all right for the moment, but the time would come when Lukas could emerge from the shadows as the owner and a legitimate businessman with influence and power.

Gus stuck his head through the open door. "Took her home."

"Thanks." A faint smile crossed Lukas's lips. Maxie Kelly's daughter was a tough little kid, lifting a wallet, and coming to him to sell what she'd stolen so she could pay the rent. Growing up with Maxie as a father couldn't have been easy. He'd keep an eye on her. Maxie might come back to town, and Lukas had business to discuss with him.

4

Chicago Dispatch, **August 7, 1914**

Out and About with Lucinda Corday

Chicago's bustling activity in the movie industry is growing! Faithful readers know when RidgeW Pictures began producing movies only four months ago, I predicted the company was going to be wildly successful. Matthew Ridgewood, studio owner and director, tells me he is about to increase the weekly production. In addition to the exciting westerns starring audience favorite Roy Emmitt, the studio will make comedies and dramas.

Rising comedy star Billy Tucker has signed an exclusive contract with RidgeW. Chicago patrons of the vaudeville theater will recognize the name, but those who don't know him will soon be able to enjoy his talents on the screen. *The Sailor and the Waitress* begins production on Monday.

For interested readers, my other good news is that RidgeW needs extra performers. Line up at the studio doors on Monday at nine o'clock, and you might be in the movies!

Until next time, dear readers.

5

Triumphant, Rae pounded on Mrs. Polsky's door just after dawn. The woman, dressed in a faded pink wrapper, her gray hair hanging in lank strands, opened her door and glared at Rae. "You knock this early?"

Rae seized her hand and slapped twelve dollars into it. "The rent," she said.

Mrs. Polsky carefully counted the money, shooting a suspicious look at Rae. "Where did a girl like you get this money?"

"That's my business. You got the rent."

"I run a respectable place," the woman said as she tucked the bills in her pocket and pulled her wrapper tighter around her thick waist. "There's only one way a young girl makes this money in one night."

"You have an evil mind," Rae snapped. "I told you I had something to sell."

She stamped up the stairs. If Lukas Krantz had told the truth, she and Lily might be out of this rundown dump before long. It was too hot in the summer and too cold in the winter. The hallways had a permanent stench from the trash the tenants left outside their doors before they got around to taking it outside to the bins in the alley. Lily had to jam pots under the windows to keep them open because the ropes were broken. Three dollars a day—for lots of days—would help them escape.

Immediately, doubt clouded her optimistic visions of the future. Maybe Lukas Krantz had lied to her. Maybe he didn't have any influence at RidgeW Pictures. Maybe she'd look like a fool on Monday.

"You come with me to the studio," she said to Lily when she returned to their rooms. "You need a job too, and you're so pretty."

Lily poured a splash of milk into her tea, took a sip, and looked at Rae over the rim of the cup. "I don't know how to act and neither do you. You're hoping for something a gangster promised you. How ridiculous!"

"We don't have to know how to act," Rae said. "He said all I had to do was stand in the background or maybe walk a little. You have to come with me—it's easy money. We might work more than one day." She bit her lip. It was hard not to hope.

Lily took the note from the table and waved it in Rae's face. "It only mentions you. I can't come with you."

"I'll tell him it means both of us."

Lily snorted, but on Monday she arranged her hair in an elegant knot at the back of her neck and put on her navy dress with the wide satin ribbons threaded along the bodice. "I have to look respectable," she murmured. Lily's wardrobe was a collection of castoff dresses her previous employer had given her whenever it was time for the season's new dresses, hats and shoes.

Rae had only her brown skirt and white cotton shirtwaist, both too tight, but fortunately the heavy cotton crushed her breasts. Lukas Krantz had said RidgeW needed young girls, so she had to look like one. The collar had a dark stain, but Lily covered it with one of her scarves.

The movie studio was in a warehouse that took up a full city block. Shreds of old posters about sausage clung to the dull, gray walls, and unevenly spaced skylights had been hacked into the roof. A slightly crooked black and white sign, RidgeW Pictures, hung over double doors wide enough for a truck to drive through. Rae's hopes for prosperity dropped to the pavement.

The building had an air of decay, but worse was the mob of people waiting in front of the closed doors. Pushing and shoving against each other to get in a good position, the waiting hopefuls spilled into the street until the driver of a passing Model T used his horn and sent them running back to the sidewalk.

"Oh," Lily said, disappointment quivering in her voice. "There must be a hundred people here. We'll never . . ."

Dark thoughts about being overlooked in the mob seized Rae. They couldn't miss this chance! "Not a hundred," she said. "Maybe fifty."

The metal doors creaked open, banging against the side of the building, and a tall man emerged. Someone yelled "Mr. Ridgewood" at him. Rae gaped. He looked only a few years older than Lily, and the sunlight gleamed on blond hair long enough to touch his collar. He wore a blue work shirt with the sleeves rolled up to his elbows, an unbuttoned tan vest, open collar, and dark work pants. A fat pencil rested behind one ear.

He gestured to the crowd. "Line up so I can see you. We're starting two productions today."

Instead of creating order, his words encouraged more pushing, and the partial beginning of a line splintered into a mob again. Rae grabbed Lily's hand and dragged her through the crowd. Two men who smelled as if they'd been drinking for days were easy to push aside. The mob surged forward, while Matthew Ridgewood slowly walked along the sidewalk, looking over people, and tapping some on the shoulders. The lucky chosen hustled into the building.

Rae tightened her grip on Lily's wrist. They were too far back—he'd never notice them. She jabbed her elbow into the man next to her. When he staggered off balance, she yanked Lily closer to the front, but an old woman, a messy pile of gray hair on her head and a figure like a block of cement, pushed past Rae and shoved herself in front of Lily.

Ridgewood nodded to the old woman and waved her into the building. "That's it for today! Thanks. Check back next week because we'll likely need new people for new pictures."

Disappointed murmurs rippled through the crowd as people straggled away. Lily wrenched her wrist out of Rae's grip. "I told you. We didn't have a chance."

Rae pulled Krantz's note from her pocket and clutched Lily's arm again. "We aren't giving up." She headed toward the metal doors. "Mr. Ridgewood! Wait!"

"Sorry, we're finished today."

She sprinted the last steps, still dragging Lily behind her. "Lukas Krantz sent me."

"Damn," he muttered loud enough for Rae to hear.

"Read this." She shoved the note at him.

He read it twice, his mouth tight, a frown cutting into his forehead. He exhaled in a hiss and looked Rae over. "How old are you?"

"Thirteen." She shook her long curls and smiled. "Mr. Krantz said you'd need someone like me."

"Krantz should let me make the movies," he said. "Does your mother know you're here?"

"My sister came with me."

He sighed. "I'll take you—just for today. One day."

"And my sister," Rae said. "He wanted both of us."

"He didn't write anything about two of you in this note." For the first time, he looked past Rae. His expression changed, and he got the overwhelmed look men always got when they saw Lily for the first time. Rae squeezed her wrist, and Lily immediately tipped her head to the side and widened her blue eyes.

He smiled at her, ignoring Rae. "Have you two had any experience?"

Lily managed to blush. "I'm afraid we don't, but we're so eager to learn. Do you imagine we could be of any use in your moving pictures?"

"I imagine you could," he said. "All right. You can both go inside."

6

Inside the building, Rae kept her grip on Lily while Ridgewood ignored them as he sent most of the men he'd just hired to the western set with an assistant he introduced as Fred Brown. Then he took the pencil from behind his ear and rolled it back and forth through his fingers while he looked at Rae, Lily, and the elderly woman he'd picked earlier.

"Call me Matt," he said. "What's your name?" he asked Lily.

"Lily Rose." She tilted her head and smiled.

"A good name for the movies. You'll be in the western—a dance hall girl as soon as you get in a costume. Ida!"

A portly woman at least six feet tall with salt and pepper hair twisted in a tight bun appeared in the hallway. She wore a long blue apron with neat rows of stick and safety pins across the bib. "You ready?"

Matt nodded toward Lily. She's in the western—a dance hall girl—give her something flashy." He looked at the older woman. "You were here last week. Ethel is it?" When she nodded, he turned to Rae and waited.

"Rae Kelly," she said instantly.

"Rae and Ethel will be in the comedy—grandmother and granddaughter in the restaurant. Nothing fancy for clothes, Ida."

Ida steered them down the inner hallway to a room filled with racks of costumes. Inside, Ethel immediately stripped to her petticoat. Her straight up-and-down figure was wrapped in a corset that had no effect on her shape.

Ida tossed a plain black dress to Ethel and turned her attention to Lily. "I hope your legs look as good as your face," she said. "Take off your dress and petticoat." She held up a red satin skirt reaching just below Lily's knees.

"It's so short," Lily said.

"Dance hall girls weren't too modest, honey." Ida took a sleeveless black satin camisole, cut low on the bodice, from a rack of costumes and pulled it over Lily's head. A ruffled petticoat and the satin skirt followed. Ida hooked them at Lily's waist and pinned a spray of feathers on one strap of the camisole. "You're just right," she said. She pulled a few curls loose from the hair at Lily's forehead. "Leave it this way," she ordered when Lily automatically reached up to tuck the curls away. Shoes with brass buckles came next.

Lily slipped on the shoes and gazed at her legs showing between the bottom of the skirt and the shoes. She made an unsuccessful downward pull on the skirt and upward pull on the camisole, but nothing changed. "It's too bare."

Ida snorted. "You'll see what's bare if you stay around." She gripped Lily's neck, holding her steady while she dabbed a red, waxy stick over her lips and hooked a glittery choker around her neck. "Perfect," she said as she stepped back. "You're gorgeous. Don't mess it up."

Snatching an ugly green cotton pinafore from a rack, Ida gestured to Rae. Grateful the dress didn't look like Lily's costume, Rae stripped to her petticoat.

Ida stared. "How old are you?"

Rae opened her eyes wide. Lying effectively required a sincere gaze. "Thirteen."

Ida chuckled. "Men don't know anything. Matt may swallow that story, but I'm on to you. Never mind, it's not my business." Once Rae had slipped into the shapeless pinafore and a plain shirtwaist, Ida ruffled her long curls around her shoulders. "A perfect little granddaughter," she said with another short laugh.

She set a hat that looked like a brown mushroom with two purple wings rising from one side on Ethel's head and steered the three of them to a back door where Lily joined the other dance hall girls. Rae and Ethel followed Ida farther along the hall into another room.

The walls in the huge room were whitewashed to add to the light coming from rows of electric bulbs hanging from the ceiling. Three wooden panels, painted to look like the walls of a restaurant, framed a wooden counter with two stools and three round tables covered in checked tablecloths.

A camera on a tripod faced the set. The background looked fake, but Rae had seen enough movies to know that wouldn't matter when the actors played out the story.

Matt gestured to a man dressed in a white sailor uniform. "Let's welcome Billy Tucker to RidgeW and our first day making *The Sailor and the Waitress.*"

Billy Tucker waved and swaggered into the middle of the set. Rae hadn't heard of him, but the crew clapped and cheered, so he was definitely famous. Billy had a wicked grin—the kind that said he'd done something wrong and wasn't sorry about it. An actress dressed in a short blue dress with a tiny white apron stood fluffing her red-gold hair while Billy bowed to the applauding crew. Rae nudged Ethel. "Is that Eve Darling over there?"

Ethel nodded. "She's usually in the westerns, but I guess she's going to play with Billy Tucker now. Shows how important this movie is. Glad I got in this one."

Matt turned to them. "Ethel, you and . . . uh . . . Rae enter from the outside through that door. Walk to the back table, and you sit down first on your right. Rae, you wait until Ethel sits down, then you sit. Got it?"

Rae nodded, a flutter of nerves seizing her. *Walk in. Sit.* Didn't sound hard. Matt muttered more instructions to a crew member he called Bud. The man nodded, took one of the chairs at the back table away and returned with a replacement.

"Eve, when Billy comes in, you walk over to get his order when I call it. Remember, nobody steps outside the strips on the floor. I'm getting all of you in the shot."

Billy joined Rae and Ethel behind the door while Rae eyed the wooden strips tacked on the floor at the edges of the set. Matt's instructions began to scramble in her brain.

"Camera, George. Billy, action!" Matt yelled. "Come in, close the door, look around, and sit at the table with the vase."

Billy entered, rolling his gait like a sailor just off a ship, took a slow glance over the tables, and sat facing the camera.

"Pick up the menu," Matt called. Billy did and pretended to read it. "Eve, take the tray and walk to the table. When Billy looks up, you are both struck with each other. Flirt for a minute. Now, Eve."

Rae watched through a crack in the plywood wall as Eve looked over Billy for a minute, fluffed her hair, put one hand on her hip, and sashayed across the floor to Billy's table. They flirted for a minute without Matt telling them what to do. Billy grinned. Eve dipped her head and giggled. He gestured to the chair next to him. She shook her head.

"Ethel, enter," Matt called.

Nervous, Rae followed Ethel too closely and almost stepped on her heels as the woman walked to the back table, pulled out her chair, and settled into it. When she pointed to the other chair, Rae pulled it away from the table and sat. The chair wobbled, teetered backward, and collapsed. Rae shrieked as she landed on the floor, arms flailing, legs kicking in the air, her skirt up to her waist revealing her cotton drawers. Ethel half rose to her feet.

"Ethel, help her up. That's it. Cut! Good take," Matt called.

"You did good," Bud mumbled as he collected the broken chair.

Rae's face burned as she wrenched her skirts down. "Was that on purpose?"

Matt grinned. "I couldn't tell you ahead of time—I wanted a fresh reaction. Not hurt are you?" He waited for Bud to return with a new chair. "Back in places. Ethel, you pretend to talk to Rae while Billy and Eve do their business." He bent close to Eve and muttered into her ear. She nodded. He clapped his hands. "George, camera. Eve, action! Bring Billy some bread. Billy, when she bends over the table, pat her."

Eve swung her hips as she walked. Billy, grinning, patted her backside when she reached the table. She stepped away, indicating shock and outrage. Then she slapped him. He leaped to his feet and made wild gestures begging forgiveness. Eve switched to coy smiles, pretended to leave him, but giggled and walked back to the table. Rae almost believed they were really flirting until Ethel leaned close.

"Pay attention," she hissed.

Pulled back to reality, Rae whispered the multiplication table for threes and fours, but she watched Billy and Eve out of the corner of her eye. They didn't need many directions from Matt. Pretending to be angry, Eve stormed off to one side while Billy slumped at the table and sent pleading glances her way. She folded her arms across her chest and ignored him. Finally, she softened and smiled. Grinning, he raised his empty water glass.

"Bring him the water," Matt said, "but make him wait while you stop at the back table and fill their glasses."

Keeping her eyes on Billy, Eve took a pitcher off the counter and walked to the back table. Across the room Billy grinned at her. She smiled seductively at Billy, twitched her hips, and poured the pitcher of water over Rae's head.

With a scream, Rae shot up, arms in the air, water dripping down her face.

"Cut!"

"You must have made a good impression," Ida remarked as she peeled off Rae's wet clothes and tossed them into a laundry bin. "Matt said to get you ready for the western this afternoon." She touched the edge of Rae's petticoat. "This is soaked too."

"I'll dry quick," Rae said, clutching the petticoat. This movie acting left her feeling she wasn't herself. Some of it was fake, but she'd hit the floor hard enough, and she was wet through. She shook her petticoat to dry it while Ida hunted through the racks for a costume.

"This might fit." Ida held up a blue and white gingham dress. "We'll put a tight camisole under it so you don't show your figure. You're going to be a country girl."

Matt and George, the cameraman, set up lights and cameras in a small park a block away from the studio, while the crew put out straggly brush to create an Old West atmosphere. Bud helped Rae climb a ladder to a good-sized branch halfway up a tree. Then he took the ladder away and left her stranded, until Roy Emmitt, the hero of *Rustlers on the Trail*, would arrive to rescue her for the camera.

"When the action starts, girls, start yelling encouragement to Rae," Matt said. "Rae, you should look frightened."

That wasn't hard. The branch swayed whenever she moved, and the ground looked far enough away for at least a broken leg. She dug her fingers into the cracks in the bark.

Roy was late. Matt swore and sent Bud to look for him, while below Rae, the crew and dance hall girls strolled around, talking and laughing. No one seemed to care she was stuck in a tree. Minutes dragged. She tightened her legs around the branch. This movie stuff was nonsense, but at least she was making three dollars. Finally, Bud returned with Roy, and Matt yelled for action. The dance hall girls jumped up and down, pretending to be worried about her. Rae kept one hand firmly on the branch and managed to press the other hand to her heart and look to the sky for help when Matt told her to.

The camera focused on her while Roy hoisted himself halfway up the tree with the aid of Bud, then hooked his leg over another branch, and reached for her. His bloodshot eyes stared into Rae's as she caught a whiff of why he'd been late to the set. "Come on, kid. We gotta get down."

In spite of Matt's directions, Rae tightened her grip on the branch. Roy looked in no condition to carry her down. Matt had to yell twice before she loosened her hold and let Roy lift her, clutch her close to his chest, and make a wobbly descent.

"Give her a little kiss before you put her down," Matt called.

She didn't want a kiss! Before she could protest, Roy jerked her closer and shoved his beer-flavored tongue between her lips.

She choked. "Get your tongue out of my mouth!" she screamed. Roy grunted and dropped her into the dirt.

Matt stepped from behind the camera. "Roy, for god's sake! She's a kid." He pulled Rae to her feet while she was still gasping. "Calm down, you're all right." He glared at Roy. "How drunk are you? You smell like a tavern. Everybody stay in place for a minute." He conferred with Bud and George while Roy swayed in his cowboy boots and leaned against the tree. Matt muttered to George for several minutes. They stared at the late afternoon sky until Matt shook his head. "That's it for today. I need everyone in this scene back tomorrow. Eight o'clock for costumes."

In the costume room, the girls from the western stripped off their ruffled skirts, tossing them to Ida. A redhead named Georgia patted Rae's shoulder. "It's a shock the first time, but if you stay in movies, it won't be the last. You'll get used to it."

Betsy, a tall blonde, snickered. "I always bite down hard when they try that. Puts them off doing it again, at least for a while."

Lily put her arms around Rae and pressed her forehead against Rae's. "Sorry about what happened, but we got another day to work," she whispered.

"I don't like this acting stuff," Rae whispered back. "It's confusing. I don't know what's going to happen from one minute to the next." She shivered. No amount of money was worth having Roy Emmitt's awful tongue in her mouth.

"It's only one more day," Lily said. "We need the money."

After the other girls drifted out of the room, Ida turned her attention to Rae. "Your sister's right. You're making some money. Don't get shaky. Roy's all right when he's sober, but he's usually drunk these days. Matt won't let anything bad happen to you."

Rae raised her arms while Ida helped her wiggle out of the too-tight dress. "I guess it's no worse than washing dishes, and it does pay three dollars a day."

Ida tilted her head to one side. "Three dollars? I thought you did stunts today." She shook out the gingham dress. "What do I know about it? I'm just saying if you did do stunts like maybe being stuck in a tree or having water poured over you, stunts get more than three dollars."

At the front entrance, Matt stood at the open double doors saying goodnight to the actors. He grinned when he saw them. "Good work, girls."

Rae twisted a long curl around her finger and put on her most innocent gaze. "Matt, was I doing stunts today?"

"You did very well. Action suits you."

"I was thinking stunts might be more than three dollars."

A crease formed between his eyebrows. "You're pretty sharp for one day at a movie studio. Stunts get five dollars. I'll tell Fred to make a note."

"Thanks, Matt."

Rae and Lily walked in silence until they'd gone two full blocks from the studio. Turning a corner, they stopped dead and looked at each other. "Five dollars!" Rae shrieked to the darkening sky. Roy's tongue was already fading from her memory.

7

att smiled at Eve as she left the studio. "You were good with Billy today."

"I'll be even better later." She caught her lower lip in her teeth, a gesture she used in all her movies and ran her fingertips along Matt's bare forearm. "Tonight?"

"I've got business to handle first. I might be too late for a decent meal."

She pouted dramatically, but the sparkle in her eyes told him she wasn't upset. "You work too hard. Come whenever you can. I can eat alone, but . . ."

"I'll hurry."

She blew him a kiss as she left. He stood in the open doorway and watched her hips swing as she walked along the street and beckoned for a taxi on the corner. Eve was exceptionally pretty, highly amusing, delightfully freethinking, and completely uninterested in permanence—the perfect woman for him, a man with no money, little time, and possibly no future.

His assistant Fred stepped out of the inner door and cleared his throat. "Matt, we've got to talk about Roy."

"Roy's getting worse." Matt leaned against the door jamb and groaned. "We have to finish the western this week. Keep him here tomorrow if you have to lock him in a storeroom. Don't let him get near a drink."

"I can lock him up all right. After that, maybe we need to dump him. Gil Owen's pretty green, but he might lead a western if we rewrote the gambler story to make it a kid on the run."

"Good idea. I'm not paying Gil much. We could try him in the lead next week. Roy's got a weekly contract, so I can tell him he's through after we finish *Rustlers on the Trail.*"

For a minute, Matt contemplated his mounting expenses and how little he paid Roy, who was, after all, the popular star of his westerns. Gil Owen might do the job, but would he bring the audience Roy did? "If I had more capital . . . Chester Slater's play is closing next week. He might be interested in making a western or maybe the story about the hotel owner. Of course, Slater will cost a lot." He rubbed his shoulder where the muscle had tightened into a knot.

"I can ask around about what he'd want," Fred offered. "If he hasn't got a new play lined up, we could strike a bargain. Actors like to keep working."

Matt didn't answer, his mind shifting from Chester's probable salary demands to RidgeW Pictures and its dwindling budget. He'd lied to the kid a few minutes ago. Stunts at other studios paid ten dollars a day, but there was no way he could meet that price by producing only one movie a week. If he managed to get out two movies this week, he still wouldn't collect enough money to pay ten dollars for stunts, and he'd used up all the cash in the bank account to sign Billy Tucker to a full year's contract. Billy's comedies should bring in some decent money, but now he was going to have to fire Roy, his well-known western star, and put an unknown nineteen-year-old as the lead in next week's western.

"Another thing," Fred went on. "Selig made a real splash with that adventure serial."

"*The Adventures of Kathlyn.*" Matt nodded. "We should be doing an action serial too. Again, I'm tight on money."

His attention shifted to a taxi pulling up to the studio. The taxi idled while Arabella Weston, her skirts making a silky rustle, walked from the curb to the RidgeW doors. "Matt, are you busy now?"

A rush of tension mixed with pleasure shot through him the way it always did whenever he saw her. She wore a narrow, royal blue, silk crepe skirt and an accordion-pleated cream silk shirtwaist with jet buttons and an embroidered collar. A cream silk hat trimmed with a single pink taffeta rose sat at an angle on her dark upswept hair. Beautiful. Expensive. Everything about her reminded him he could not afford what Theodore Weston could afford.

Fred mumbled a polite greeting. Arabella acknowledged his presence with a barely perceptible nod and waited until he'd excused himself, closing an inner door firmly behind him.

"This is a surprise," Matt said softly. "What brings you here?"

She moved closer in the dim light, her dark eyes fixed on his. "Mother wants to invite you to dinner next month," she said.

"Next month? You had to deliver the invitation in person so far ahead?" He kept his tone light, as if she weren't standing too close to him, as if he couldn't inhale her lavender scent.

"I wanted to ask you myself—to persuade you to come. I wanted . . . we miss you, Matt. Mother thought . . . we haven't seen you in months."

"I've been busy. Your calendar must be filled with demanding social obligations as the wife of an important city council member. Does your husband know about this invitation?"

"We used to see each other all the time," she whispered.

"We used to be children whose families lived within a couple hundred feet of each other," he countered.

"Not just children," she said. "We promised we'd always be true to each other. You remember."

She put her cool hand on his bare arm, burning his skin where she touched. He caught her hand intending to pull it away, but instead he held it for an instant, sliding his thumb over the thin pulsing vein on the inside of her wrist. Her breath caught in a slight gasp, the way she'd sounded when they weren't children any longer and he'd stroked her wrist before kissing her for long, feverish minutes in the gazebo behind her parent's mansion. Deliberately, he ran his thumb across her soft skin again, pleased to feel her shiver before he let her hand drop.

"We were young enough so any promises we made don't hold," he said.

She shook her head. "Nothing changed between us. It was that terrible financial mess—our fathers died—disgraced—money gone—but we didn't change."

"Luckily," he said, "you managed to find a new fortune rather quickly—or your mother did. Perhaps you found a new father too," he added unable to resist a cruel jab.

"You were free to go off to New York and learn how to make movies. I had no choices, and Mother did not intend to starve."

He gave a short, humorless laugh. "Starve? Was the situation that dire?"

"Mother thought so at the time," she said, a touch of frost entering her voice. "I can't change what's been done."

"No," he agreed. "We can't."

She glanced over her shoulder at the street. "The taxi is waiting. Will you come to dinner?"

"Will your mother send me an invitation?"

"Yes."

"Then I'll send her an answer."

She stepped closer and made a pretense of brushing lint off his shoulder. "Mother will be delighted to see you," she murmured, her warm breath skimming over his jaw.

She turned and walked slowly toward the street where the driver held open the door of the taxi.

Matt chewed his lip while he watched the taxi pull away from the curb.

Damn it.

8

B y the time Matt reached Gus's Motor Shop, his mood was as dark as the streets.

"Mr. Krantz ain't here," Gus announced when he opened the door. "He stepped across the street." Gus pointed to Madam Yvonne's lighted windows and grinned. "If you don't find him right away, you can take it easy over there for an hour or so—on the house."

"I'll wait here," Matt growled, "and you can track him down." He stamped through the shop to Lukas's office. He was in no mood for a visit to Madame Yvonne's, and he'd lost any inclination to see Eve tonight because Arabella's lips so close to his flickered over and over in his consciousness like an image stuck in a movie projector. He used the brass telephone on the desk to call the Brimfield Hotel and leave a message for Eve—*so sorry, but business has taken over tonight—forgive me.* Then he dropped into a plush leather chair and let his emotions boil.

He hated knowing all the money for RidgeW Pictures came from a man most people considered to be a gangster, but he hadn't had any choice in the end. Every bank in Chicago had turned down his loan request because every financial man in town knew he had no collateral with his parents dead and the family fortune gone. He'd even humiliated himself by asking Theodore Weston for a loan after the banks said no. Weston had refused at once, claiming he didn't have any faith in the movie business and advising Matt to find a solid business position in Denver or San Francisco.

"Get out of Chicago and try your luck out west," Weston had said with a false hearty chuckle.

Resolutely pushing Arabella out of his thoughts, Matt took a long breath and forced his body to relax. Maybe getting the money for the studio from a gangster was the better choice in the end. A straight business arrangement.

The door opened behind him. "Gus said you wanted to see me." Lukas walked in wearing a dark blue pencil-stripe linen suit. When he unbuttoned the jacket to sit behind his desk, the white silk lining shimmered in the lamp light. Matt was suddenly conscious he had on the same wrinkled shirt and pants he'd worn all day. He clenched his jaw as another stab of frustration went through him. He was twenty-eight, only a year younger than Lukas, and by rights, he should be the one in the expensive suit. Instead, he was here to beg for money from a man who probably should be in jail.

"If you're worried about getting the film stock this week," Lukas said, "Gus and Otto will deliver it tomorrow night. I had to get it through Cicero this time. That damned Motion Picture Patents Company has film stock in this city locked down—no new studios getting any film. The bribes are big enough to keep it tight. My boys . . . you might say they found a shipment, and they'll be around to your place."

"Thanks. There's a lawsuit—it could break up the monopoly."

Lukas waved his hand in dismissal. "Yeah, a lawsuit. A man can grow old waiting for justice." He grinned and leaned over the desk toward Matt. "I got something the other day on Theodore Weston." His grin faded, replaced by a questioning look. "Did a kid show up at the studio?"

"Yes, she did," Matt said. "Look Lukas, I put the two of them into what we were shooting today, but don't send me people off the streets to put in my movies."

"What two of them? I gave the kid a note for her."

"She brought her sister and said you meant both of them. It turned out all right. The kid was good in comedy, and the sister," Matt paused, "the sister is dazzlingly beautiful. I can use them both."

"Dazzling, huh?" Lukas relaxed in his chair.

"Do you want to see the stuff we did today? I started the Tucker movie and a western."

Lukas shook his head. "No, the only pictures I'm interested in are the ones they print on money." He stroked the paperweight on his desk. "The kid picked Sean Rogan's pocket and sold me his wallet. Wallet had a paper showing what Weston's been collecting around town. I might use that to get him to loosen the film supply. Hell, maybe I can get him to cut the boxing squeeze that's been getting tighter. He's on every damn committee the City Council has."

"I need more money," Matt said abruptly.

"More money," Lukas repeated softly.

Matt shifted awkwardly in his chair. "The thing is, Lukas, I have to drop Roy Emmitt—he's a drunk—and I want to hire Chester Slater if I can. He's got lots of stage experience. He can play western or drama. RidgeW also needs to do a serial—stay competitive." He tried to read the other man's face, but it was a blank. "That kid you sent me—Rae—she could do a serial if it was mostly action and didn't call for much else." He warmed to his topic, aiming to get a glimmer of interest from Lukas. "We've got Billy Tucker for comedies, and if we could get Slater for dramas and do a serial with the kid, maybe ten or twelve chapters, we could really break through and start making real money."

Lukas let the silence grow for a minute. "I like making money," he said finally, "but the movie business has something else I want. It's legitimate. You come from society. You could introduce me to the right people—the better people."

Matt frowned. "I'm nobody, Lukas. My father lost everything, and my parents are dead. I've got one uncle in New York."

"You still know people around Chicago. You never lose all your connections. I'm not saying you can bring me in tomorrow, but when the opportunity comes, I want to be included. Parties. Celebrations. Dinners at the fancy clubs. Serious business meetings. You understand what I'm saying?"

"Yes, I understand. I'm not sure—"

Lukas smiled. "How much money did you want, Matt?"

9

Chicago Dispatch, **August 28, 1914**

Out and About with Lucinda Corday

RidgeW Pictures has a real winner in Billy Tucker. His first comedy for the studio, *The Sailor and the Waitress,* has audiences laughing all over Chicago. Special comedy moments are added by a young girl in the restaurant scene.

RidgeW's new western, *Rustlers on the Trail,* with the popular Roy Emmitt has lots of action as usual. The girl from the Tucker comedy also has a small part in this movie. One wonders if she will be more prominent in future productions. A bit of sad news is that Roy Emmitt has had to step away from acting to visit his elderly mother in Oklahoma. We do hope he will be back in Chicago before very long.

RidgeW released two movies this week for the first time, indicating to Chicago audiences that the fledgling studio is on the rise.

Until next time, dear readers.

10

The letter arrived ten days after Lucinda Corday's glowing report appeared in the newspaper. Ida answered the pounding at RidgeW's front doors and tried to take the envelope, but the messenger insisted he had to hand it directly to Mr. Ridgewood. The boy waited patiently at the door, handed Matt a light blue envelope addressed in dark blue ink, said Mrs. Horace Graham did not require an immediate answer, and lingered until Matt dug a coin out of his pocket.

"Fancy paper," Ida commented, not hiding the curiosity in her voice. "A lady friend?"

"A friend of my mother's," Matt said. Arabella's mother still used an old-fashioned wax seal, dark blue with an oval imprint containing a *G*. Stuffing the envelope in an inside pocket, he ignored Ida's disappointed expression. "Put Lily in ruffles today. She's the banker's daughter, and it's the last scene so she needs to look especially beautiful.

Rae is the kid working in the blacksmith shop so she gets overalls." He thought a minute. "And braids."

"Using those two girls a lot, aren't you?" Ida asked.

"They look good on the screen," Matt said, running his fingers over the outline made by the envelope under his jacket. "They don't cost much."

"You going to sign them to contracts? Selig or Essanay could snap them up. If we lose them . . ."

Matt gave her a sharp look. "Getting rather motherly, aren't you, Ida?"

"I'm thinking of the business, that's all," she said, smoothing her apron in a show of indifference before a smile crept over her lips. "I confess, Matt, I do get a bit protective with those girls. Lily, she's a beauty. Billy's sniffing around, and it's clear what he's after. Don't know if she's given him any encouragement. Rae is tough, but—"

"She's a kid," he finished for her. "All right. I'll sign them today, and you can hover over them."

She snorted, hands on her hips. "As if I'd have time for mothering, the way you have me scrambling between two movies every day."

Fred opened the hallway door. "Matt, we're set up for the final shootout and Gil's ready." He shot Ida an accusing look. "We're waiting for the girls."

"I'll be there in a minute," Matt answered and looked pointedly at Ida until she spun on her heels, heading to the costume room.

Alone, Matt pulled the envelope out of his pocket, split the wax seal, and lifted the flap. Lavender scent wafted into the air. For a moment he weakened and inhaled deeply, allowing Arabella's face to take over his imagination. She might as well have been standing in front of him as he unfolded the thin blue paper.

> *Dear Matthew,*
>
> *I was so delighted to read Lucinda Corday's column. Your late mother was my dearest friend, and I know how very proud she and your late father would be of the way you have succeeded. I do hope you will allow me the honor of arranging a reception at our home to celebrate your work and success in perhaps three weeks. A convivial mix of your actors and some of our local society, including Mr. Weston's colleagues on the City Council, would make for a most enjoyable evening, and, dare I say, increase the visibility of RidgeW Pictures in the Chicago business community. Please do say yes to my little reception, Matthew, and allow me to send formal invitations. I would so enjoy seeing you again.*
>
> *Yours, Most Affectionately, Emeline Graham*

Emeline might have written the words, but the reception had Arabella's stamp. He'd intended to refuse a dinner invitation, but she'd found a way to hook him into a commitment he'd be a fool to decline. He closed his mind to thoughts of what she had to do to persuade Weston to allow it.

This reception might have a more interesting mix of people than Emeline or Arabella could imagine. He rubbed the back of his neck while he calculated the potential for social disaster. Lukas was not entirely unknown around town. Weston and many of the men at Arabella's reception would know his name. No doubt some of them had patronized Madame Yvonne's establishment. How long would it take for someone to tell Arabella who Lukas was and what he did? Lukas would cause a stir just by his presence. What mattered was the kind of stir he caused—impossible to tell beforehand.

Before going to the set for the final scene in *Wyoming Kid*, he stopped in his cluttered office and rang Lukas. "It's exactly the kind of affair you wanted," he ended after stating the details.

A low chuckle on the other end. "Theodore Weston?"

"The invitation is from his mother-in-law who lives with the Westons."

"But it's his house, so he'll be there," Lukas said. "I might have a talk with him about loosening up on the film supply in this town or . . . other things."

"Too much business talk is frowned on at these events," Matt warned. "Lukas, anything out of line will give RidgeW Pictures a bad image."

"Don't worry." Another chuckle. "By the way, Matt, after I read Lucinda Corday's column, I went ahead and made another deposit in the company account. We don't want to skimp on production now, especially since we'll be mingling with the big shots in town." Lukas rang off without saying goodbye.

Matt slowly hooked the receiver back in place. In spite of his misgivings about bringing Lukas to the reception, a rush of energy went through him. Amazing how powerful a man could feel with money in the bank. Reaching the open yard behind the building where the western shootout was about to take place, he beckoned to Fred. "I've got the money for Chester Slater. Set up a meeting so I can talk to him."

Fred nodded. "He's staying at the LaSalle Hotel. I'll find him."

"I want to talk to the girls for a minute. Send them over here."

Rae came from behind the horse trough where she was supposed to be hiding during the shootout, stepped over the edge markers, and joined Lily. Ida had braided Rae's hair and dressed her in baggy overalls, making her look younger than usual. Lily was the ideal movie heroine in a soft pink dress with a full skirt and ruffles on the sleeves. Her light hair was tied loosely behind her head, long pink ribbons trailing down her back.

Matt fixed his attention on Lily for a minute. She'd be stunning in color. Some studios spent money to have certain scenes hand tinted, but that cost would eat into his budget, and he needed Chester Slater more than he needed a pink dress in his western. The sisters smiled at him, caution flickering in their eyes. Actors always looked like that—hopeful but afraid at the same time.

"You've both done a good job here, and you're doing more than background stuff," he said. "I want to stop paying a day at a time and put you on weekly contracts—let's say twenty-five dollars a week even if you don't work every day." He probably could have paid twenty, but paying Rae less than he should for stunts pricked at his conscience, and the money from Lukas gave him the sensation of being flush.

Lily gasped and Rae's mouth opened into a small O.

"Oh yes, we accept," Lily said at once. "Thank you, Matt."

"A weekly contract," Rae repeated. "That's the same as if we were real movie stars, like Mary Pickford or Blanche Sweet."

He laughed. "Those two are paid a lot more than twenty-five a week, but you're on the way. Now let's get this scene finished." He snapped his fingers. "Oh, I forgot. Rae, you'll need to cut your hair short next week."

11

Cut her hair?

Rae clutched her braids as if Matt were coming at her with a pair of scissors, but she couldn't ask questions now. The set for *Wyoming Kid* stretched along the outside wall behind the studio—a dirt street with a hitching post and fake doorways. Playing the blacksmith's daughter, she crouched behind a water trough while Gil and the villain, a nice fellow named Bert, faced each other for the shootout. Lily, the banker's daughter, waited inside the painted wooden flat representing the bank.

"Ready, let's get this while the light's good. Camera! Action," Matt called. "Gil, take a step forward and offer to go into the saloon. Bert, you shake your head and step back. Put your hand on your gun. Gil, you realize he's determined to fight."

Rae tried to concentrate on the action, but Matt's casual announcement about cutting her hair was a shock.

The baggy overalls Ida put her in concealed her figure, but her long curls kept her looking young enough for the parts Matt gave her. He'd told her over and over she was exactly the age he needed. He might fire her if he knew the truth. Lies were tangles, and she was caught in this tangle for sure.

"Keep staring at each other," Matt called to the two men. "On the count of three, both of you draw. Gil, make sure you point the gun directly at Bert. Bert, struggle to get your gun out of your holster and point it to your right. You're going to hit his arm. One, two, three—draw!"

A crew member sent puffs of smoke into the air when the two cowboys shot at each other. Bert clutched his chest, spun around, and flopped on the dirt, arms spread wide. Gil dropped his gun, grabbed his arm, and grimaced as if he were in terrible pain.

"Gil, you're wounded, lean against the hitching post. Lily, step outside the bank, look at Bert, scream, and drop your package."

Lily managed to look terrified and beautiful at the same time. When she dropped her package on the wooden platform outside the bank doors, she screamed, put one hand to her throat, and sank back against the door.

"Rae, grab the bucket and run over to Bert. Stop and look at him. He's dead. Go to Gil, pick up the wet towel in the bucket, and press it against his wound. Gil, sigh with relief and give Rae a little kiss to thank her."

Not again!

Rae's skin turned icy as she flashed back to the horrible moment when Roy Emmitt's big, ugly, beer-flavored tongue pushed into her mouth. The other girls had laughed and said she'd get used to it, but no one could get used to something that disgusting. She opened her mouth to tell Matt she couldn't endure another kiss, but closed it. She was a real movie actress now with a weekly contract. Serious actors probably always did what the director wanted. Having her back to the camera for this scene was an advantage because she couldn't keep the horror out of her eyes when she looked up at Gil.

He winked at her. Bending closer, he slid his free hand around her waist while she scrunched her eyes shut, so she wouldn't see his tongue coming at her. Then he brushed the lightest kiss over her lips, like feathers touching her mouth. She barely felt it, but the oddest shivery feeling went through her body. Her eyes snapped open, and Gil winked at her again.

"All right, Gil, straighten up and walk a little unevenly over to Lily—remember you're wounded. Lily, step away from the door and run to him. Take his hand. Cut. Hold there. George needs to move the camera."

George shuffled the camera, pushing it close to Lily and Gil and adjusting the lights while Ida fluffed the ruffles on Lily's sleeves and smoothed her skirt.

"Ready again. Lily, lean on Gil's shoulder and smile at him. Gil, smile at her and rest your head on the top of her head. Hold it. Great! Cut!"

Rae waited for Lily to finish, her head buzzing with the odd sensation caused by Gil's kiss. When Roy jammed his tongue into her mouth, she'd wanted to throw up, but Gil's lips had been warm and pleasant.

Matt beckoned to Rae and Gil. "I've got a great story for a serial—ten chapters—Gil joins Theodore Roosevelt's Rough Riders in 1898. Rae's his sister and wants to go with him, so she cuts her hair, puts on boy's clothes and follows Gil. You'll both go through the fight with the Spanish in Cuba while Rae is always in danger of being found out. After the Battle of San Juan Hill, Gil will get malaria, and Rae will nurse him. Plenty of action. It's what audiences want these days." He took a closer look at Rae's face and made a clumsy attempt to pat her shoulder. "Sorry, about your hair. We'll have a big scene of you cutting it off when you decide to follow Gil to war. It'll be a giant moment in the story. Audiences will love it. Do you think you could cry for the camera?"

He looked so excited, she wanted to please him. "Sure I can cry."

Gil grinned at her. "We'll have a good time, Rae."

In the costume room, Ida shook out Lily's pink dress and hung it on a rack. "Did Matt give you both contracts?"

"Yes, he did," Rae answered. "Lily's going to be in Billy Tucker's movie next week, and I'm going to be in a serial with Gil."

"I'm glad to see Matt has some sense." Ida pulled Rae's braids apart and fluffed her curls back into shape.

On the way home, Lily took Rae's arm. "Let's find a new place to live. If we're each making twenty-five dollars a week, we can get a nicer apartment."

"Matt could fire us any time," Rae said. "He fired Roy Emmitt fast enough."

"He's not going to fire you. You're his favorite. He puts you in every kid part he has, and the serial will be good for ten weeks."

Rae grinned. "You're right. Mrs. Polsky's rat trap is no place for two movie stars."

Lily went a little crazy in the next weeks. She informed Mrs. Polsky they were leaving her crumbling excuse for an apartment and tossed in a lot of complaints about garbage in the halls and broken windows. Then she poured over the notices for rentals, visited apartments, and interviewed landladies. To those who didn't want *movie girls*, Lily snapped back that their rooms didn't meet her standards anyway. She finally settled on a first-floor apartment in a new building conveniently near the studio. Rae had to admit the new place was pretty grand. There were three bedrooms, a sunny front parlor, a big bathroom with a clawfoot tub, and a small back room for whatever they wanted. The kitchen was freshly painted bright yellow with shiny, yellow-and-black-checked linoleum. It also had a brand new Glenwood cook stove and a two-door ice box set against a little door in the wall that opened onto the side porch, so the iceman could slide the ice block in every day—best of all, the ice came with the rent.

After they moved in and unpacked what little they had, Lily went shopping and came home with three new dresses, a hat, two pairs of gloves, and three pairs of shoes.

Watching her open packages sent a nervous shiver through Rae. "Twenty-five dollars a week is more than we've had before, but we can't spend it all. We need to save some in case this movie stuff doesn't last."

Lily twirled around the room holding a powder blue dress with white lace cuffs and collar against her shoulders. "I had to have this dress. Blue looks so good on me. Anyway, we're going to keep making more money. I just know it. I'm going to have a mansion someday and live in the most exclusive neighborhood." She stopped spinning, her blue eyes dark with intensity. "Of course, you'll be with me. My husband will be happy to have you with us."

"What husband?"

"The husband I'm going to meet once I'm famous enough. Eve told me lots of men are eager to meet actresses—rich men."

"Are they eager to marry actresses?"

"Don't be a spoilsport. I've got a happy feeling about what's coming for us."

12

The day the first episode of *Danger for Dora* started filming, Rae's insides twisted into a knot. She'd promised Matt she'd cut her hair for the serial, but she didn't want to. The closer the moment came, the more she wanted to run back to being the girl with long curls who knew how to pick pockets. Doing stunts in front of the camera was one thing, but cutting her hair would make her a different person.

Ida put her in a gingham dress with a wide ruffled collar. "This dress is loose enough to keep your figure out of sight," Ida remarked as she pulled the dress over Rae's head.

"Please don't tell Matt."

"I'm not saying anything to anyone. Matt needs someone he can rely on, and you're it." Ida fluffed Rae's curls around her shoulders. "Go on now."

The set looked like a young girl's bedroom—ruffled pillow cases and dolls on the bed. A mirror hung on the opposite wall above a low vanity table. A large pair of shiny scissors rested on the top. Matt had decided to use two cameras, so one would show Rae as she came into the room, and the other would follow her actions in the mirror.

The day was sunny, and the sunlight streaming through a skylight above the set created a faint haze in the air. "The sun will put a halo on your hair when you're at the table," Matt said. "You'll look like an angelic little girl sacrificing her hair so she can follow her brother into battle."

She couldn't suppress a shudder when she looked at the scissors. The metal blades gleamed in the light.

Matt touched her shoulder. "I know cutting your hair is hard, and we have only one shot at getting it right. I thought about using a wig, but it wouldn't look real on the screen, and you'll be in ten episodes with short hair. I guarantee this scene will make you a heroine to everyone in the audience, and if this serial is as popular as I think it will be, we'll have more *Danger for Dora* stories, and the long hair won't be right for those stories either."

"I can do it."

Matt stepped back. "Stand outside the door. When I tell you, open the door, close it, walk over to the vanity, sit down, and pick up the scissors. Whatever you do after that is up to you. I trust you to know how to make it all look natural—show the audience how a girl would feel about cutting her hair."

She stood in the dark space behind the door to the bedroom waiting for Matt's signal while her heart pounded. George said something. Matt answered him, but she couldn't distinguish the words. Not that she cared what they said. She focused on those shiny scissors and what she had to do with them. Voices died out, feet shuffled and then stopped. Finally, Matt called to her.

She opened the door, glanced around the room, and walked to the vanity. Although Matt had told her to pick up the scissors next, she didn't. Instead, she sat and gathered a handful of long curls in each hand. Staring in the mirror, she pressed the curls against her cheeks, and without any effort, tears streaked down her cheeks. Her breath sounded ragged in her chest.

Lifting the scissors, she stretched a handful of curls nearly straight and quickly slashed through the hair. It was done. Panting, dragging in air, she cut off the rest of her curls until all she had left were uneven wavy strands. The scissors dropped out of her hand, skidded across the vanity, and fell to the floor. The girl in the mirror was a stranger. Clutching one long severed curl, she put her head down and cried.

Matt called *cut*, but Rae stayed at the vanity, crying, until Matt patted her and muttered how sorry he was but also how good the scene had turned out. "You're the best, Rae," he said in her ear. "You did everything right."

"Good job, Rae," George called.

Lily and Ida pushed Matt out of the way and threw their arms around Rae. "I'm so proud of you," Lily whispered. "You had me crying in sympathy. We'll trim these strands, and you'll look adorable with short curls."

Not much chance of that.

13

Chicago Dispatch, **September 22, 1914**

Out and About with Lucinda Corday

As I reported earlier, RidgeW Pictures is on the move to become another giant of the movie industry. Last week, noted stage actor Chester Slater signed an exclusive contract with RidgeW. Mr. Slater, who appeared in *Hamlet* on the London stage last year, will be acting in dramatic roles. His first movie for RidgeW is *Pathway to Sin*, the story of a husband's deception.

Equally exciting is an exclusive reception Mrs. Horace Graham is giving this Saturday for Matthew Ridgewood to celebrate his success with RidgeW. Mrs. Graham was a close friend of Mr. Ridgewood's late mother, and she is now the mother-in-law of Theodore Weston, prominent businessman and member of the City Council. Mrs. Graham's daughter Arabella Weston and Mr. Ridgewood were childhood companions, and they remain close friends. The reception will be at the Weston mansion, which Chicago architecture aficionados know combines gothic and medieval design. Guests will include the RidgeW actors, members of the City Council, and leaders of Chicago's business and social circles.

Readers, you will not miss one detail about this lavish event because yours truly is also on the guest list, and I promise to report absolutely all news of any interest.

Until next time, dear readers.

14

Three days before the reception, Lily opened the kitchen cabinet and took out her mother's milk glass bowl. She circled the rim with one finger, assessing the bills and coins Rae put in the bowl every week after they paid rent and other expenses. The bowl was the only keepsake her mother left behind when she ran off with *the damn limey* as Pa always referred to him. She'd never blamed her mother for abandoning them. Having a husband like Pa would be a horror, although Rae never held him responsible, as she did, for driving away their mother and keeping them on the ragged end of poverty.

She counted the money in the bowl daily, not that the amount changed much, but she liked to run the bills and coins through her fingers. She and Rae were finally on the path to better things. Scooping the money out of the bowl, she jumped nervously when Rae entered the kitchen.

"What are you doing?"

"I'm going to Marshall Field and get proper clothes for us. If we're going to a reception at a mansion full of rich, important people, we have to look as though we belong there." Lily put the money in her handbag and slung the bag over her arm. "I'm not going to wear an out-of-date dress to the Weston mansion. Society people always have music at their parties, and a rich gentleman might ask me to dance. This could be the time when I meet my future husband." She closed the front door behind her with a decided thump.

Four hours later, she came back, swinging shopping bags from both hands. "Look!" She ripped open a package and shook out a swirl of an aqua silk crepe dress with an ivory silk and lace bodice and matching lace on the three-quarter sleeves. "And shoes!" Holding up a pair of black patent shoes with Cuban heels and silver buckles, she giggled. "And these!" A pair of black stockings with embroidery up the sides fluttered in the air.

"Fancy," Rae agreed. "The color nearly matches your eyes. You'll look beautiful. Any rich gentleman would be lucky to have you."

Lily held the dress against her and studied her reflection in the bedroom mirror. "Let's hope so. This movie business might not last." She turned quickly. "Maybe it will for you. Matt says you have a knack for acting. He never says that to me. I just smile and faint into the hero's arms. We both have to think about the future. I'm not going to make Delia's mistake and fall for a handsome fellow just because he makes my skin tingle." She carefully arranged the dress over the tissue paper on the bed.

"Did you spend all the money?"

"Yes, but don't worry, I didn't forget you." Tearing into another package, Lily shook out a light green chiffon dress with a round lace collar, a huge bow at the waist, and a matching lace overskirt. "Do you like it?"

"It's pretty," Rae said, taking the dress and holding it up to her shoulders. "It looks a little young."

"You told everyone you're thirteen. How old do you want to look?" A half-smile curved Lily's lips. "Are you sweet on someone? Tell the truth."

"No." Rae avoided Lily's gaze and stared at her image in the mirror. "This dress is perfect for me. I wish Matt hadn't made me cut my hair—it's so short and awful."

"I told you—short hair is going to be the fashion." Lily searched in one of the bags and held up a ribbon. "I got ribbons for our hair. I'll pin yours in for you." She hugged Rae. "Don't frown. The reception will be fun. When we get to the Westons, we'll go through a receiving line, and all you have to do is smile and say you're pleased to meet them." She held the ribbon up to her hair and twirled in front of the mirror to see all possible angles. "Who knows what might happen on Saturday?"

15

Rae pulled at the collar on her dress as they rode in the taxi Matt had sent for them.

"Is it too tight?" Lily asked.

"I feel trapped in it."

"Don't be ridiculous. You look like a sweet young lady." Lily peered out the window of the taxi as it slowed to a stop outside the Weston mansion. "Billy and Eve are ahead of us. Let's catch them."

Billy made a joke about the medieval tower looming on one side of the house as they climbed the front steps, sending Rae into giggles. The Weston vestibule was a small, round space opening on a corridor leading to the reception room where Matt and two women stood greeting guests. Rae fell a step behind the others, gazing at what Lily had promised would be sophisticated and elegant decoration. The hallway walls were covered in paintings of Greek gods, and a statue of a boy with wings stood on a tall white marble pedestal next to the inner door. The floor was black marble with swirling white threads. She decided it looked like the entrance to a bank.

Matt smiled at her. "Mrs. Graham, I want to introduce my rising star, Raeanne Kelly. Rae, this is Mrs. Horace Graham, your hostess."

Emeline Graham's dark hair was threaded with silver, and her short, round figure was wrapped in a peach satin gown with a line of black embroidered roses across her bosom. She smiled, spidery lines crinkling at her eyes. "My daughter took me to see *Danger for Dora,* and I can barely contain my impatience to see the next episode. You know, a dear friend of mine was one of President Roosevelt's officers when the Rough Riders went to Cuba, so I have a special interest in your adventures."

Rae shook hands. "I'm very pleased to meet you, Mrs. Graham. I'm glad you like our serial."

Matt shifted to the woman on the other side of him. "Mrs. Theodore Weston—"

Arabella held out her hand without waiting for him to finish. "So lovely to meet you, Raeanne. Matt's very proud of you. I'm sorry my husband isn't here to greet our guests. I suspect he's been detained by business."

Her voice was pleasant, cool, and uninterested. Her gaze drifted away from Rae and turned to the next guests, while her hand rested lightly on Matt's arm, keeping him so close her skirts brushed his pants leg. Her dark hair, looped at the back of her head, held a feathered comb firmly tucked into one side. The black and cream striped silk gown had rose-colored ribbons that tied under her bosom, shaping her figure.

Rae smoothed her skirt as she waited for Lily to join her. Arabella Weston's dress was much more expensive than the dresses Lily bought for them, and the three red stones in her silver necklace must be rubies. Lily had been right when she said they were in a new world. Now they hovered somewhere between the bottom of Chicago society where they'd always lived and the upper layer they were allowed to visit. Wherever they were, it was better than the life they'd had.

The Weston reception hall was lined on one side with tables holding platters filled with cakes, chicken and ham salads, tiny rolls, strawberry and orange gelatin molds, fruit, and dozens of champagne glasses. Musicians in one corner created a soft musical background for the rising voices as guests filled the room. Billy motioned to a servant who immediately poured champagne into glasses. "Take advantage," he said, handing a glass to Rae. "It's all free tonight." He drained his own glass and gestured for a refill immediately.

She'd never had more than a taste of Pa's beer. Champagne was the drink sophisticated people enjoyed. Tentatively, she took a sip. The fizzy taste was pleasing, and she tipped the glass for a longer swallow.

Lily pinched her. "Remember, you're only thirteen— no more than one glass."

The musicians played a flourish, and Mrs. Graham clapped her hands for attention. "Friends, I am so happy we can gather tonight to recognize Matthew's success. As many of you know, his late mother was my dear friend. She would be so pleased at this moment." Acknowledging a polite round of applause, she pointed to the frosted glass doors at the far end of the room. "Please do visit the conservatory and enjoy my collection of orchids. My generous son-in-law has graciously indulged my hobby. Several exotic species arrived this week from South America."

Another round of applause. Two couples headed for the conservatory at once. The musicians resumed playing, and several couples began dancing. Billy whirled Eve around until an elderly gentleman interrupted them with a bow. Eve tossed her head with a flirty laugh and before long a series of older men took turns steering her around the dance floor. Lily accepted an invitation to dance from a gray-haired gentleman while Rae waited uncertainly at the edge of the dance floor.

Gil tapped her on the shoulder. "Sorry, I didn't see you sooner. You look different tonight, all dressed up with a ribbon in your hair."

"You look different too." A blush crawled up her throat, and that odd shivery feeling went through her again.

She'd only seen him in western outfits, dusty with fake bloodstains on them. He wasn't dressed in a tuxedo like the society gentlemen in the room, but his navy blue suit looked smart, and his grin said he was glad to see her. She searched desperately for something to say, but fortunately, Gil didn't notice her silence because he rattled on about what a spectacular house it was and how meeting these business people might help Matt get his movies into the theaters as fast as the other studios did. Whenever he paused for breath, Rae murmured agreement, but she couldn't concentrate on what he said because of the way thick eyelashes framed his brown eyes and dimples cut into his cheeks when he smiled.

Lily interrupted them, her hand on the arm of a young man. "Rae, this is Edmund Gordon Carleton III."

He laughed. "Call me Eddie. Say, I saw that adventure you're in. It's a good one. Making movies must be a lot of fun. My father says movies are a fad for the working classes, but I think they're swell." He looked at Gil. "You're the western fellow. I've seen most of those movies too. See one or two almost every week." Lily brushed her fingers lightly over his sleeve, and he slipped his hand over hers pressing it against his arm. He radiated friendly, easy confidence. "I like the gunfights, but watching Lily is the main attraction. I couldn't believe my luck that she came tonight." He directed a wide grin at Lily, who fluttered her lashes as if embarrassed. Rae recognized that flutter. Eddie was close to being caught.

"Eddie is in the hotel business," Lily said, with a significant glance at Rae.

Eddie shrugged. "It's my father's business. Nothing exciting like making movies. I'll run it all someday—the hotels and the printing companies—when he retires. For now, I'm just an employee."

Billy had taken over the piano, banging out a ragtime tune, raising the noise level in the room. Next to the piano, a girl in a pink taffeta dress bounced in time to the music.

"That's Marigold Gregory," Lily said to Rae in a low voice. "She went to London for the season last year and an earl became quite attached to her, but her parents put a stop to any talk of marriage because Mrs. Gregory couldn't bear to part with Marigold."

Billy's vigorous playing encouraged the musicians to join him, and ragtime replaced the softer music. Stepping away from the piano, he grabbed Marigold. Arms flying and legs kicking, they danced around the floor.

"Say, it's the Turkey Trot," Eddie said. He took Lily's hand. "Come on. Let's dance."

Gil reached for Rae, but she resisted. "I don't know how."

"Turkey Trot is easy," Gil said, drawing her to the dance floor. "Not like a waltz."

He was right. She eyed the other couples, and no matter how she kicked and shook her arms, her movements seemed to match Gil's well enough.

"I wish I had a little sister like you," he said as they kicked.

She kept a smile frozen on her face, so he wouldn't see disappointment crashing through her. The humiliation would be unbearable if he guessed how often she remembered his lips against hers.

When the music changed, Billy and Marigold shifted to what Gil called the Grizzly Bear. Arms in the air waving like claws reaching for a prey, they danced closer, rubbing together.

Gil shrugged. "Let's get something to eat."

They piled sandwiches and sweets on plates and sat at one of the little round tables along one wall. Gil's remark had blasted away Rae's romantic notions, so she relaxed as they laughed and sampled as many cakes and tiny sandwiches they could stack on their plates.

Three men at the next table lingered over coffee and liquor. "The morning paper said the Germans are digging trenches," one remarked.

"The British and French are doing the same," said another. "If both sides dig in, this war could last for a long stretch."

"Don't think we'll get in it," the third man commented. "Nothing to do with us. There's a big ocean keeping that conflict in Europe."

Gil frowned. "I've been thinking I should sign up. My family's in Ottawa, and my brother wrote to me that he's joining the army."

A chill shot through her. "Why should you go? The war has nothing to do with us."

"I'm Canadian, and Canada will be in it with the British before very long. That's probably enough reason to go now."

"But the war is so far away." Rae searched for a better argument, but a low murmur of conversation swept through the room and heads turned toward the entrance.

Lukas stood at the open doors talking to Matt. He'd visited the most expensive men's clothier in the Loop, determined to have the same quality suit other men would wear for an evening at the Weston mansion. He'd succeeded with the clothing, but the comfortable look of ease and luxury the rich always carried had escaped him. The older men's soft bellies under the fine cloth revealed indulgences their comfortable lives allowed. The younger men were casually self-assured. Lukas was hard, all muscle, and intensity radiated off him while he surveyed the crowd.

Matt introduced him to a few businessmen—none of whom showed interest in prolonged conversation. Then Arabella Weston interrupted, pulling Matt aside, and leaving Lukas alone in the crowd. He took a glass of champagne from a servant and wandered across the room, pretending he had a destination. Standing close to some tables and watching the dancers, he kept his face expressionless although some low whispers reached him.

"I can't imagine why Emeline Graham or Arabella Weston would invite his sort."

"I doubt the ladies know who he is, but surely Matt Ridgewood knows better."

"I admit I've visited Madame Yvonne's a time or two, but I never expected to drink with the owner."

Lukas fought the urge to retreat. He would not give up his first attempt to reach a higher level in Chicago society. Pretending to focus on the swirling dancers, he didn't instantly sense the women at his elbow.

"Mr. Krantz." Emeline Graham was accompanied by a middle-aged woman swathed in puce satin, diamonds sparkling at her throat, on her ears, and on her fingers. "I promised Mrs. Gregory I would introduce you. She's a dear friend of mine and so dedicated to the community. Perhaps you know she's the founder of the Chicago Home for Wayward Girls."

Lukas's muscles relaxed. He turned a flashing smile on Mrs. Gregory, and when she extended her hand, he bent slightly over it for an instant as if he had to resist a longing to press his lips on her plump fingers. "I'm delighted to meet you, Mrs. Gregory. I've heard amazing reports of your project on behalf of these tragic young women." Thank god, none of those girls had ever worked at Madame Yvonne's. He'd been careful about ages, and most of the girls had come with Madame from St. Louis. Emeline smiled, murmured something about the other guests, and left them.

Mrs. Gregory moved closer and looked up at him, intense purpose in her gaze. "I am dedicated to saving these poor creatures from a catastrophic fate. Many are innocent farm girls coming to the city to work, and they are tricked—kidnapped—into a life of degeneracy. Once they fall into sin, they lose all natural sense of morality, and their actions inevitably prevent them from ever entering a decent marriage or respectable employment."

"Shocking circumstances," he murmured while she rattled on about honest work, religious training, and expenses. When he heard her mention *expenses,* he understood why she pressed her fingers against his sleeve to hold his attention. "Mrs. Gregory," he cut in smoothly over her description of sewing instructions, "I feel compelled to support your noble venture. Please tell me what I can do."

She made a helpless gesture. "So generous of you, Mr. Krantz. I'd never thought to ask."

He'd bet good money she'd solicit funds from Genghis Kahn without a second thought. "Perhaps, if you'll allow it," he said, "I might contribute to your cause. Would three hundred dollars be of any help?"

She sucked in her breath and visibly relaxed, her fingers slipping from his coat sleeve. "I can't begin to tell you, Mr. Krantz, how useful such a donation would be. These girls are completely without personal funds, depending entirely on—"

"One of my . . . assistants will deliver the money on Monday," he said.

She poured out her passionate gratitude and kept him captive for another few minutes. When she finally hurried away, he wondered how much money his climb to respectability was going to cost him.

Glancing around, he relaxed when he saw Rae in the crowd. She waved and headed his way. "Did your pa come back?" he asked when she reached him.

"No, he's gone for sure."

"He'll be back. When he shows up, you tell me." His smile softened the command.

"I promise I'll tell you, but Pa isn't likely to come back if he owes you a lot of money." Rae grinned up at him. "Thanks for sending me to Matt. You helped me out when I needed it. I've got a weekly contract now. Have you seen me in the Dora serial?"

He shook his head. "I don't see the movies, but Matt told me you're doing a good job and making money for the studio—and that means you're making money for me."

"Matt hired my sister Lily too. I want you to meet her. Wait here."

Lukas watched Rae join a group gathered at the piano and seize the arm of a young blonde woman. Rae gestured toward Lukas, but the blonde was reluctant and shook off Rae's hand. They had some kind of argument with the sister clearly resisting efforts to drag her across the room. Lukas studied the champagne left in his glass. The last thing he needed at this damn reception was a fight between sisters over whether to talk to the gangster in the room. When he looked again, Rae, a smile of triumph on her face, was steering her sister toward him.

After introductions, Rae chattered about working at RidgeW, and Lily murmured a few polite comments indicating gratitude for helping Rae. His mind didn't register their words. *Dazzling,* Matt had said. Matt was an idiot. Lily was beyond dazzling—long, dark lashes flicking against white cheeks and framing dark blue almost violet eyes, velvety pink lips ideal for kissing, golden hair swept away from her face. Her looks, her voice, everything about her was soft, tempting, and yielding—waiting for him.

He mumbled something, not sure what came out of his mouth. He'd always prided himself on logical thinking, but after the sisters said a final thank you and left him, only wild, unreasonable ploys to capture Lily for himself spun in his mind. Deaf to the music and laughter in the room, he looked around until he spotted her laughing up at Eddie Carleton as they whirled on the dance floor. Wavy tendrils of her hair had escaped her hair ribbon, so she looked like a painting he'd seen in the Art Institute. He couldn't remember the name of the painting or the painter. Irrational jealousy gripped him. He'd known Eddie for years—a nice enough fellow—but not for Lily. Watching them, Lukas clenched his jaw so hard it ached. He put his champagne glass on a tray offered by a servant and strode toward the table where stronger liquor was available.

16

Lucinda Corday surveyed the room from an inconspicuous spot near some potted ferns. The Westons would never ordinarily invite a newspaper columnist to their home. Matt had pressured Emeline Graham to put Lucinda on the guest list to ensure good publicity for the studio in her next column. She understood and intended to do her part. She also intended to convince Matt to buy some of her screenplays. Tit for tat. Still, she couldn't gush about RidgeW in her column without adding something spicy about the guests to entice her readers and keep her editor happy.

Her roving glance fixed on Billy Tucker and Marigold Gregory. They stood near the terrace doors, heads together, obviously well provided with champagne. Billy bent over Marigold, his lips touching her ear, while she giggled at whatever he whispered to her. Those two would bear watching.

Lucinda seized a second glass of champagne from a passing waiter and made a note to chat with cute Rae Kelly talking to Gil Owen. Young people often babbled indiscreetly without knowing it. Watching the guests, she saw Eve Darling apparently asking Matt to dance with her, but Matt pointed to the conservatory where Arabella Weston waited at the frosted glass doors. Guests at Emeline's receptions were expected to admire her orchids, and Matt, the guest of honor tonight, certainly had to visit the conservatory, but Eve glared at him and stalked away. Another bit of drama Lucinda needed to keep track of.

For several minutes she roamed, sampling food, and collecting what gossip she could. Her brief chat with Rae and Gil produced only wild praise of Matt and excitement about the serial they were making. She could get a charming quote out of their remarks but certainly not a full column.

She raised her champagne glass to her lips but stopped before taking a sip. Theodore Weston entered the reception room, scandalously late for an event held in his house. And he was drunk. A casual observer might not notice, but Lucinda's long departed husband had been a drunk, and she recognized the signs. He walked a little too stiffly and held his head a little too carefully. A rosy flush colored his nose and cheeks. She wasn't close enough to see his eyes, but they'd be streaked with red. As she watched, Weston approached Emeline, who glanced nervously at nearby guests. Weston, scowling, was obviously questioning Emeline, who shook her head, perhaps pleading ignorance. Lucinda shifted her gaze to the frosted conservatory doors and then back to Weston. A rustle of satin at her side caught her attention.

"I don't know where she is. I'll have to search for her." Mrs. Gregory's voice had begun as a whisper but ended in a shrill cry. Her husband muttered something and walked away.

"Excuse me." Lucinda put her glass on a tray and moved closer. "Could I be of any assistance, Mrs. Gregory? Are you looking for your daughter?" She remembered Billy Tucker whispering in Marigold's ear. Please let there be a bit of shocking disgrace tonight!

A fluttery laugh came from Mrs. Gregory as she twisted the diamond bracelet on her arm. "Yes, I need to find Marigold. I can't imagine where she's gone, and my husband is ready to leave."

Lucinda mustered a comforting smile—the one she used to persuade unsuspecting society matrons to confide their deepest secrets. "I believe I saw her near the terrace. Perhaps she's gone out for a breath of air. The evening is very warm for September. I'll go with you. Two sets of eyes will find her more quickly."

The terrace jutted into the gardens, lit only by the glow coming through the diamond-shaped glass panes in the terrace doors. Huge potted bushes inside the low stone wall surrounding the terrace created odd shadows. Lucinda peered into the darkness. Her sharp ears caught a faint sound, and she turned toward the shrubbery blocking the garden view.

"I thought I heard," she began, but Mrs. Gregory pushed past her, thrusting her way through the bushes.

Marigold sat on the terrace wall clutching Billy's shoulders. Her pink taffeta bodice was unbuttoned, and Billy's hand moved under the taffeta while he pressed kisses along her throat. Marigold gasped into the night air.

Mrs. Gregory screamed, an agonized shriek, loud enough to be heard behind the closed terrace doors. The music inside faltered for an instant and then resumed. Billy and Marigold straightened, still clinging to each other, confusion on their faces. Marigold looked dazed, but when she saw her mother, her eyes cleared. She snatched at her bodice, pulled it together, and fumbled with the buttons. Billy stepped back, a drunken smirk on his lips.

Lucinda touched Mrs. Gregory's arm. "A scene here simply won't do," she said in a low voice. Thrilled with the situation she'd fallen into, she was already writing the story in her head. Could she possibly name names?

Mrs. Gregory pulled free of Lucinda and jerked Marigold off her perch. An awkward struggle began between mother and daughter as they both fought to loop thin pink taffeta bands around pearl buttons on Marigold's bodice. Billy started to speak, and Mrs. Gregory screamed again. "Get away, you animal." He swayed on his feet before lurching sideways to lean on the terrace wall.

The second scream brought shadowy figures to the terrace doors. Lucinda placed her hand on Mrs. Gregory's arm again. "I'll find Mr. Ridgewood. He'll take care of this situation. Pretend you've only stumbled, and take Marigold out the front door."

The terrace doors opened. Eddie Carleton peered into the darkness. "Is everything all right out there?"

Lucinda rushed up the three steps to the doors and forced him back into the room. "Just a stumble into one of the bushes," she said. "A scratch, that's all."

She waited just long enough to see him nod before she started across the floor toward the conservatory. To her right, Weston intently questioned a servant. The servant gestured, and Weston swung his head to look at the conservatory doors. He had to walk carefully upright, giving Lucinda the opportunity to speed ahead of him.

17

The conservatory air was heavy with scent. Tall palms flanked the narrow path through the orchid displays, the large palm leaves drooping into the pathway, masking the view ahead. The heady fragrance from the orchids combined with the steam heat created a jungle atmosphere, the humidity putting a light sheen of moisture over exposed skin. The early visitors had left, and at the back of the conservatory, Arabella abandoned her standard hostess commentary about the orchids and moved close to Matt, her perfume surrounding him so he could no longer distinguish the other aromas.

"Do you remember," she whispered, "my mother's garden and the gazebo the night before you left for Harvard?"

He remembered. The warm August night seven years ago. Sighs and kisses. Arabella's dark eyes closing, lips parting, reaching for him as she sank back on the bench.

Breathless promises and reckless embraces amid the flowers, the darkness, and the moonlight through the lattice roof of the gazebo creating silver patches around them. Two months later—the bank panic—both fathers dead—Harvard ended—all promises erased.

She was so close he felt her breath against his cheek. He clenched his fists to avoid reaching for her. "I'm sorry I was harsh when you came to the studio. It wasn't fair of me. It's no good to look back."

"I wanted to wait for you. Mother was desperate after father died. She said we had to be smart about our options, accept whatever was possible."

He shook his head. "You did what was best for you. I had nothing after the bank failed." A harsh laugh broke from him. "I still have almost nothing."

"I want . . . to help you succeed." She placed her palm lightly on his chest.

He could feel her hand burning through his suit. Knowing that she'd had to marry a man like Weston to keep her mother and herself in suitable circumstances infuriated him even after years of trying to forget. The regret in her voice echoed his own, and he touched her shoulder. "You have helped. You've done me a great favor with this reception, and I'm intensely grateful."

Without thinking he moved his hand from her shoulder to the edge of her necklace and stroked her warm, moist skin. Her breathing quickened as she swayed toward him. He should leave. Instead, he pulled her close and kissed her. The years dissolved. He was in the gazebo again with Arabella warm in his arms. He felt her tremble and sanity returned, but when he broke the kiss, she pressed against him and wrapped her arms around his neck. He held her tighter and kissed her again, drifting into a fog of memory.

The conservatory doors opened so forcefully they smacked against the walls. The noise barely penetrated Matt's consciousness, but Arabella stiffened and drew back. Footsteps pattered on the tile floor. Hands swatted at the overhanging palm leaves.

"Matt, are you in here? Billy's gotten himself in trouble." Lucinda was breathless when she reached the rear of the conservatory and found them. They stood a few feet apart as if examining different plants. Arabella's carefully arranged hair was now somewhat disordered, tendrils falling around her temples. She drew quick, uneven breaths as she looked at Lucinda.

"What's happened?" Matt asked.

"Billy has trifled with a young lady," Lucinda answered with a cautionary glance at Arabella. "He's had too much to drink. You need to handle the situation."

The doors banged again as Weston pushed them open, entering somewhat unsteadily. He slapped violently at the palm leaves in his way. Before he was halfway along the path, Lucinda intercepted him. "Mr. Weston, there's been a small incident. I believe Mrs. Gregory is extremely upset and needs attention."

He ignored her, continuing to walk in a lurching gait toward the rear of the conservatory. Arabella emerged from behind the orchid displays. Matt came a few steps behind her.

"I want to talk to you, Arabella." Weston's voice slurred.

"We must see to the guests," Arabella said. "Apparently, the Gregorys are having difficulties."

"Where's Billy?" Matt asked Lucinda.

"I left him on the terrace. Hurry." She pulled his arm.

"I must find Mother," Arabella said.

The multiple voices distracted Weston. His eye caught something colorful lying on the floor, and he bent to retrieve it, giving Arabella the chance to step past him and follow Lucinda and Matt.

In the reception hall, one of the musicians was pulling Billy away from the piano. Jarring notes from the keyboard added to the struggle. Matt caught Lukas's eye, and both men started for Billy, but before they reached him, he slid off the piano bench and stumbled toward a table filled with champagne glasses. Reaching for a glass, he pitched forward, grabbed the white tablecloth, and pulled the cloth, glasses, and champagne over him as he sank to the floor. Several women released fluttery screams when champagne splashed their dresses. Voices rose in the room.

Matt quickened his pace and while he and Lukas bent over Billy, Mrs. Gregory and Marigold came through the terrace doors into the room. Seeing the mess scattered across the floor and Billy lying senseless, Mrs. Gregory began to whimper. Half sobbing, she gripped her husband's arm and babbled her distress until most of those around her heard some of the story. Marigold, her bodice unevenly buttoned, her hair hanging free of her combs, unsightly bruises from deep kisses forming on her neck, and Billy in a stupor on the floor told them the rest.

As if obeying a signal, husbands and wives found each other, located Emeline or Arabella, and murmured excuses for leaving. Comments from the departing guests floated in the air, reaching Matt and Lukas as they pulled Billy upright.

"What do you expect from movie people?"

"Frankly, I was shocked when Emeline arranged this reception and invited actors."

"I knew Matt's parents—upstanding until that banking mess—but why he would get involved with movies is beyond me"

"I'm sorry for Arabella. Weston will be furious."

Weston stood between Arabella and Emeline as the last of the guests straggled to their autos or waiting taxis. He was closer to sober now, his fury at Arabella and the evening's social disaster rising to a pitch. He let Emeline handle the farewells while his hand closed over Arabella's wrist in a viselike grip. He felt her wince and squeezed harder.

"The evening started so successfully," Emeline murmured as she walked inside the house with them. "I'm distressed for the Gregorys. Who could have predicted such an incident?"

"Anyone with sense could have predicted movie people would not behave," Weston snapped. He had to admire Emeline's ability to maintain a façade of serenity. The vestibule positively throbbed with tension, yet she kept her smile.

"I'm simply exhausted." Emeline sighed. "You were so good to allow this small reception for an old family friend, and this movie business is so important in Chicago, isn't it?" She put her hand over her mouth to cover a small yawn. "My eyes won't stay open another minute. We'll chat in the morning, Arabella."

When Emeline's footsteps died away, Arabella struggled to pry his fingers open. "You're hurting me," she hissed.

"Not enough." His voice was a low growl. "You and your mother pressured me into allowing this reception. It's been a disaster, and we'll be blamed for that drunken actor practically ruining Marigold Gregory on our terrace." He tightened his hold on her. "Why was that gangster Lukas Krantz here? He's not an actor."

Arabella made another unsuccessful attempt to escape his grip. "There was a list of people to invite—people who were connected to RidgeW Pictures. How do you know he's a gangster?"

"Connected with the studio?" He hesitated, his mind working through the alcoholic fog still clinging to him. "Must be money. That's it. Matt couldn't get any money from a bank or respectable investors, so he must have gone to Krantz. The man runs a brothel!"

Arabella pressed her free hand to her throat and took deep breaths. "You should have invested when Matt asked you. He's going to be successful, and you could have made a good deal of money. Please, Theodore, you're hurting me."

Weston laugh cracked into a snarl, but he released her wrist. "Successful. Is that what you were hoping for? He hasn't got a chance of competing with Selig or Essanay." He leaned closer, a grim smile on his lips. "Frankly, when I agreed to this ridiculous evening, I hoped someone would make him an offer to go to California. Instead, we have a high embarrassment on our hands—and the newspapers—that columnist will attach our name to that drunken comic." His fury took possession of him as he glared at her. "I'm not an idiot, Arabella. I find you in the conservatory alone with Matt, and I haven't any doubt about your actions."

"Mother's orchids—"

"Orchids be damned." He searched in his pocket and brought out her feathered comb. "Did you lose this while you looked at orchids, or did your lover pull it out of your hair?"

She reached for the comb, but he held it away from her. "You think you can have my money and a lover. Well, you can't. I've never had any illusions about why you married me. You wanted my money after your father lost everything. At least he had the decency to die quickly. Your mother dangled you like a bon-bon in front of me. I admit I divorced poor Nellie fast enough when I knew I could have you."

"I haven't been unfaithful." Her lips trembled.

"If that's truly the case, I must commend Matt for his restraint. But I think you were willing to attempt a seduction in my own house—in your mother's conservatory—during a reception attended by some sixty people." He bent closer, the whiskey on his breath hot against her cheek. "I'm not satisfied with my bargain, Arabella. You have my money, but I've gotten shortchanged. Nellie was always willing, but you've been reluctant too much of the time. All those headaches. I expect to get compensated for your extravagances."

Arabella drew in a ragged breath. "I won't—"

He seized her arm, pulling her toward the stairway. "Yes, you will. Tonight."

18

Chicago Dispatch, **October 4, 1914**

Out and About with Lucinda Corday

The very elegant reception given last week by Mrs. Horace Graham and Mr. and Mrs. Theodore Weston to celebrate Matthew Ridgewood's success with RidgeW Pictures brought together Chicago society and the studio's lively acting ensemble. The reception also was attended by members of the Chicago political world along with business owners in a wide variety of enterprises.

The fabulous orchids in the Weston conservatory and the delightful music provided by the Music Institute Ensemble created the perfect atmosphere for romance. Edmund Carleton III appeared utterly entranced with the lovely RidgeW actress Lily Rose as he kept her on the dance floor all evening and shrugged off attempts by other gentlemen to cut in. The two have already been seen dining at the Bavarian House. Billy Tucker, the talented comedian, paid ardent attention to Miss Marigold Gregory. Alas for this budding romance, Mrs. Albert Gregory confided to me that she and her daughter plan to spend the winter in Savannah and will leave immediately for the warmer climate.

Eve Darling, leading lady in many RidgeW movies, seemed disconcerted when RidgeW's owner begged off dancing because he was intent on seeing the orchid displays in the Weston conservatory with Mrs. Weston. However, the adorable actress did not lack for dance partners as numerous gentlemen twirled her around the floor throughout the evening.

An unfortunate incident involving spilled champagne produced an earlier conclusion to the evening than expected, but the departing guests all agreed the evening was a memorable one.

My own good news is that Matthew Ridgewood has persuaded me to write several screenplays for RidgeW Pictures, and he assures me my stories will be on the movie screen as quickly as he can put them into production. We expect to have a long and mutually satisfying collaboration.

Until next time, dear readers.

19

Rae knew Matt well enough now to recognize his emotions, and his temper was at a boil on the first day filming Chester Slater's drama. Several businessmen who'd been close to investing in RidgeW had backed out after Billy's embarrassing exhibition at the reception, so Lukas remained the only source of production money, and Matt had spent most of what he had on fancy sets and costumes for *Pathway to Sin*. The set had been transformed into a lavish drawing room with plush furniture, wood paneling, and velvet drapes.

Chester didn't look like much of a prize to Rae. He was forty, big and burly, with hard lines in his face. Rae watched from the side while he paced, paused to stare at the ceiling, and then paced again. Eve sat in a chair on the side, hands curled into fists in her lap, one foot tapping on the floor.

Matt raked his hand through his hair. "Chester, the audience will know why your character is attracted to Eve—she's gorgeous. We have to shoot some scenes today. I've got the party scene scheduled in two days with thirty people and lots of action. It'll take all day or more to shoot. We have to move ahead." His voice sounded calm, but Rae saw the vein throbbing in his temple.

Lily was in the costume room when Rae came in after finishing her last scene for a Dora episode. "We did almost nothing today," Lily said as she slipped into her wool skirt and white shirtwaist. "Chester has to know the reason for everything we do. He says he has to get in the mood. He steps over the floor strips all the time and gets out of the shot—how hard is it to remember to stay inside the strips? He argues about how to enter the scene. Matt keeps saying, *It's not the stage, just come through the door.* She finished dressing and sent a pleading glance at Rae. "I can't walk home with you because Eddie's picking me up here. You don't care, do you? I told Eddie you'd be fine."

"I don't care," Rae answered.

Walking alone would be a relief. Lily, jittery with nerves, had driven her half crazy after the Weston reception wondering if Eddie would forget her, or abandon her for a society girl, or fall in love with her. When he'd come to the studio to see her again and asked her to a fancy restaurant, Lily had danced around the apartment.

Bud knocked and opened the door, holding a bouquet of red roses. He put them in Lily's arms. "There's a card."

Lily buried her nose in the flowers and inhaled slowly. "Eddie is so sweet. Two dozen roses!"

Rae plucked the card from the tangle of stems. *With great admiration, Lukas Krantz.*

Lily jerked her nose away from the roses. "That gangster," she said, holding the flowers away from her as if she'd discovered spiders among the petals. "Ida, take these and do anything you want with them." A distant horn tooted outside. "It's Eddie." Lily snatched her coat and dashed out.

Ida sniffed the roses. "Must be love," she muttered.

Rae shrugged. "It's Eddie Carleton she wants."

"Lukas isn't a man who gives up easily."

"He won't get Lily. She's good at discouraging fellows."

Walking toward the corner where Lev usually sold his papers, Rae imagined Gil going to war. The thought put an empty feeling in her chest. The late October wind was chilly, and by the time she found Lev, she was shivering.

His nose red from the cold, Lev hitched his collar tighter with one hand while he handed Rae his last paper with the other. "Saved one for you."

"Thanks, Lev." Rae checked the front page. *Canadian Troops Sail for Great Britain.*

She sucked in her breath. If she went back to the empty apartment, she'd conjure up dark images of Gil and bullets. "Let's eat, Lev. I'll pay."

Ma Fischer's Diner was warm and well lit. Lev ordered meat loaf, potatoes, and green beans, and Rae did the same. The plates came heaped with big portions and flaky biscuits with butter. Lev dug in. Rae avoided thinking about Gil and war by describing Chester Slater and the way he drove Matt crazy.

Lev wiped his mouth on his sleeve and buttered a second biscuit. "I seen your *Dora* episode yesterday. Everybody stood up and cheered when it ended."

"They cheered?" She'd be sure to tell Matt first thing in the morning.

"You're the best, Rae. That Gil fellow is good too. Don't think this Chester person sounds right."

"He's not used to working in the movies. He'll get better," she said, hoping she was right for Matt's sake.

Lev finished his meat loaf, ate Rae's biscuit, and added a slice of apple pie. When they stood to leave, he burped and patted his stomach. "Thanks, Rae. Ma didn't get much laundry work this week, and we ain't eaten as good as usual."

Rae ordered another meal of meat loaf and handed Lev the bag. "Remind your ma who I am," she said.

"She knows. She tells everybody she knew you when you were nothing."

In the apartment, Rae made tea and spread the newspaper on the kitchen table. Germans, Russians, Turks— far away but too close if Gil enlisted in the army. She let the pages drift to the floor, so Lily had to sidestep them when she came in.

"Did you have a good time?" Rae poured a cup of tea for her.

"Wonderful." Lily sighed and wrapped her hands around the cup. "Eddie's so much fun. We went to a French restaurant and had lobster and wine, and afterward he took me for a drive. He has an Oldsmobile—it's amazing, Rae. It has leather seats, carpet on the floor, and a real clock in the front." She inhaled sharply. "He has to like me, Rae!"

"Anyone could love you. Did you kiss him?"

A blush. "Yes, I did." Lily took a sip of tea. "We kissed a lot."

"Does Eddie make you quiver when he kisses you?"

"Quiver?"

"Delia always said she knew she loved Hal because she quivered all over when he kissed her."

"Delia was always earthy," Lily said with a sniff. "Eddie's nice and thoughtful, and kissing him is fun."

"But you don't quiver?"

"It's not necessary to quiver in order to like kissing." Lily put down her tea cup. "Have you been kissing someone?"

Heat rose in Rae's cheeks. "No, except when Matt tells me to for the movies."

Lily's gaze narrowed. "It's Gil, isn't it? You blush when you're around him." She shook her head. "Gil's not going to be romantic with a girl he thinks is thirteen. You need to tell him the truth. You'll be seventeen in another month."

"Matt needs me to be thirteen, so I can play all his kid parts. That's why he liked us when we showed up. You're pretty and I'm young. Matt wants to do another adventure with Dora when we finish this one."

"Ida knows you aren't thirteen. If Matt wasn't so busy, he'd have noticed by now. What happened when Gil kissed you?"

"I got a strange, shaky feeling all the way to my toes. Isn't that how you feel when Eddie kisses you?"

"No. Kissing Eddie makes me think all my dreams might come true. Shaky, quivering—sounds as if you're sick." Lily laughed. "Maybe we should call a doctor."

The front door knocker clanged, the sound rattling through the apartment. "Don't know who'd be knocking this late," Rae muttered.

Delia stood in the doorway, arms spread, a smile on her face. "Look who's here! I've come home to you. Let me in."

20

Delia pulled Rae into a bear hug. "I missed you both so much," she said. She pushed Rae away to look her over. "You cut your hair—it's so cute." Their voices buzzed at the same time. Questions from two of them and answers that weren't really answers from the other. Rae dragged Delia's suitcases inside, made another pot of tea, and opened a tin of Oreo biscuits.

"Why didn't you write and say you were coming?" Lily asked.

Delia stared into her tea cup. "I made a sudden decision. Didn't have time to write. Do you have room for me?"

"We've got an extra bedroom," Rae said, "and Lily bought furniture for it last month, so you can have a nice room."

"I left Hal," Delia announced. "I left him, and I'm not going back." Her lips trembled for an instant until she caught her bottom lip in her teeth.

Rae gaped at her. "You left him for good?"

Delia's body sagged. "You can't imagine how awful it was living on a farm! His mother never left me alone. She told me what to do every second. We had to share the house with her and Hal's two brothers. There wasn't any time to be together. Hal and I could hardly—" She glanced at Rae. "We couldn't enjoy ourselves at night. Or any time."

"I didn't think you'd like it on the farm," Lily said.

"I'm a city girl. Look at this dress!" Delia plucked at the sleeve of her blue and white striped cotton dress, faded at the hem. "It's horrible, but there's no reason to dress smart if all I'm going to do is collect eggs in the morning. The whole family went to a tractor auction today, but I said I felt sick. Then I packed, left a note, hitched a ride to Racine, and caught the next Milwaukee Road train to Chicago. Are you sure you can take me in?"

"Of course," Lily said. "We stick together, no matter what happens."

"Don't you care for Hal anymore?" Rae asked.

"I love him, but I can't stand living on a farm—especially with his mother." A tear shimmered in Delia's eye. "He can't live in the city."

Lily sighed dramatically. "It's tragic." She brightened. "You can get a job with us—at RidgeW. Rae will get you in."

"Can you, Rae?" Delia held her breath.

Rae jerked to attention. "What?"

"Delia needs a job," Lily said, "and Matt has that big party scene in Chester's movie this week. He'll hire her for the backgrounds if you ask him. He pays three dollars a day, Delia."

"I didn't take any money when I left," Delia said. "Can you fix it for me?"

"I don't know." Rae glared at Lily.

"Don't be modest," Lily said. "He doesn't care if I leave him, but you're his star in *Dora*. Matt doesn't want you to move to another studio. You can get him to hire Delia."

"I won't embarrass you." Delia had a pleading note in her voice. "Can you get me on?"

"I guess I can ask," Rae mumbled.

The day of Matt's party scene, Delia rose at the first flicker of light through the bedroom window. Nerves had taken hold of her in the middle of the night, leaving her sleepless, but she'd kept her eyes shut for hours to ward off dark circles or bags. She simply could not fail at this chance to rush into a new life. It galled her to think she had to rely on Rae, the baby, to grease her way into a job in the movies. She was the oldest, but somehow the other two had left her behind. They were making money in glamorous jobs—a realization that nagged at her. She had to catch up with them somehow. Shivering in the morning chill, she pawed through a suitcase and shook out her wine-colored velveteen dress with a white silk chiffon sash and matching collar. It was two years old and suddenly looked frumpy. If she could get this job, she'd buy new clothes.

She found Rae in the kitchen eating a muffin. Smoothing her dress over her hips, she twirled in front of her sister. "I haven't worn anything fun since I married Hal," she said. "There's always work to do on a farm. His mother gave me the most awful chores . . . will this dress look right?"

"Ida said the girls in the scene will wear silk, taffeta, or velveteen. You look fine."

Delia twisted her long dark hair into a double loop at the back of her head and checked herself in a hand mirror Lily kept on a shelf. "I'm going to get my hair cut as soon as I have the money. You look adorable. Lily should cut her hair too."

Rae finished her muffin and took a sip of tea. "Lily's not going to cut her hair. Eddie told her she looks like a goddess with her hair down, and Matt uses Lily as a sweet heroine in the westerns." She studied Delia for a minute. "Are you ever going back to Hal?"

"You can't imagine how boring . . . how utterly impossible it was." Delia forced a smile. "It's over now. We're all together again. We'll have fun."

"I guess so." Rae put her cup in the sink. "Let's go. We need to find Matt before he starts the party scene."

When they reached the studio, Rae took Delia's hand as they walked through the front doors. Bud was watching the entrance, but he was chatting with a pretty redhead and barely looked up as Rae waved to him. Downstairs, the set was decorated as a ballroom with a piano in the center. The extra performers, dressed for a party, strolled around the set, their voices rising in a disorderly roar as they waited to begin the scene.

Delia kept close behind Rae who headed toward a tall man with unruly blond hair standing at the edge of the set and grabbed his sleeve to catch his attention. "My sister Delia is in town, Matt. Can you use her in the party scene?"

Matt glanced over Rae's shoulder and frowned. "How many sisters do you have?"

Delia lost hope for an instant before she saw the faint grin on his lips. Lily had been right—Rae had more power than she realized. Matt's expression was the look of a protective older brother who wasn't likely to say no. Delia's nerves abruptly ended. She was in.

"Just two sisters," Rae said. "Please, Matt?"

His grin widened. "All right." He turned to the man standing near him. "Fred, put Rae's sister in the scene. Where's Ida?"

"She's coming," Fred said. "I told Ida we wanted Eve in something transparent. This wild party can't look like a church social. We need some bare flesh."

Ida arrived, carrying a black chiffon shirtwaist trimmed with black lace. It was sheer enough to show every detail of the girl wearing it. "Eve won't wear this," she announced. "I told her you wanted her in something enticing, and she said you usually looked for *enticing* in the Weston conservatory—whatever that means."

Matt grimaced. He and Fred mumbled to each other. Delia couldn't hear the words, but she sensed the urgency in both men. This filmy shirtwaist must be important.

Matt listened to Fred mutter for another minute before he turned to the background actors on the set. "I need a woman to wear a costume that's transparent. Who's willing?" He waited a beat and added. "Five dollars for the day."

Delia shoved past Rae. "I'll do it." She seized the shirtwaist from Ida and held it up to her chest. "I guess this will fit well enough."

Matt hesitated, glancing sideways at Rae. "Sorry, I've forgotten your name."

"Delia Kelly," she said, erasing two years as a married woman.

"Delia," Rae whispered. "What are you thinking?"

"You'll have to sit on the piano, and the camera will be close." Matt lowered his voice. "Everyone in the audience will see your . . . bosom."

"I'm not shy. Maybe I'll become famous."

Rae exhaled in a whoosh. "Delia!"

Matt waited another beat before he shrugged. "Ida, help Delia get ready, and put Rae in dungarees for her scenes with Gil." A stern look settled on his face. "Don't come back to this set today, Rae. When Fred finishes your scenes, go home or wait with Ida."

In the costume room, Delia giggled as she slipped out of her dress and stepped into a taffeta skirt that buttoned down the front. Ida opened the last six buttons, so Delia's legs in black stockings showed up to her knees when she walked. The shirtwaist, open down the front, had no buttons. Only the tie at the throat held the two edges together. Delia slipped it on and was more or less naked from the waist up. When she moved, the filmy edges separated, revealing flashes of her breasts.

Rae cringed. "Are you really going to wear that?"

Delia preened in front of the mirror, turning so the skirt swirled around her knees, adjusting her shoulders in various ways to see how far the shirtwaist opened. "Don't worry about me. Matt needed someone to wear this. I'm only trying to help."

"I expect your sister knows what she's doing," Ida commented.

Delia laughed. "I certainly do, Ida."

On the set, Fred lifted her onto the piano and told her to cross her legs. "You'll be up here for the whole scene," he said and left her.

Delia glanced around the room, anticipation thrumming in her. Atop the piano, she was higher than anyone else. The camera had to notice her. Crossing her legs, she swung her foot just strongly enough so her skirt fell open and revealed her black stockings up to her garters. Thank goodness, she'd borrowed Lily's fancy garters today.

An excited murmur raced through the room as a man with a touch of gray at his temples entered the basement. He strolled across the floor exuding an air of importance. "Chester Slater," mumbled a woman close to the piano.

Delia watched the star consult with Matt for a few minutes before he walked to the center of the room not far from her piano. Surely, he'd notice her. She leaned back far enough to make her breasts jut forward under the gauzy shirtwaist.

Matt clapped for attention. "We're going to start with the general party atmosphere. Talk to each other. Chester will walk around the room. He may stop and talk to you. If he does, pretend to answer him. Don't step over the floor strips. George, camera! Action!"

Chester turned away from the piano and wandered a few feet in the opposite direction. He stopped to talk to two women. They smiled and lifted their glasses. Delia watched—he had to come her way next. She swung her foot.

"Chester, turn toward the piano. Notice the girl sitting on it. Smile at her." Matt waited while Chester strolled toward Delia. "Smile at each other. Swing that foot higher, Delia. Now untie the bow on your shirtwaist and let it hang open. Slowly!"

The camera fixed on them. This was the moment for her to shine. Delia kept her eyes locked on Chester's as she carefully pulled at one end of the bow, opening the loop. She twitched her shoulders and leaned back another inch so the transparent material separated revealing one breast. She recognized the spark in his eyes, and it had nothing to do with Matt's directions. Chester leaned against the piano and ran his gaze over her body.

"Chester, say something to her. Delia, laugh as if it's funny."

Chester leaned closer. "I like what I see."

She touched her tongue to her bottom lip, forgetting Matt wanted her to laugh. "There's more to see," she whispered. Expectation crackled between them. Victory was nearly hers. She remembered Matt and tossed her head as if she were amused.

"Wait for me later," Chester murmured.

Rae was in the costume room when Delia rushed in hours later. "How did you—"

"I'm in a hurry," Delia said as she slipped out of her costume. "Chester Slater is taking me for a drive and then to an expensive restaurant. You don't mind going home alone, do you?" She snatched her dress off the side rack and frowned at it. "Ida, could I borrow a coat or fur? Matt said I'd be working tomorrow again."

Ida grunted deep in her throat. "We can't afford furs, even fake ones. I guess you can take this." She pulled a black and ivory wool cape off a rack, handed it to Delia, and folded her arms across her chest. "I know where you live, so you can't disappear with it."

Delia laughed and smoothed the cape over her shoulders. At the door, she paused and looked at Rae. "Tell Lily," she said and flounced out the door.

21

Out and About with Lucinda Corday

RidgeW Pictures has expanded its talent list recently with the three Kelly sisters. Rae, only thirteen years old, is the star of the popular *Danger for Dora* serial. Now that the Rough Riders story has ended, RidgeW is launching an adventure set in the frozen North to take advantage of Chicago winters for background. Many young girls in Chicago are copying Dora's short curly hair style, another sign that the serial is more popular every day.

RidgeW Pictures also is the place to go for romance—on screen and off. The oldest Kelly sister, Delia, has been emoting in some daring roles, primarily working with Chester Slater, and my spies tell me the two have found romance. They have been seen around town, dining, dancing, and racing through the countryside in his red Stutz-Bearcat. Their romance looks as sizzling as their scenes in RidgeW dramas.

The third sister is Lily Rose, a regular in Billy Tucker's comedies, and she has found romance with Edmund Carleton, III, heir to the Carleton hotels and printing companies. The two appear inseparable and completely smitten with each other. With the young Carleton about to take on an important position in his father's firm, perhaps marriage is in the future for Lily Rose and Eddie, as his friends call him.

My own thrilling news is that I'm writing the screenplay for RidgeW's new production of *Barriers Burned Away,* the tense drama based on the best-selling novel by E. P. Roe. The story features the problems of two unlikely lovers against the background of the Great Chicago Fire in 1871. Lily Rose will star with Chester Slater. This story will be RidgeW's most dramatic and costly production yet.

Until next time, dear readers.

22

Matt pushed open the studio doors at the loading entrance. He'd already checked the alley to make sure no one was close enough to see the special deliveries coming after dark. Clouds covered the moon, leaving no light except what spilled into the alley from the open doors. A cold, sharp wind stirred the air, signaling the coming winter. He took a long pull on his cigarette and tossed the nearly untouched butt into the alley.

"Coffin nails." Lukas said.

Matt stepped inside, rubbing his hands. "That's what my father always called them." He grinned.

"My old man said the same," Lukas said. "I suppose the old boys knew something." He reached inside his overcoat and produced a flask. After taking a swallow, he offered it to Matt. "Brandy. Good for cold nights."

Matt took a longer swallow and returned the flask to Lukas. "Thanks. If we didn't have to wait in the cold to sneak in film stock—and don't tell me where you got it— we'd be eating in a warm restaurant by this time."

Lukas slipped the flask into his coat pocket. "Gus is driving the truck himself tonight. I needed Otto at the boxing match. I've had to move the matches three times in the last two weeks. Our city fathers have had an attack of morality lately. Very unlike them," he added.

The two stood silently for a few minutes, staring into the darkness beyond the doors. Gus would be driving without headlights when he reached the studio, so they'd hear the tires rattle over the bricks before they saw the truck.

"I saw the new Billy Tucker comedy," Lukas said, breaking the silence. "The audience liked it."

Matt glanced at him in the dim light. "You said you weren't interested in seeing our movies, only in counting the profits."

Lukas shrugged. "I've been more interested lately. Seen a few comedies and a couple of those westerns."

"Billy has a knack for comedy," Matt said. "He's behaved himself since the reception. He works pretty well with Lily Rose."

"I noticed. She's . . . something."

"If Lily's the reason you're suddenly interested in watching movies, you can forget about it. Eddie Carleton is here every night in his Oldsmobile waiting to pick her up. According to Rae, Eddie's wild about Lily, and he's ready and willing to be caught."

Lukas hitched up his collar. "So the kid has it all figured out. She's smart, but she's young—thinks she knows more than she does. You can never be sure how things will work out."

Matt shook his head. "You haven't got a chance—not with Lily."

Lukas turned his back to the wind coming through the doors. "Is that Slater fellow doing good for you? He cost enough." He pulled out the flask again. "Damn, it's cold tonight."

"Slater got off to a rough start, but my big trouble's with the Chicago Censorship Board over nudity." Matt took another gulp of brandy after Lukas offered it. "The other studios have girls running around wearing less than my girl wears, and if we have to cut our nude scenes, we're behind again." He shifted on his feet and put his hands in his pockets. "It's another sister."

"What?"

"The girl who does the nudity—she's Rae's sister. Rae brought her in, and Delia—the sister—volunteered the first day to show her breasts."

Lukas laughed. "The kid's a real operator. Keep an eye on her, or she'll take over the studio." He thought a minute. "Who appoints the censorship board members?"

"It's a police board, but Theodore Weston controls it." Just saying the name made Matt clench his jaw. "The board doesn't object to the westerns or the *Dora* serial, but they've been hard on Billy's comedies and now Slater's dramas."

"Men like seeing naked women," Lukas said. "If politicians and society types pretend to be horrified, it's to calm their wives. Maybe I can come up with an angle for that censorship problem. Weston doesn't strike me as too virtuous. He dumped his first wife for a good looking young one."

"Yes, he did."

"Got the feeling at the reception Weston wasn't too fond of you. Couldn't have been his idea to throw a party for you."

"Mrs. Weston and her mother arranged the reception," Matt said. "Our families lived next door for years." Not exactly the entire answer, but good enough for Lukas.

A clatter at the far end of the alley alerted them to Gus's truck. Lukas pulled his watch out of his vest pocket. "Right on time. Tell Gus to do something, and he does it."

Gus pulled up to the doors, and the three men worked quickly, hauling boxes into the building and stacking them inside the store room. The temperature had dropped again, and their breath hung like frosted clouds in the night air.

"That's all?" Matt took another look in the truck. "I'll need more by next week."

Gus coughed. "Hard to get this time." He glanced at Lukas. "The Selig truck was—"

"Matt doesn't want to know the details," Lukas cut in. "Let's concentrate on getting another supply."

Gus mumbled something, stamped to the truck, and drove off. The sound of the tires faded as he reached the end of the alley and turned into the main street.

"I'll get more film," Lukas said. "Don't worry about—" A movement in the dark hallway leading to the store room stopped him. When a figure came into the light, he inhaled sharply and made a slight bow. "Good evening, Mrs. Weston."

"Good evening, Mr. Krantz." Arabella barely looked his way. She fixed on Matt. "I thought I could find you here, and the front door was unlocked."

Lukas smiled. "A pleasure to see you, Mrs. Weston. I was just leaving." He shot a warning look at Matt. "I might have a solution to that board problem. Let me look into it." He tipped his hat to Arabella and disappeared down the hallway.

Matt gazed at Arabella until he saw her shiver from the chill wind coming through the open doors. Murmuring an apology, he pulled the doors closed. "I'm surprised to see you here," he said.

"Theodore is in New York for a conference—a political meeting," she said. "Mother went to bed with a migraine, and I took a taxi here, so no one knows . . . where I am," she finished in a breathless rush, a soft flush marking her cheeks.

If he had any sense, he'd call a taxi and send her home. His father, during an awkward talk when he was fourteen, had warned him not to give in to temptations offered by married women. *No good can come of it,* his father had said. But he'd loved Arabella with adolescent fervor until his yearning and hers had flamed into more mature passion. When he returned to Chicago after years in New York, he was sure the fever had ended, but every time he saw her, his resistance shredded a little more, like a net with weak threads.

Arabella shivered again. "Is there some place warmer?" He abandoned the idea of calling a taxi. "We can go to the office."

In the office, he cleared papers off the worn leather chair, adding them to another stack on the cluttered surface of his desk. Arabella ignored the chair. She strolled around the office, running her fingers over Lucinda's latest screenplay, gazing at the wall calendars full of scribbled notes, and examining the publicity photos lying on a table.

The wind had ruffled her dark hair, and stray wisps fell around her neck. She looked excited, nervous, almost shaken. Matt closed his eyes for a second to stop himself from touching her. When he opened his eyes, she'd unbuttoned her coat and tossed it over a chair. Her wool dress, cream-colored, with a black satin collar, reminded him of a dress she'd worn when she was fifteen and he'd kissed her for the first time.

"I'm sorry about the reception," Arabella said in a soft voice. "I wanted to talk to you the next day, but Theodore was very angry, and I couldn't get away until now." She clasped her hands in front of her. "I wanted the reception to be a triumph for you."

"Did he hurt you?"

"He blamed me for embarrassing him."

"Billy made a mess of it. Not your fault. You know I'm grateful for anything you and your mother do for my business." He realized he was speaking awkwardly, not certain what they should say to each other. He gritted his teeth at the thought of Weston mishandling Arabella. "I don't want you to have problems, especially because of me."

She smoothed her skirt and smiled at him. "People become rich making movies, don't they, Matt? You'll surely be rich again."

"Maybe," he said, his mind flitting briefly to censorship, supplies of film stock, actors, and payrolls. He deliberately smothered those grim concerns. "Yes, I can be rich again—with luck."

She stepped closer, lifting her face at a perfect angle for a kiss. "You can be rich again, and we can leave Chicago. The papers say the important movie studios will be in California before long. We could be together again in California."

A surge of pleasure at the word *together* caught him, and desire jolted through his senses. "What does that mean? Would you leave Weston?"

Her arms slid around his waist. "Yes," she murmured. "I don't want to lose you again. We can be together in California. I don't care about anything else." She rested her forehead against his shoulder, fitting her body to his as if they were two edges of a broken plate.

The threads in the net holding him back shredded completely. He put his finger under her chin tilting her face up and stroked her cheek. He kissed her softly, then more feverishly, making up for years without kisses.

Finally, she broke away with a gasp and leaned back, locking her arms around his neck. "Promise me you'll be rich, promise me we'll be together. I have to know I can escape."

"I promise," he murmured, not caring what he promised. He fumbled with her hair, pulling out enough pins so her dark locks fell past her shoulders. He ran his fingers through the silky waves and inhaled her perfume. He kissed her again, pleased to feel her lips part for him while a tremor rippled through her body.

She twisted in his arms, presenting her back to him. "All the buttons are out of reach," she said with an uneven laugh. "You'll have to help me."

He kissed her neck, resting his lips on soft skin below her ear, while his fingers slipped along the row of onyx buttons. "Help is on the way."

23

Lukas rattled the RidgeW front doors to be sure he'd locked them. No good would come from allowing anyone else to wander into RidgeW Pictures tonight because he could predict fairly well what was going to happen once the two inside were alone. He'd known the instant he saw her standing in the dark hallway Arabella Weston had come to offer herself to Matt. She had the look of a woman caught up in longing, excited at her own courage, and determined to betray her husband. A man had to have a will of iron to resist a beautiful married woman who wanted him. Apparently, Matt had omitted some details about the old family friendships. His partner wouldn't be the first fool to take a chance with another man's wife, Lukas thought as he slid behind the wheel of the Pierce-Arrow. Of all the married women in Chicago, however, Arabella Weston had to be the worst possible choice.

Resigned to eating alone, Lukas parked in a small dirt lot close to the Bavarian House, his favorite German restaurant. The sauerbraten here was nearly as mouthwatering as his mother's had been, and when he ate in the warm, family atmosphere of the restaurant, he felt close to his mother's smile and his father's laugh at the table when he was a boy and times were good.

"Mr. Krantz, good to see you tonight. Are you alone?" The manager stood at the door as Lukas stepped inside.

"Good evening, Herman. Yes, I'm alone." Lukas answered, slipping off his coat and handing it to the dark-eyed girl working at the coatroom.

She was dressed in Bavarian style—a dark blue dirndl, tightly laced in the front, with a light blue apron edged in tiny white bows. The skirt was short enough to display her ankles and the bodice low enough to reveal the beginning of a generous bosom. She smiled at him. He couldn't recall her name, although late one evening in the past summer, they'd enjoyed a brief but close acquaintance.

Herman seated him at his favorite table, somewhat out of the way and at an angle allowing him to watch the room. He ordered the sauerbraten and a glass of red wine, and when the waiter walked away, he leaned back and glanced at the other tables. In a moment, acute frustration knifed through him. Eddie Carleton sat at a table for two on the other side of the restaurant near the windows. He was laughing as he reached for the hand of the woman he was with.

Lily Rose.

Lukas watched while Lily smiled beguilingly at Eddie and whispered to him across the table. Frustration gripped him. Seeing the two flirt with each other triggered a possessive surge demanding he disrupt their connection. Rising, he strolled over to their table.

Eddie looked up and grinned. "Lukas," he said, rising to offer his hand. "I didn't see you."

"Just arrived," Lukas answered, shaking his hand. His gaze shifted to Lily, but when Eddie started to introduce him, Lukas shook his head. "I met Miss Kelly at the Weston reception."

Lily sent a cool glance his way accompanied by a polite nod.

He felt the chill and after a few remarks to Eddie, he retreated to his table. Tasting his wine, he considered his situation and gestured to Herman. "Send Bennie to me. I have a job for him." Herman nodded and disappeared in the direction of the kitchen. Keeping his gaze on Lily and Eddie, Lukas waited.

Lily stole a quick glance at Lukas under her lashes before she slid her hand into Eddie's. "How do you know him? He owns—" She paused, and ended with "a house where . . . you know what I mean."

He squeezed her hand. "I don't know him from that house. Honest, I don't. His father worked for Carleton Printing. We hire mostly German immigrants. About fifteen years ago there was a robbery. A gang burst in, and Lukas's father was killed. I was only seven, but I remember it. My father was horrified. He paid for the funeral and gave Lukas's mother some money, but she died a few months later, and Lukas was on his own when he was fourteen."

"He's a gangster," Lily murmured.

Eddie stroked her hand. "After his parents died, he did odd jobs for a while, but you can't live on selling newspapers. I confess I rather admire his grit in finishing school and finding ways to make money without any serious business connections. He never blamed my father for the killing, and he's always cordial when we meet." He lowered his voice. "I suppose you know he owns most of RidgeW Pictures. I'm sure that's the only reason the Westons invited him to the reception. You're absolutely right—he's not socially acceptable."

"You accept him."

"We've known each other a long time. Once, I got into some trouble., and he made it go away. I was grateful. We shake hands and say hello when we meet. That's the extent of it."

They murmured to each other, drank wine, and pushed the chocolate torte around their plates without eating much of it. They stopped gazing into each other's eyes when the manager came to their table and muttered into Eddie's ear.

Eddie got to his feet. "It's about the Oldsmobile," he said. "I'll be back in a few minutes." He followed Herman out of the restaurant.

Like a hunter focused on his prey, Lukas rose from his chair. Lily sat with her hands folded on the table, her head turned away from the room, looking toward the windows. She must know he'd come to the table the minute Eddie left. No matter how intent she was on charming Eddie, she couldn't have been unaware of his desire for her when their eyes met. As he walked across the room, the window caught his reflection.

She turned when he came near. "Mr. Krantz," she said.

"Call me Lukas," he said. She didn't invite him to sit down, but he did anyway, sliding into Eddie's vacant chair. "I saw Eddie leave, and I was sure he wouldn't want you to sit here alone."

"He'll be back in a minute," she said, a sharp edge in her voice.

"I've been watching your movies," he said, ignoring Eddie's inevitable return. "None of the other actors matter when you're on the screen. You look like an angel. Beautiful. I was hypnotized." In business and with women, he always moved quickly to overwhelm any resistance. Confident, he leaned toward her and lowered his voice. "I want to see you again. Tell me when."

Lily's mouth tightened into a thin line while her blue eyes turned icy. "I don't want to see you again. And I don't want you to send flowers. I gave the roses away."

He paid no attention to her words, barely hearing them. Inhaling the faint perfume she wore, he plunged on. "We could go away for a weekend—wherever you'd like."

"That will never happen."

This time her tone registered with him, and he straightened in the chair. She looked soft and lovely on the screen, and his first impression when they met had convinced him she was a fragile beauty needing his protection. He'd never seen a woman more beautiful, but she didn't look especially angelic now. Her cold gaze sparked with anger—her jaw was rigid—nothing about her seemed fragile.

"What's more," she continued, "Eddie regards you as an old friend or at least a man he trusts. So you aren't being very honorable making advances to me when he's gone for a minute." She tapped her nails on the tablecloth for emphasis.

He'd misjudged her. She wasn't a gorgeous, passive creature waiting to be swept off her feet. She was like her little sister—bold, tough, focused on what she wanted, which at the moment was Eddie Carleton. Competition didn't bother him, but how to reach her was a puzzle. She didn't offer a sliver of encouragement. No matter. He intended to win the game.

"Lukas!" Eddie slapped him on the back. "Thanks for keeping Lily entertained. Some idiot dented my fender. Have to get it fixed. Highly irritating."

Lukas rose, muttered something about his repair business, and gave Eddie a card. "Gus can pound out that fender for you. No charge." He sent a vague pleasantry in Lily's direction. She glared at him without answering, and he retreated to his table.

He had to be patient. He watched them leave the restaurant, Lily's hand on Eddie's arm. Her cool resistance had increased his appreciation of her. She'd never be boring. He drained his wine glass. A half-smile of self-pity touched his lips as he remembered what Matt and Arabella Weston were most likely doing while he was looking at a plate of cold sauerbraten.

He declined Herman's nervous offer of another meal and went to the coatroom to collect his overcoat. The girl fetched it, but before handing it over, she stroked the collar and ran her hand along the sleeve, looking up at him. He gazed at her, the way he knew women liked to be looked at. "I've misplaced your name, Fraulein."

"Karin," she answered with a giggle. "We close the restaurant in an hour." She waited. When he didn't move to take his coat, she smiled and slipped it back over the hanger.

Lukas turned to Herman, standing a few feet away. "I might have pork and dumplings—while I wait."

24

"It's too slippery," Rae yelled at Matt from her perch on a rock at the edge of Lake Michigan. "It's icy already."

The new *Danger for Dora* adventure was set in Alaska. Rae didn't think the story made much sense, but Lucinda had written in lots of action so the audience wouldn't notice the confused plot. The day was sunny but frosty enough so Rae was half frozen before she'd reached the edge of the rocks on the beach near Waukegan. Matt said the place was perfect for the opening scene. Dangling over the choppy surf in the frigid wind, she'd lost feeling in her fingers almost at once.

"Just a few more minutes," Matt yelled to her. "Crawl up the rock you're on and shift over to that flat one." He pointed.

Rae tilted her head to scan for the rock he wanted. Her fingers were sure to slip if she shifted her body even an inch. Why couldn't Matt fake this scene like he faked so much of the action? Instead, in this cold, he'd decided on realism. She squeezed her eyes shut for an instant to clear the fear out of her mind. "I see it," she called to Matt, leaning over the bluff above her. George had anchored the camera just beyond them at an angle to capture Rae, the rocks, and the water below in one shot. "I'm moving now," she yelled above the noise of the crashing waves.

Slowly, she reached for a deep groove in the rock, but her fingers slipped on the icy surface. Struggling to find a hold, she swayed awkwardly, and her foot lost its place in the notch she'd found earlier. Losing all contact with the rock, Rae flapped her arms like a bird beginning flight.

"No, no," she screamed in a long, high-pitched shriek. Looking into Matt's shocked face above her, she tumbled backwards, still flailing her arms, and sank below the splashing waves. Coughing, she surfaced, but her thick wool jacket soaked through, and she couldn't paddle enough to keep above the freezing water. She went under again, fighting to rise above the waves, but her arms were so heavy they didn't move the way she needed, and her legs didn't kick. She lost connection with her body. The cold stopped her thinking. Desperate, she reached for the surface one more time, gasped for air, choked, and sank into the darkness.

A hand grabbed the collar of her jacket and pulled her up. "Rae!" Matt yelled in her ear. "I've got you! Keep breathing."

He hooked one arm around her waist and dragged her to shore. They knelt together on the sand coughing, spitting, trying to pull air into their lungs. The November wind quickly turned their clothes into stiff, frozen fabric. Holding on to each other, they staggered to their feet as George tossed down a blanket and Matt's coat. Rae clutched at the blanket, but she was shaking so violently, she couldn't keep it in place. Matt pulled on his coat, draped the blanket around her shoulders, and hooked his free arm around her waist while they staggered across the sand to the path leading up the bank.

"Get in the truck," Matt said. "We've got costumes in the back. Put on anything."

Scrambling under the canvas cover, she sucked on her fingertips to get some feeling back, ripped off her wet clothes, and grabbed whatever she could find—thick pants and a wool shirt. On second thought, she added another shirt over the first one, and a heavy jacket.

Matt's teeth were chattering by the time she emerged and he took his turn in the back. George packed the equipment, and Rae settled into the front seat, wrapping her arms across her chest. When Matt came to the passenger door, he wore one of the trapper costumes with an enormous fur hat pulled down so far only the ends of his blond hair stuck out beneath the fur.

"You look—"

"Like a fool," Matt finished for her. "Move over."

Shivering, Rae made room for him while memories flashed in her head—the water, the ice on the rocks, losing feeling in every part of her. "You saved my life." She fought tears. "Thank you."

He ruffled her damp hair and put his arm around her shoulders. "You're welcome. I couldn't let Dora drift off into the lake—I need her for more episodes."

His joking tone helped. She shoved her hands in the pockets of the jacket and focused on warming her fingers while George drove back to Chicago, rambling nonstop about the great shot he'd gotten of Rae clinging to the rocks and then falling into the lake. "We do a little cutting to get Matt out, and the audience will be thunderstruck with the realism."

"Great," she mumbled. Did movie people care about anything except if the shot was good?

"We won't get that realistic again for a while," Matt commented.

When they reached the studio, Matt insisted on driving her home. "It's dark and cold, and you had a bad scare. I want to be sure you get to a warm place." They were close to the apartment when he spotted Ma Fischer's Diner and swerved his Model T into a parking place. "Let's eat. I'm starved." He tossed the fur hat onto the back seat and ran his fingers through his still-damp hair.

Rae vouched for the meat loaf, so Matt ordered two full dinners with hot coffee. When it came, they bent over the food and ate silently. The plates were empty before they both leaned back, took in long, satisfied breaths, and relaxed. "I want to explain what happened to your sisters when I get you home," Matt said. "I'll go inside with you."

Rae sipped her coffee without answering. How much should she tell Matt about Delia and Lily? "Delia isn't at home very often," she said. "She's with Chester a lot of the time."

Matt frowned. "Chester doesn't have the best reputation with women."

"She says Chester's exciting." Rae stared into her coffee cup, thinking about Delia's bruises, which she always claimed came from a fall. "Do you mean Chester's dangerous?"

"The rumors say he's rough with women. Delia should be careful," Matt answered. "Look, Rae, don't be upset about Delia not wearing much in her scenes. We have to compete with the other studios."

"Delia does what she wants," Rae said. "She doesn't care what people think."

Matt grinned. "Like you. Is Lily serious about Eddie Carlton?"

I guess so. He's all she talks about. How can you tell if someone's in love?"

"I think it's different for everyone. You don't have to worry about that yet." He cocked his head to one side. "Or do you?"

"Not me."

"Good—you're too young. I don't need my players tangled in romantic problems. Lily starts working on *Barriers Burned Away* next week. It's our biggest project yet, and she'll get a lot of attention from the press."

"I guess Lucinda will write some columns about it."

"You bet she will," Matt said with a laugh. "*Barriers Burned Away* was a best-selling novel. It's old now, but Chicago audiences will be interested. People are still alive who remember the big fire. I want you to play the spunky girl who sounds the alarm and rescues a family. It's only a few scenes, but you're perfect for it. Audiences will recognize Dora, so you'll be advertising the serial too."

The apartment windows were dark when they pulled in front of Rae's apartment. "No lights," she said with a little sigh of relief. "You don't have to come in. Lily and Delia probably aren't home. I'll tell them about falling in the lake in the morning."

"I'm coming up with you just in case one of them is there," Matt said.

Rae made a show of calling out when she unlocked the apartment door. "Lily? Delia?" She didn't expect an answer. Delia hadn't slept in the apartment for days. She switched on the light. Matt followed her inside and waited while she shouted again and shook her head. "They aren't here."

He frowned. "I promise I'll keep you safe in the next episode. Nothing risky."

"I'll tell them." Rae slipped off her jacket and tossed it over a chair. "I'll tell them you saved my life." Her head ached, and the meat loaf sat like a rock in her stomach. If only Matt would leave, maybe she could block out the memory of icy water closing over her head.

He was nearly out the door when they saw the white envelope on a table. Rae read the note, drew in a deep breath, and silently handed the paper to Matt.

> *Dear Rae,*
>
> *I'm so excited, and I want you to be happy too. Eddie and I have gone away to get married. We couldn't wait—and there was no possibility we could have a big wedding right now. We'll be gone at least a week, and then we'll probably move into the Carleton mansion. Please tell Matt I'm sorry, but I won't be able to start the movie next week as planned. I'm moving into society!*
>
> *Love, Lily*

Matt and Rae stared at each other. "Now what?" he muttered.

25

"Are you happy?" Lily slipped her hand through Eddie's arm as they entered the elegant lobby of the Pfister Hotel in Milwaukee.

Eddie squeezed her hand. "Yes, I am, Mrs. Carleton."

The bellhop followed them into the lobby, set their suitcases on a luggage cart, and pulled the cart to one side while he waited for them to register. Lily stood next to Eddie at the desk, trying to look as if she were accustomed to checking into an exclusive hotel, but she couldn't resist glancing around the ornate lobby, admiring the plush leather chairs, the thick carpet under her feet, and the crystal chandeliers directly above the curved registration desk. Every dream she'd indulged in since she'd met Eddie at the Weston reception was coming true. From this moment on, her life would be one of luxury and sophistication.

Hearing Eddie register them as Mr. and Mrs. Edmund Carleton sent a shiver of delight through her, and she glanced down at the ring on her finger. The thin gold band had been somewhat of a disappointment, but Eddie had promised a more elaborate ring once they settled into their married lives. She pressed against his side and sent a dazzling smile at the clerk behind the counter. She rather wished his bland expression would change into a questioning look, so she could display the marriage certificate she'd tucked into her bag. However, the clerk remained politely disinterested, snapped his fingers for the bellhop, handed him a key, and murmured the room number in a discreet tone.

On the fifth floor, the bellhop opened the door to the suite, carried the bags inside, pulled open the curtains facing Lake Michigan, and placed the room key on a table. He returned to the hallway where Eddie and Lily waited and lingered just long enough to accept the dollar Eddie handed him before he rolled the luggage cart back to the elevator.

As soon as the bellhop was out of sight, Eddie swept her into his arms and over the threshold. He pressed a kiss on her lips before setting her down in front of the double windows. "Look at that." He pointed to the white-crested waves rising on the lake.

They stood at the window silently admiring the view, arms around each other, her head nestled against his shoulder. After a moment, Lily straightened. "Where should we go first when we get back to Chicago?"

She wanted to settle immediately into the Carleton family's lavish chateau-styled mansion. Of course, she'd arrange small dinner parties there as soon as possible to enhance Eddie's position in business and her position as a leader in society. Eddie's mother wasn't likely to give up control over the household, but she'd charm his mother into a shared arrangement for social events, and eventually, she'd be the true lady of the house.

He glanced around the room. "Isn't this place great?" He shrugged off his coat, took Lily's, and hung both in the closet.

"Yes, but when we get back to Chicago, where are we going?" Lily smiled up at him and evaded his attempt to take her in his arms

A slight frown came and went. "I thought we'd go to the Palmer House first. It's really fine, Lily. You'll love it, and my father has an account there, so we can get a suite and order just about anything we want."

She had to be careful not to dim his cheerful enthusiasm. "The Palmer House would be grand. I'm sure the suites are wonderful, but shouldn't we go to see your parents right away?" She tilted her head and smiled up at him in the beguiling style she'd developed for her movie roles. Moving closer, she put her arms around his waist. "Hotels are wonderful for honeymoons, but houses are for marriage."

He dropped kisses along her cheek and down her throat while his fingers tugged gently at the sash around her waist, reminding her of what was expected on honeymoons. She sighed, and pulled back. "Where will we live— after the honeymoon?"

"We can think about it later," he mumbled as he reached for her.

She gracefully twirled into the center of the room. "Let's have champagne—and food. I'm famished, Eddie!"

He grinned, defeated for the moment. "All right. Let's get champagne. We can go downstairs."

The stylish elegance of the hotel dining room thrilled her. They were early for the evening meal, but a few families and couples were already seated. Lily sank gracefully into the chair held by the waiter and couldn't resist running her fingertips over the white linen tablecloth. A rush of affection for Eddie flooded her. He was exactly the kind of husband she'd wanted since she was old enough to think about husbands. She held out her hand and he took it, threading his fingers through hers.

"Happy?" he whispered.

"So very happy," she whispered.

Eddie ordered champagne and the lamb with asparagus tips and baked potatoes. "And the brandied fruit," he added as the waiter took the menus.

Lily sighed with pleasure. She was warm, safe, cared for, and delightfully free of worries. The waiter came with champagne. They toasted each other and sipped the sparkling drink while they held hands under the table and gazed into each other's eyes.

She murmured appreciatively about the lamb as they ate, but food was not uppermost in her mind. "Don't you think we should see your parents the minute we get back to Chicago even if we do stay at the Palmer House for a few days?"

Eddie moved his fork aimlessly around his plate. "There's no rush. We should enjoy ourselves. After all, we're on our honeymoon. We can visit my parents later."

"You're their only son. They'd surely want to meet his bride right away. I certainly want to meet them." She watched him cut a piece of lamb while a vague suspicion took root in her mind. Her hand trembled slightly as she put a dab of butter on her potato. "They must have been terribly surprised when you told them we were getting married. I'm sure they'd appreciate a long visit as soon as we're back in Chicago."

He drained his champagne glass and stared at it for a minute. "Actually, Lily, I didn't tell anyone we were getting married. When I said I was going to Milwaukee for a couple of days, they probably assumed I was visiting my college friend Walter Bagley. He lives here, and I come up occasionally to see him. My parents aren't expecting me to bring home a bride."

Lily put her fork down, a chill creeping through her. "You didn't tell them? We agreed we'd tell our families before we got on the train. I left a note for Rae and Delia. Why didn't you tell your parents?"

He reached for her hand but could only pat her clenched fist. "At the last minute, I didn't think it was a good idea. My mother . . . she's very delicate and gets emotional over surprises. Don't be angry. Everything will be fine when we get back. I'll tell them then. They'll love you."

He pried her fist open and kissed her fingertips. "They'll love you as much as I do."

"How can you be sure?"

He laughed. "Of course, they're going to love you. You're enchanting." He kissed her hand again. "We might want to get our own house right away. You can decorate it."

His confidence flowed over her, and she grew calmer. His parents certainly must want a daughter-in-law to keep the family intact and provide grandchildren. Eddie had said a hundred times she'd be the most beautiful hostess in Chicago, and the wives of his friends would be wild with jealousy. She'd planned to join one of his mother's volunteer organizations, perhaps even take charge of it eventually. But Eddie might be right about getting a mansion of their own. She'd momentarily forgotten her promise to Rae about living with her once she caught a rich husband. Gradually, she relaxed and listened to Eddie's lively descriptions about parties and trips. Under the table, she put her hand lightly on his thigh.

He inhaled sharply and covered her hand, pressing it firmly against him. "Let's not wait for dessert," he said, a touch of hoarseness in his voice. "Why don't you go to the room ahead of me? I'll have another drink and come up in a few minutes." He put the room key in her hand.

In their room, she slipped out of her clothes and slid her new ivory satin nightgown over her head. She'd spent too much on it, but the giggling salesgirl had told her it was perfect for her wedding night. The square neckline was edged in heavy ivory lace threaded with ivory ribbons.

The lace sleeves ended at her elbows. She let her hair down and studied herself in the mirror. Her heart was pounding in anticipation of what was about to happen. Without a doubt, she'd soon be a real married woman.

The door handle turned, and when she looked over her shoulder, Eddie stepped into the room. He sucked in his breath at the sight of her. "So beautiful," he murmured. "My wife."

He locked the door behind him.

Lily glanced at Eddie, his face half-buried on the pillow next to hers, his arm flung heavily across her waist. He snored softly, unevenly, lips slightly curved in what could be a smile if he were awake. Thank goodness he looked happy. She wanted him to be happy, especially if his parents didn't know about their marriage yet. She should have insisted on more concrete plans. Eddie's passionate declarations had convinced her their future would be golden. She stared at the ceiling for another minute and then carefully slid out from under his arm.

Picking up her nightgown lying discarded on the floor, she padded to the bathroom. The soreness between her legs wasn't as painful as she'd expected. She filled the sink with water and washed. A little blood. Not much. She rinsed the washcloth and dried herself with a fluffy hotel towel. Staring in the wide mirror, she looked for changes in her face, but saw none. Aside from knowing a great deal more about what Delia always called *intimacies*, she was the same Lily.

So this was what men wanted so desperately. Five or ten minutes of grunting and pushing, and then they fell asleep. It was all rather ridiculous. Still, Eddie had whispered over and over that he loved her, and hearing those words was highly reassuring. She was Mrs. Edmund Carleton III, and the Palmer House would be a wonderful place for a honeymoon. Once his parents welcomed her into their family, she'd be socially important. Eventually, she'd find the right husband for Rae. They could forget everything about their past.

Shaking out her satin nightgown, she slipped it over her head and opened the bathroom door. She tiptoed into the bedroom, but Eddie was awake, grinning, an eager expression in his eyes. She smiled at him.

26

Matt rubbed the space between his brows. He'd had a raging headache for two days—because of his icy bath in Lake Michigan—or because the Chicago censors demanded he cut the nude scenes—or because he had to recast his biggest movie because his leading lady decided to get married. He searched in his desk for aspirin and washed one down with a cup of black coffee while he contemplated rearranging his actors. Billy's next comedy, *The Barbershop*, had only three characters—all men—so that one could stay on schedule. Lily's absence would delay *Barriers Burned Away*. Swearing under his breath, he rose and headed to the back of the building where Fred had put up a set for *Lost Husbands*, Chester's latest drama. He'd probably have to cut the nude scenes again.

When he reached the set, Chester was arguing with Fred about entering the scene from the left or the right.

"It's not a Broadway show," Matt snapped, his headache pounding in his temples. "The camera will catch you staggering into the room and threatening to shoot Delia. Left or right doesn't matter." He looked at Fred. "How much have we got to do on *Husbands?*"

Fred checked his clipboard. "Should be able to finish on Friday, if the trial scene isn't a problem." He glanced at Chester's sullen expression. "Friday could be tight. We'll finish next Tuesday at the latest."

"Good enough." He noticed Delia perched on a chair out of the way. "I'm sorry," he said when he reached her. "Rae probably told you she's all right. She fell in the lake, but we got her out, dried her off, and nothing's broken."

Delia didn't look particularly concerned, but she wrinkled her brow in a semblance of worry. "Thank you for telling me. I . . . haven't been at the apartment much. Haven't seen Rae for a couple of days. As long as she's all right— that's what matters."

Matt had a dark opinion of sisters who left a thirteen-year-old alone overnight, but he refrained from sharing it. Instead, he focused on a long purple bruise on Delia's arm. "Where did that come from?"

"I slipped and fell. I can keep it covered even if I'm not wearing much."

"I'm not sure what you'll be wearing. We had to cut some of your shots in the last two movies with Chester."

She pouted. "I want to be noticed. Chester says bare skin catches the audience's attention."

He rubbed his temple. "Unfortunately, it also catches the attention of the Chicago censors, and once they start cutting scenes, other city review boards do too. Other studios are doing nude scenes and getting away with it. Must be something we can do," he added more to himself than to her.

While George positioned the camera, Matt cornered Chester. "No more bruises. I don't care what you were used to doing when you were on the stage and what the audience could or could not see from the upper balcony. On the screen, bruises and cut lips show. Got that?"

Chester glowered at him. "What a man and woman do together—"

"I don't want to hear what you do," Matt cut him off. "No more bruises!"

Chester turned red and hurled his prop gun at the back of the set, shattering the lamp on the table. Bouncing off the table, the gun crashed into the mirror on the back wall. "I have finished for today," he announced before marching out of the room. Delia left her chair and, casting an uncertain look at Matt, hurried after Chester.

Matt waved away Fred's attempt to follow Chester. "Forget him for today. Where's Eve?"

He found her in the costume room where Ida was fitting her into costumes for Gil's next western, *Aces and Eights*. They'd barely spoken in weeks, but he thought talking in front of Ida might make it easier for both of them. However, Ida took one look at his face, gathered up an armful of dresses, and mumbled she had to do some stitching. The door banged behind her, leaving them alone. Eve shot a cold glance at him and waited.

He attempted a smile but abandoned the effort. "Lily has left us to get married," he said. "I want you to take her place in *Barriers Burned Away*. It's the lead. You should do well in it. We'll have to delay the start a couple of days while you finish *Aces* and get costumes, but you're experienced. You'll catch up quickly."

"I should have had the lead from the beginning."

He ignored her barb and launched into a description of the opening shots and what kind of person she'd be playing.

When he paused, Eve moved close to him. "I'll do a good job. You can count on me." She smoothed a wrinkle in his shirt. "I'm sorry things didn't work for us, Matt. We used to have fun. When I saw you with Arabella Weston, I imagined I knew what was going on, but Lucinda told me you two grew up together. So maybe I didn't have the right idea." She put her lips close to his. "Come back to me," she whispered.

Eve had always made everything simple. Simple was especially appealing right now. He bent his head the small distance required to touch her lips and kissed her. She put her arms around his neck while he deepened the kiss. As Eve pressed against him, Arabella floated into his thoughts, and he pulled back. "Eve . . ."

Her eyes darkened. "Never mind," she said, anger crackling in her voice. "You do what you want to. We won't try to go back." She brushed her fingers across her lips as if wiping away his kiss. "You're a fool, Matt. Get out of here and let me change out of this costume."

Later, when the studio was empty, Matt swallowed two more aspirin and washed them down with whiskey. Dealing with the actors today had been more difficult than leaping into a freezing lake and saving Rae. Heavy pounding at the back doors brought him to his feet still holding the whiskey bottle. Snow swirled through the air and flew inside when he pulled open the heavy doors. Lukas and Gus stood there, shivering, a hand cart with a packing crate behind them. As soon as the doors were sufficiently open, the two wheeled the cart inside.

"More film," Lukas announced while Gus maneuvered the crate into a corner.

"Thanks," Matt said. He offered the whiskey bottle to Lukas, who took a gulp and handed it to Gus. The bottle was nearly empty when Gus returned it, and Matt took the last swallow while Gus wheeled the empty cart back to the parked truck.

"Rough day?" Lukas removed his leather gloves.

"I got a notice I have to cut the nude scenes in Chester's last two movies."

"I asked around. Some of the other studios in town make payoffs to the censor board so they can keep the hot stuff in the movies. Most of the money ends up in politicians' pockets eventually."

"Do you want to make payoffs?"

Lukas shook his head. "This movie business is already costing me too much." He leaned against the wall. "I've got something Weston might want more than a payoff. Give me a few days, and I'll test it on him."

"Maybe I should talk to him," Matt suggested.

Lukas laughed. "Not a good idea. What would you say if he told you he knows about his wife's visits here? Me—I can lie whenever I need to. You don't lie so good, Matt. Stay away from Weston." He smoothed the fingers of his gloves. "How's the big production coming along? I thought I might drop in and watch you do some scenes."

"It's delayed for a while. I had to recast." Matt sent a sharp glance at Lukas. "If you were planning to watch Lily, you're out of luck. Eve is replacing her."

"Why?"

"To be correct, she replaced us. She married Eddie Carleton."

Lukas's jaw tightened. "Rotten luck."

27

"Good day, Mr. Carleton." The man behind the desk of the Chicago Palmer House, wearing a tag identifying him as the assistant manager, glanced at Eddie's registration and failed to conceal a twitch of surprise before he looked intently at Lily. She smiled and placed her hand on Eddie's arm.

"Good day, Stanton. Just put our stay on my father's account, would you?" Eddie smiled at Lily. "I'm on my honeymoon you see."

The assistant manager ran a finger over his mustache and dipped his head. "Let me offer my congratulations, Mr. Carleton, and my best to you, Mrs. Carleton. I imagine you'll want a large suite on the seventh floor."

Eddie squeezed Lily's hand. "We'd like a view of the lake if you would. Could you send up a cart with coffee and something for lunch? We had a hasty breakfast in Milwaukee." He squeezed Lily's hand again. "A bottle of wine too—something light. Gerard always has a recommendation for me."

A thin smile came from the assistant manager as he glanced at Lily again. "Of course, Mr. Carleton. I'll have him select his best. Let me know whenever you need anything more." He snapped his fingers for the bellhop.

In the suite, Lily waited until the bellhop disappeared before she spun around, touching the plush upholstery on the chairs, the marble tops of the dressers, the elaborately curved faucets in the bathroom, and the ornate embroidery on the thick drapes. "I want this embroidery on our drapes when we furnish our own rooms."

He laughed. "Anything you want." Catching her in his arms, he pulled her toward him for a kiss. "You tell me what you want, and I'll get it for you."

The food and wine arrived within minutes. Eddie was inclined to be romantic before lunch, but Lily insisted she was faint with hunger, so they ate at the small table next to the windows, holding hands and gazing at each other.

"I'm so happy," Lily whispered. "Shouldn't we see your parents today? We don't want them to think we're neglecting them."

Eddie shifted to look out the window. "We have plenty of time."

"I do want your mother to like me."

"I'd better see the family alone first. You know—get them prepared for a new bride."

"They must have suspected we were serious about each other."

Eddie cleared his throat. "I—my mother dislikes change and excitement."

"I'm sorry I didn't meet her at the Weston reception."

"She avoids social events with a lot of people. I didn't mention you to her because she prefers," he winced, "a stable family life. My sister's marriage upset her although Mother liked Reggie well enough, and he brought a title into the family. Vivian and Reggie moved to London after the wedding, and Mother was inconsolable for weeks."

Lily slowly withdrew her hand from his. "What did your father say about me?"

"I never . . . my father's at the office or his club most of the time, so I don't see him too often outside of business."

"You only talk to your father about business?"

"That's generally right," Eddie said. "I'll inherit the companies someday, and he wants me to know them from top to bottom."

She rose from the table, walked to the center of the sitting room, and folded her arms across her chest. "I can't believe you never said a word about me to your parents. Have they seen me in any of Matt's movies?"

"God, no! They don't—my mother wouldn't consider— movie people aren't of much interest to them. That's why I'd better talk to them alone before I take you home. You understand— to explain things."

He stepped close and wrapped his arms around her stiff body. "We can't just pop in and shock them," he said in a soothing voice. "I'll go home and see them first. After I explain that we're in love and couldn't wait to be married,

I know they'll be thrilled to meet you." He bent to kiss her neck in the space where her collar fell open.

She gradually relaxed against him. "Do you promise?"

"I promise."

She shifted in his arms so he could easily kiss her throat. He plucked at the top button of her dress when a discreet, but persistent, knocking at the door interrupted.

Stanton, the assistant manager, smiled weakly and sent a slight bow in Lily's direction. "So sorry to trouble you, Mr. Carleton. Perhaps I could see you for a moment."

Lily stared out the window and counted slowly in her head. When she reached two hundred and twenty-six, Eddie came back into the suite, his face pale.

"What is it?" she asked.

"There's a little problem with my father's account." He looked around the sitting room and found his overcoat tossed across a chair. "I'll need to see my father in his office right away."

"What problem?"

"He . . . he refused to allow our stay to go on his account. Stanton said Father was confused, and if I explain the situation, he'll certainly approve our stay here." Eddie pulled on his coat.

"I'll go with you."

"No!" Eddie's hands shook slightly as he fumbled with the buttons on his coat. "It's best if I go alone. It's rather like a business talk, you see." He sent her a weak smile. "No ladies. My father can be rather abrupt. I'm sure he was confused when Stanton checked with him." He dropped a kiss on her cheek. "You wanted my family to know about us, so here's an opportunity come right away. I'll be back before you know it."

Lily paced around the sitting room. Eddie's bravado didn't fool her. He'd made extravagant promises, but for the first time, she faced the possibility his family might not accept his choice of a bride. All those society women were snobs. The men were worse. They didn't blather about clothes or etiquette rules the way their wives did, but women outside their social class could only be useful as office clerks or in tawdry affairs.

She took a sip of the now cold coffee, sank into a chair, and waited for Eddie to return. When he finally put his key in the lock and stepped inside, she rose and met him in the center of the room. His face was pale, and he avoided her eyes while he unbuttoned his coat and tossed it on a chair.

"It's been over four hours," Lily pointed out unnecessarily. She clasped her hands in front of her to keep them from shaking.

He nodded, still avoiding her gaze. "It took longer than I expected. I went to my father's office, and then we went to the house to see my mother." He heaved a long, drawn-out sigh and raised his head to look directly at her. His normally cheerful expression had vanished, and his eyes had a dark, haunted look. "My mother became hysterical.

We had to call the doctor to give her something to sedate her."

"Because we're married?" A chill ran along her skin although the room was warm.

Eddie licked his lips. "Is there any water?" He spotted the carafe on a table and poured a full glass, draining it in two gulps. "My mother's very emotional. I told you she doesn't like change. When my father told her the news, she . . . she began to scream."

Lily's sight blurred for an instant, and she grasped the back of a nearby chair. Her fanciful notions about dinner parties with Eddie's mother dissolved. Mrs. Carleton was shocked today, but by tomorrow her shock would harden into hatred.

"I'm sorry, Eddie," she murmured. "I didn't realize your mother would be so surprised. If I'd met her before—"

"She wasn't surprised. She was frantic," he cut her off bluntly. "She collapsed and wouldn't—couldn't—stop screaming." He rubbed his eyes.

Lily slipped her arms around him under his suit coat. She ran her hand over his back the way he liked while she abandoned any idea about moving in the Carleton mansion even temporarily. They would have to find their own house immediately.

"Perhaps when she calms down, she'll feel better about us," she suggested.

"Not likely," he answered. The finality in his voice increased her rising panic.

"What did your father say when you went to his office?"

"He was furious. He said I'd behaved like an immature dolt." He groaned. "He said an acceptable marriage was expected of me—was my duty actually—and I should have discussed any marriage plans with him beforehand."

"Didn't he understand when you explained how much we love each other and wanted to be married." She felt him shudder.

"He said we have to get an annulment."

For an instant, she didn't grasp his words. When she did, alarm shot through her. "An annulment?"

Eddie caught her hands in his. "Listen, Lily, an annulment isn't like a divorce. It wouldn't be disgraceful for you. An annulment just erases what we did—as if nothing had ever happened. It could be done quietly. No one has to know besides our families."

She tried to pull away but he kept her hands firmly clasped in his own. "An annulment! How can you even say that?"

"It's not like a divorce," he repeated. "My father could arrange it."

Shock turned to fury. "Your father? How convenient!" Her gaze became suspicious. "Did you agree to an annulment?"

"I . . . I told him I had to discuss it with you." He grimaced. "I don't see much choice, Lily. My father said he'd disinherit me if we stayed married."

"He doesn't know me." Lily's voice trembled. "Why does he hate me?"

"He doesn't hate you. To my father, making the right marriage is part of business."

"He doesn't think I'm suitable."

Eddie hesitated. "He was quite definite about my future. He and Mother planned for me to marry someone from our social circle. You work in the movies, so they . . ."

"If you loved me, you wouldn't give me up." Her voice trembled.

Eddie groaned. "I do love you. I loved you the instant I saw you at the Weston reception." He kissed her frantically.

She let him kiss her for a moment before she tried another tack. "Your parents will get used to our marriage. They're upset now, but in a few weeks, they'll adjust to our being together."

" My parents—you don't know them. They won't change their attitudes." He made a helpless gesture and walked in a circle before coming back to stand in front of her. "My father said I won't have a position in any of his companies if we don't get an annulment. No job. No inheritance. What would we live on? How much do you make at the studio?"

She stared at him. "The studio? I told Matt I was leaving to marry you. I don't know if he'd take me back."

"If he did take you back, how much would he pay you? A hundred dollars a week?" Eddie shook his head. "How could we live the way we should on a hundred dollars a week?"

Lily turned white. "Twenty-five a week," she blurted. "That's what Matt pays me."

They stared at each other in silence. Lily fought an urge to shriek, to cry, to beg.

"I tried to negotiate," he said. "I bargained to keep my job and you. I said we'd keep the marriage a secret for a year until we found a way to introduce you in our circles. He said no to everything. I would be his son and heir as he always expected, or I would be nothing." He put his hands on her shoulders. "I have no particular skills, and I'm hardly suited to the life of a laboring man. We have to let my father arrange an annulment." He caressed the side of her face, letting his fingers trail down her throat. "We can still be close," he whispered.

She stepped out of his reach. "Close? You mean keep me as a mistress? You'll have your inheritance, your position, and me. What will I have?" She drew a ragged breath and crossed her arms. "I gave you . . . everything. What kind of man abandons his wife because his father threatens him and his mother's upset?"

He pressed his palms against his temples. "There's nothing to be done," he said at last in a flat voice. "I tried, but I couldn't move my father. The annulment is the only answer for us. I love you, I do, but we have no way to live comfortably."

"You should have persuaded your father before we married. You could have told him we'd never give each other up," she said.

"He wouldn't have believed me. Be reasonable. He knows perfectly well neither of us expected to be penniless after we married." His gaze mixed despair and blame in equal parts. "You knew I was rich. You didn't marry me because you wanted to live in poverty."

"No, I thought . . . we'd . . ."

Eddie glanced around the suite. "My father said we could spend the night here—leave in the morning."

"How thoughtful of him." Lily's eyes sparked dangerously. "I'm not staying here with you."

Eddie's shoulders sagged. "I'll leave then. Stay as long as you want." He struggled into his overcoat. "You might feel differently tomorrow, Lily. An annulment doesn't mean we have to split apart completely."

"Get out! I won't be your mistress!" She threw a sofa pillow in his direction. "You're a coward, and I don't want to see you anymore."

The door closed behind him. She stood frozen in the middle of the room barely breathing. She'd known their marriage would be a shock to Eddie's parents, but she'd never imagined they had the power to destroy it—and all her dreams with it. Hot tears sprang to her eyes, and she collapsed into a chair, weeping over her lost chance.

28

Lukas unlocked the safe in his office at the back of Gus's Motors and took out the red leather wallet Rae had sold him months ago. He held it next to the lamp on his desk and studied it. The leather was high quality, but the paper inside was more valuable. After his mother died, he'd run errands for a Chinese bookie who told him a wise man didn't squander an advantage but waited for the best time to use it.

Gus opened the office door without knocking. "Trouble at the tannery," he announced.

Lukas frowned. "What trouble?" He glanced at the clock on the desk. "The fight is starting in an hour."

"Otto sent word. Rudy says he wants more money to throw the fight. He says he has a reputation to uphold."

"His only reputation is that he's an over-the-hill boxer. He's paid plenty just to keep on his feet for six rounds."

"Otto said Rudy's holding out. He's not stepping into the ring. The crowd's getting restless. If they get too noisy, the police could show up." Gus shifted his feet. "Should I tell Otto to pay him more?"

"No." Lukas took another look at the wallet, tossed it back into the safe and spun the dial. "I'll handle Rudy." He shut off the desk lamp. "Let's go."

Gus drove. Lukas stared out the window while his thoughts wandered to Lily. He'd let her become an obsession. Matt's news about her marriage had jolted him. She was out of reach now, but his mind still drifted into random thoughts of soft lips, silky hair, gowns undone, and smooth bare skin.

Gus slowed the auto as he turned a corner. "Something's going on," he said, pointing to a group of newsboys, their papers strewn on the ground, four of them throwing punches at another boy crouched below them.

"Stop," Lukas said as he twisted the door handle. "Hey," he yelled.

The boys on their feet turned, hesitated in the headlights, grabbed their newspapers, and ran. The boy on the ground sat up, blood running down his face. Lukas pulled him upright.

"Thanks Mr. Krantz." Lev tried to catch some of the blood dripping from his nose on his sleeve.

"Do I know you?" Lukas dug in his pocket for a handkerchief. "What's your name?"

Lev mumbled his name and dabbed at his nose. "I'm Rae Kelly's pal. Told her where to find you when she had something to sell." He offered the bloody handkerchief to Lukas.

"Keep it. Why were you getting the worst of it?"

"I tried selling on a new corner, but they said this corner was theirs and I'd better not come back." Lev groaned. "They took my papers too." The handkerchief went back to his bleeding nose. "My ma lost her laundry job, and I need to sell more papers."

"Invading somebody else's territory is always a risky business." Lukas flicked clumps of dirt off Lev's jacket. "Want to come to a boxing match while we consider what to do next?"

Lev gaped at him. "I ain't never been to one."

"It's always good to try new things." Lukas steered him to the auto. "Climb in."

The matches were in an abandoned tannery where odors from dyes and polishes lingered in the air. The floor was stained and slick in places from old grease mixed with animal blood and oils. The crowd, a collection of laborers and clerks, generated a rising din as they cursed, made their bets, and argued about their prospects for winning. Smoke rose thick in the stale air, forming a hazy gray umbrella over the makeshift boxing ring—canvas pulled tight over a raised platform.

Lukas kept his hand on Lev's shoulder while he signaled to Otto. "Get the two Irish boys in the ring. I'll talk to Rudy." He waved a couple of middle-aged men off the bench closest to the ring and steered Lev to a seat. "Wait for me here." He and Gus headed for the door leading to a back room where the boxers changed clothes.

Lev took a deep breath dragging in as much of the smoke from cigarettes, pipes, and cigars as he could before he had to cough and gasp for air. His cut lip was swollen and so tender, he winced if he touched it with his tongue, but more important than any aching, bruised part of him was having a seat in the front row of one of Lukas Krantz's illegal boxing matches. His nose had stopped bleeding. Carefully, he folded Lukas's bloody handkerchief and stashed it in his pocket—a physical memento. He fixed his eyes on the Irish boxers—punching, backing up, and then coming together to punch again. When they lurched close to his side of the ring, he thrilled as a fine spray of sweat from their bodies fell across his face. He'd describe it all to Rae later, of course, but he wouldn't tell his ma exactly how he spent a few hours before he arrived home. The younger boxer dropped to the canvas, bringing a roar from the crowd and yells of "Get up, Red." The boxer took a count of eight before staggering to his feet. Lev's mouth went dry, and his racing heartbeat pounded in the same rhythm as the blows that knocked Red to the canvas again.

"Who's winning?" Lukas slid onto the bench beside Lev.

"Not sure," Lev mumbled, without tearing his gaze from the boxers.

After wobbling around the ring, Red suddenly landed a string of hard blows, sending the other boxer down to his knees and then flat on his face. Lev rose, yelling and shaking his fist along with the crowd, until the referee had counted a full ten. He sank back on the bench and grinned at Lukas. The flesh around one eye had turned dark, and his eyelid was swollen to twice its size. "That was swell," he said. "I thought Red was done for. He went down twice."

"Red's popular—he wins most of the time." Lukas was silent while the boxer jogged around the canvas waving his arms in triumph. "Listen Lev, I have a proposition—your mother can have a laundry job at my . . . establishment. It's across the street from my motor shop."

"You mean the house with the red—"

"That's the place."

"My ma—she's kind of religious," Lev began slowly. "I don't know if she'd feel right."

"There's a small house in the back where all the laundry and cooking are done. She'd never have to go in the main house, and she could work in the daytime when it's not very . . . busy." Lukas waited while Rudy climbed into the ring and waved at the cheering crowd before adding, "There's a lot of laundry. She could work every day."

Lev's swollen lips curved in a smile. "I guess she'd be all right with it then. Thanks, Mr. Krantz. This was my lucky night after all."

29

Since her sisters had deserted her for husbands and lovers, Rae usually stayed late at the studio helping Matt until he sent her home. On the way to her apartment, she picked up newspapers and food from Ma Fischer's. While she ate, she read the newspapers.

Austria occupies Belgrade
Royal Navy fights Germans in Falkland Islands
Canadian Light Infantry heads to France

The last headline put a stab of panic into her. Gil hadn't talked about the war lately, but she knew he hadn't forgotten about it.

She was in her nightgown ready for bed when Lily burst through the front door of the apartment—nose red, dried streaks from tears on her cheeks. "Eddie's abandoned me!" she wailed. She flung her coat on the floor and dropped into a chair while huge, gulping sobs shook her body.

"What happened?"

"His father said he'd disinherit Eddie if we were married," Lily said between sobs. "Eddie swore he loved me, but he couldn't stand up to . . ." Her weeping muffled whatever she was trying to say.

Lily wept unceasingly for over an hour. Rae made tea but she didn't touch it. She shrugged off Rae's attempt to rub her shoulders. Offered a piece of apple cake, she said she'd never eat again. What few words Rae could understand between Lily's hysterical sobs gave her a general idea of the situation.

"His mother would never—disinherited—no company position—no money—annulment." This last brought louder shrieks and wails followed by another gush of tears.

"So you left him at the Palmer House?"

Fresh wails. "He . . . he left me there. I cried for hours." Lily drew a long, shuddering breath and seized Rae's hand. "We were married for over a week. I gave him my . . . he and I were . . . I've been used!" She peered at Rae through red-rimmed eyes. "Do you know what I mean?"

Listening to the other actresses chatter in Ida's costume room had broadened Rae's education considerably. "I know what you mean, but you weren't married very long. His parents aren't going to say anything, so only a few of us will ever know it happened." She drew up a chair and put her arm around Lily. "No one will know you were used."

More sobs. "He promised me—his family's mansion—his mother—my dreams and plans." Lily put her head on her arms and soaked her sleeve with more tears. Finally, she seemed to run dry.

"You need to rest." Rae went through Lily's suitcase and pulled out a soft batiste nightgown with lilac ribbons. Lily shrieked when she saw it. More tears. Hunting through the dresser in Lily's room, Rae found a plain cotton nightgown. "Get in bed and try to sleep." Tucked in bed under a quilt, Lily continued to cry, and Rae finally lay on top of the quilt and put her arm around her sister.

"Everything was going to be perfect," Lily whispered once her sobs faded. "I'd make sure you lived with us—on Lake Drive in a mansion. We could have been in society."

Rae tightened her arms around her. "We don't have to live in a swanky house and be in society," she whispered. "Ida says I'll get plenty of money from making movies eventually. She said I might have to leave RidgeW and go to a different studio, but there's lots of money to be made."

"Do you want to leave Matt?" Lily pushed herself up on the pillows and turned a questioning gaze on Rae.

"No. Matt took us in when we didn't have anything. I owe him." Memories of the icy lake and Matt's arm pulling her to safety flashed in her mind.

"Still," Lily murmured. "You might have to change studios to advance yourself."

A thump on the door brought Rae to her feet. Delia dashed inside, pushed past Rae, and threw herself on Lily.

"I heard about what happened! You poor darling. You must be crushed."

"What did you hear?" Rae asked.

Delia rose to slip off her muskrat coat, a present from Chester. She smoothed the fur with a long caress before sitting back on the bed and taking Lily's hand. "You must not think about Eddie. He's not worthy of you."

"What did you hear?" Lily repeated Rae's question.

"He deserted you at the Palmer House—without any money. Ida knows one of the maids there, and the maid told the story. Of course, the hotel staff knew all the details because Eddie went back and forth between his father and the hotel manager about the bill and then checked out." Delia stroked Lily's hand. "Everyone's on your side. Eddie's a weakling."

"So everyone knows?" Lily's voice cracked. "Everyone at the studio?"

Delia hesitated and threw Rae a cautious glance. "Yes, but they're all completely sympathetic. I suppose the superior busybodies in town will side with the Carletons, but Chester says it's the twentieth century, and no one much cares about marriages that don't work out."

"Have you told Chester about your marriage?" Rae asked, unable to resist a jab.

"Of course not," Delia snapped. "It's a mistake to tell men too much." She turned back to Lily. "Matt promised he wouldn't let Lucinda write another word about you and Eddie."

"Another word?" Lily turned white.

"She hinted in her column you and Eddie were getting married. Lily, you have to concentrate on the future and forget this terrible episode. I'm staying here tonight. I won't leave you alone." Delia sighed. "It's so tragic."

Lily sank back on the pillows and stared at the ceiling. "I suppose I should focus on my career—my role in *Barriers Burned Away*. Work helps heal wounds—or so I've heard."

Delia shot a meaningful glance at Rae and continued to pat Lily's hand.

Left to share the bad news, Rae sat on the other side of the bed. "You said you weren't coming back, so Matt had to recast the movie. Eve is playing the lead role now."

Lily looked stricken. "Will he take me back at all?"

Rae and Delia exchanged uneasy glances. Then they uttered a stream of reassurances—Matt would be happy to take her back—he'd put her in a movie the minute she was ready—she looked gorgeous on the screen—she'd be working with Billy—or in a western.

Lily sniffled on and off while Delia continued to murmur advice in her ear, but Rae stared at the ceiling thinking about Matt. Maybe she'd have to threaten to quit in the middle of a *Dora* serial. Ida had said over and over Matt needed her more than she needed him now that she was a success. She felt his arm again, pulling her out of the lake, back to life.

In the morning, Rae woke first, dressed, made a pot of extra strong tea, and heated corn muffins in the oven. The aroma brought Delia and Lily to the kitchen. Lily sipped her tea and sighed heavily. Her nose was red, and her eyes were so puffy, they'd turned into narrow slits.

When Rae answered the vigorous knocking on the door, a man in a dark suit asked for Lily, accepted Rae's word Lily was in the apartment, and handed Rae a large envelope. He nodded and quickly disappeared into the street.

Lily gasped when she unfolded the papers inside. "It's the annulment."

"Well, well," Delia said. "Eddie's father certainly wasted no time. He must have a judge in his pocket." She peered across the table at the papers. "I hope the lawyer put a check in there—for your trouble—for your—" She glanced at Rae. "After all, Eddie did have his enjoyment with you. Mr. Carleton ought to know he has to compensate."

Mute, Lily held up a pale blue check.

Delia snatched it from her. "Five hundred dollars," she announced. "Cheapskate. I wonder—could you demand more?"

Lily gave a little shriek, and her tears started again.

Rae put her arms around Lily and shot an irritated look at Delia. "Be quiet, Delia. Lily's upset. Her marriage is over."

Delia shrugged. "It was just a thought."

"Rich people do get what they want fast," Rae muttered.

A soft chuckle came from Delia. "A good reason for the three of us to get very rich."

30

"Rudy's skipped town." Gus stood in the doorway of Lukas's office.

"I told him to go," Lukas said. "He's not a big loss, but I need a new boxer—a fresh face, somebody younger to get the crowds excited."

His boxing matches made money no matter who was in the ring. Madame Yvonne's had a steady business. Card games were profitable. RidgeW Pictures was the enterprise sucking up his profits, and now the Chicago censor board was interfering with the productions. The red leather wallet was back on his desk, propped against the base of the lamp. He'd been considering how to approach Weston with the contents. He tapped the wallet with his finger. "Find Sean Rogan for me. I want a meeting with his boss. Tell Rogan it's to Weston's advantage to meet. I'll come to his city office—he can set the time."

Gus tipped his head in the direction of the street. "Rogan's across at Madame's. I saw him go inside a few minutes ago. He likes to visit Sadie."

"Let's not interrupt him. After an hour with Sadie, he'll be relaxed, even accommodating. Sit in the parlor over there until he comes out and talk to him then." Gus turned to leave, but Lukas stopped him. "Did you find out where Eddie Carleton's taking his honeymoon?"

Gus paused in the doorway. "Sorry, I forgot to tell you. I heard this morning Carleton isn't on a honeymoon. He's back with his family, and Miss Lily is back with her sisters. Word is old Mr. Carleton didn't take to having a movie girl in his family." Gus lingered in the doorway, but Lukas made a dismissive gesture.

A piano rendition of "Oh, You Beautiful Doll" drifted through the closed, but drafty, windows of Gus's Motors, Lukas let the music flow over him while he considered the ramifications of Gus's information. He wasn't entirely surprised. Old man Carleton wouldn't have had much patience with Eddie's romantic inclinations—especially regarding a young woman with no background who worked in the movies. What was surprising—astonishing— was the powerful flash of relief he'd felt when Gus told him the news. He drummed his fingers on the desk. He'd tried to shut Lily out of his mind, but he'd failed. He didn't believe in fate as a rule, but the instant she'd lifted her blue eyes to meet his at the Weston reception, he knew she belonged to him. The sooner she realized it, the better. Various possible approaches occurred to him—flowers, jewelry, invitations to fancy restaurants. Nothing seemed right. It was too soon. She'd be devastated over Eddie Carleton's betrayal and angry at herself for making such a mistake. He'd have to wait for her—again.

Lukas parked the Pierce-Arrow on a side street a half block from Weston's mansion. He'd been told not to come to Weston's city office—too public. Weston didn't want to be seen dealing with a man who ran illegal businesses. Lukas was to come to the house, after eleven, and knock at the back entrance where tradesmen delivered their goods. He didn't mind the late hour, but being told to use the delivery entrance stirred his deep-seated hostility to Weston and his kind—rich politicians who pretended to be offended by mercenary dealings.

He stepped onto the curb and walked down the street, ignoring the iron gate and stone path leading to the mansion's back entrance where Sean Rogan would be waiting for him. Climbing the front stairs and pausing between the nymphs on each side of the double doors, he lifted the heavy knocker and let it drop with a clang. Knowing Rogan would need an extra minute to leave the back door and rush to the front to answer, Lukas dropped the knocker again and then once more. He was about to drop it a fourth time when Rogan wrenched open the door, panting slightly from his run through the house.

"I told you to come to the back," he snarled. He looked at the empty street. "Did anyone see you?"

Lukas pushed past him. "Who cares? Nobody's robbing a bank. Tell Weston I'm here."

Weston was seated behind his desk in his library. He didn't rise when Lukas entered, but his glance indicated a chair in front of the desk. His tie was undone, and he'd taken off his suit coat, revealing the soft flesh around his middle sagging over his belt. After taking a swallow from the tumbler of whiskey on his desk, he lit a cigar and leaned back in his chair, without offering either to Lukas. "Sean says you need to see me about something. Can't imagine what we have to discuss."

If they'd met in a location under Lukas' control, he'd have smacked Weston around to teach him respect before starting the conversation, but here, he smiled coldly and leaned back in the leather chair. "RidgeW Pictures," he said. "We have censorship problems I think you can help us eliminate."

Weston rested his cigar on the edge of a silver-rimmed ashtray. "Matt Ridgewood owns RidgeW Pictures. Why are you here?"

"I'm sure you know I finance the studio. Matt is the creative partner." Lukas lowered his voice. "I'm concerned with the money situation. The Chicago censorship board is making Matt cut all the scenes in which the ladies are not fully covered. Every studio in town has those scenes, but for some reason Matt gets a weekly notice from the board telling him to cut his." He flicked a tiny piece of lint off his pants. "This situation is costing me money."

Weston leaned forward. "Matt needs to leave town. I've advised him to go to California. I hear all the big studios are going there. Chicago's no place for him. You should persuade him to move on."

Lukas shook his head. "We need to make money now. I've invested in RidgeW, and I want it to pay off."

"Your investment could pay off in California. You don't need to sit next to your money." Weston took another swallow of his whiskey. "In fact, I could make it worth your while to send Matt to California. An extra bonus up front, let us say."

"California is hardly in my territory, and I like to keep my investments all in the same area," Lukas said. He studied the man across the desk. Weston seemed relaxed, but a trace of desperation flickered in his eyes. If Weston wasn't certain his wife was visiting Matt whenever he was out of town, he had a strong suspicion she was. The push for California was a dead giveaway. "Matt isn't going anywhere," Lukas added.

"What kind of bonus would persuade you to get Matt out of town?"

"Bonuses are for employees. I'm concerned with my investments."

Weston drained his glass. "I want him out of Chicago for good. He's . . . his presence creates obstacles for some of my interests."

"Obstacles," Lukas said in a philosophical tone, "can be difficult, but every man has problems. He has to face them and solve them. That's why I'm here. You control the members of the censorship board—most of them anyway. Put pressure on the board, so they'll let RidgeW keep those scenes with the naked women."

"Not a chance," Weston replied. "Why should I help you? You aren't offering to help me."

Lukas put his hand inside his coat. "Rogan, come in here," he called.

Sean popped through the door so fast he'd obviously been listening outside. Lukas held up the red wallet. "Tell your boss what this is."

"It's—It's my wallet—and the paper I lost."

Weston's face reddened. He smacked the top of his desk with the flat of his hand. "Get out!"

Lukas waited until the footsteps in the hallway faded. "As you can see, I'm prepared to offer you something rather valuable. You'll have new obstacles in your life if I show this list of names and bribes to the right people."

"Just a bunch of numbers on a sheet of paper."

Lukas smiled. "The numbers aren't that hard to interpret. I'm sure the police commissioner could do it, or, even better, the editor of the *Chicago Tribune*. It might go hard for you." He glanced around the room. "You might lose your mansion—or more."

"How much do you want?"

"I don't want your money. I want you to fix the censorship problem."

Weston sat breathing heavily for a long moment. "I could speak to a few people. Naturally, I can't guarantee—"

"I like guarantees."

"All right, I'll fix it." Weston picked up his glass, noticed it was empty, and put it down. "Matt can put as many naked women in his movies as he wants. The board won't send any more notices." He reached for the wallet. "I guess that concludes our business."

Lukas tucked the wallet in his inside pocket. "For the moment, it does. I don't want to have to come back here and complain your boys on the censorship board didn't do what you told them to."

"I said I'd fix it. What about the wallet?"

"It's safe for now." Lukas rose from the chair, pulling his gloves out of the pockets of his overcoat. "I'll make sure no one sees it."

As Lukas closed the door behind him, Weston hurled his empty whiskey glass against the fireplace.

31

Rae pulled the last cranberry through the heavy thread, tied off the end, and handed the string to Ida who draped it over the branches of the official RidgeW Christmas tree, a short, scrawny pine set up in the back studio that usually served as the saloon for the westerns. Rae had offered to help with the arrangements for the Christmas party, but Ida had taken charge and settled on the food, drink, and decorations. She'd ordered Bud up on a ladder to loop green and red crepe paper around the doors and windows and tie red ribbons to the overhead lights. Finally, she'd insisted on a sizeable cluster of mistletoe tied to a low-hanging light in the center of the room.

"That's for Billy," she said, winking at Rae. "He won't have to strain too much to catch someone under it."

Rae took a paper angel out of a box. "I thought you warned the girls away from Billy."

"It's Christmas. Even Billy deserves a little present." Ida chuckled as she poked the angel over the twig sticking up near the top of the tree. She glanced at the opposite end of the room where Lily was filling cups with punch and adding a splash of gin when requested. "Wasn't sure Lily would come to the party. She's been gloomy."

"She's still suffering over Eddie," Rae said, "but I told her we needed help. I don't know where Delia is—somewhere with Chester."

Ida arranged the red cotton skirt around the tree stand. "Lily's lucky Matt took her back. He was furious—doesn't show it much, but I can tell when he's boiling."

Rae was silent. Luck had nothing to do with Lily's return. She'd had to beg Matt to give Lily another chance and suspected she'd only succeeded because he wanted "Dora" to be happy.

The outside door opened. Wind and light snow swirled into the room for an instant as Lukas entered, carrying a box marked Krauss's Bakery. A thin layer of snow covered his overcoat, and his black hair glistened with melting flakes. He shook his head, sending a cold mist over Rae. Opening his coat to shake off the snow, he grinned. "Merry Christmas, Rae. Heard from your old man?"

"Merry Christmas. You know Pa won't be back in town." His question and her answer were the same every time they saw each other—a running joke. She'd stopped being nervous about Lukas and Pa months ago.

"You never know. *Danger for Dora* is in a lot of theaters. I'm betting Maxie will see you and think you're rich."

Rae gave a mock groan. "I wish I was rich."

Lukas slicked his hair back into place. "What's Matt paying you these days?"

"Twenty-five a week, same as always."

"Not much of a deal maker, are you? You ought to have fifty a week at least. I'll talk to Matt." He winked at Ida. "Run away with me, Ida. We need some sun. Miami sounds good."

Ida put her hands on her hips and cocked her head. "You couldn't handle me."

He laughed. "Maybe not, but I could die trying."

"All this talk must be holiday fever," Ida said. "Billy kissed me under the mistletoe the minute we put it up."

Lukas glanced up at the white berries and then around the room. "If I can't have you, Ida, I'd better see who else I can find."

"I'll take the bakery," Rae said, reaching for the box.

"No," he said, his gaze on Lily at the opposite end of the room. "I'll carry it over there."

Apprehensive, Rae trailed after him. He was going to talk to Lily, and she was in no mood to be nice. If Lukas said the wrong thing, she might erupt into tears the way she did at home. Lukas put the box at the end of the long table with the punch bowl. Taking side steps as she unpacked the gingerbread cookies, Rae managed to edge close enough to hear their voices over the noise in the room.

"I hoped to find you under the mistletoe."

Lily looked at him, her face blank. "Do you want punch?"

"The mistletoe would suit me better. Maybe it would suit you too if you gave it a try."

"I'm not interested in trying it."

"Why not? Let's enjoy the holidays." She glared at him without answering, her fingers curled into fists. His smile faded. "I'm glad you came back to RidgeW after . . . you were missed."

Lily filled a cup with punch and held it out until he took it. "Anything else?"

"The mistletoe."

"Never," she snapped.

"Never?" He looked at the red-orange punch and put the cup on the table without tasting it. "I'm sorry you were hurt. Let me take you somewhere tonight. We'll have a good time. They can manage here." He made a vague gesture at the room.

"I don't believe you."

"About what?"

"That you're sorry."

"I'm not sorry Eddie Carleton gave you up," he said, a rough note slipping into his voice. "I'm sorry for the way it happened. Come out with me now."

"No. You think because Eddie Carleton left me I've fallen to your level like those women in . . . I haven't. I'm not going to compromise."

He straightened and buttoned his overcoat. "I'm patient. I can wait for you."

Lily glanced at Rae while Lukas headed for the door. "I wasn't harsh. I was truthful."

"I guess so," Rae mumbled.

Leaving Lily at the punch bowl, Rae focused on the mistletoe activity. Eve was under the white berries, kissing every man who came near. Billy stood next to her, and most of the women in the room lined up for kisses. Even Lucinda, having had two cups of punch with the extra splashes of gin, went straight for Billy to get a holiday kiss. Apparently, just standing under the mistletoe was enough to capture a kiss. How to avoid the unwelcome kisses and get the kiss she wanted was the question. Gil and Matt were talking on the other side of the room—nowhere near the crucial spot. She couldn't drag Gil under the mistletoe.

Matt knocked a metal rod against a post for attention. "Merry Christmas, everybody! We've had a good year, and I expect next year to be even better."

Billy gave a somewhat drunken hurrah, bringing laughs from the crowd. "Billy's got it right," Matt said. "Unfortunately, we're going to lose one of our own. Gil's leaving RidgeW to join the Canadian army. A round of applause would seem to be in order."

A hard pulse started in Rae's throat. The last time she and Lev had gone through the newspapers, they'd read terrible descriptions of deep water in muddy trenches—waist high in some places—barbed wire, and hopeless attacks by the British in driving rain that left half a battalion dead or wounded. When she'd asked Matt, he said a battalion was about a thousand men. Five hundred bodies on a field was beyond her imagination. She watched the men slap Gil on the back and predict the war would be over before he got to France. Eve kissed him. Rae's feet felt nailed to the floor.

"He'll be all right," Ida whispered, putting her arm around Rae's shoulders.

"Of course, he will," Rae said. But everybody lied about war. Nobody ever said *don't volunteer—my god, you'll be killed.*

At last after many slaps on the back and hugs, he smiled in her direction and walked toward her. "Are you surprised?"

"No, I knew you'd volunteer someday." A long, ragged breath. "Promise you'll come back to . . . all of us."

"Sure I will," he said. "I'll write to you, but I'll be back before I write more than one or two letters. People say the war can't last long." He took her hand. "I'm getting a train tonight for home. Don't get in trouble while I'm gone."

She let out a shuddering sigh and hugged him. "Be careful." Her cheek rested against his chest where she could hear his heartbeat. In spite of her best effort not to cry, her tears made a damp spot on his shirt. "I mean," she whispered, "don't do anything dangerous."

He laughed. "I'll do my best. Take care of yourself, Rae." He put his hands on either side of her face and dropped a light kiss on her forehead.

Without any plan, Rae rose on her toes, locked her arms around his neck, and pressed her lips against his. She was awkward. She was desperate. She hung on even after she felt him freeze in surprise.

Then his arms circled her waist, and he kissed her the way she'd imagined he would, sending that shiver of excitement through her again. He broke the kiss first and smiled down at her, flicking away the tear sliding down her cheek. "Hey, that was nice, but don't grow up too fast. Stay out of trouble until I get back." Another minute and he was gone, taking his coat, waving to Matt, and closing the door behind him.

Rae ran her finger over her lips, tracing her first real-life adult kiss. If only the warm feeling running through her would last forever. If only Gil would come back and kiss her again.

The door to the outside banged against the wall. Arm in arm, Chester and Delia pushed into the room. A bottle of champagne slipped out of Chester's hand, shattering into bits of glass, frothy liquid spilling across the floor. "We have an announcement!" Chester hiccupped and looked at Delia.

She giggled. "We're married!" she called out. "Surprise!"

Stunned silence exploded into cheers, sounding increasingly drunken as they continued. Matt kicked the glass shards under a table. Fred found a towel and soaked up the champagne. One of the crew handed Chester a glass of gin without any punch, and a great deal of back-slapping began along with low jokes about wedding nights. Women surrounded Delia, who giggled and simpered as if she were a nervous virgin about to fall into the hands of her ravisher.

It's the best acting she's done, Rae thought as she watched. In a minute, Delia rushed toward her, arms outstretched, shrieking excitedly as she flung her arms around Rae. Lily followed.

"Are you crazy?" Rae said in a low voice. "You can't marry Chester. You're already married."

"What are you thinking?" Lily hissed.

Delia managed to look offended. "I'm not crazy," she said, matching Rae's low tone. "Chester's planning to go to California, and I'm going with him. We'll be in the movies together." She glanced over her shoulder. "He doesn't know about Hal and doesn't need to. That's in my past. I'm thinking of the future."

"You can't cross off a husband as if he doesn't exist," Rae said.

"Hal's on an onion farm in Wisconsin."

"You said you still loved him," Lily said.

Delia made a face. "Maybe I do, but love isn't everything. I know Chester's not exactly the best . . . but he says the movies in California can make us rich. Our careers will soar."

Rae sneered. "Are you going to work half-naked in California too?"

"Don't act smart with me," Delia snapped. "You're in that stupid serial playing a twelve-year old and telling everyone here you're only thirteen."

What if Chester finds out about Hal?" Lily cast an anxious look at the men joking near the liquor table. "How are you going to explain yourself if—when—Chester finds out what you've done?"

"He's not going to find out if you both keep quiet. I'm not the only one with secrets. What would Matt say if he knew Rae turned seventeen a month ago? Dora's been sleeping in that Alaskan cabin with the three fur trappers for most of the episodes so far. How will that play with the audiences who think she's such a little darling?" Delia heaved a sigh. "I thought you'd be happy for me. I have a famous husband now."

"Be careful," Lily whispered. "Just be careful."

More toasts. More jokes. Smirking, Chester announced he and Delia needed to start their honeymoon in his suite at the LaSalle Hotel. More laughter—a final toast—and people drifted into the cold December night.

Ida shook her head. "Can't tell what will happen next," she muttered to Rae as they cleared the table of dirty glasses.

"Whatever it is, it won't be good," Rae mumbled.

Lucinda pulled on her gloves and looked around the empty room. "Are you coming, Matt? I'll walk out with you."

"I want to check the prop list for the saloon in *Guns Along the Red River*. I'll lock up later."

"You work too hard. Isn't one western saloon a great deal like every other western saloon?"

Matt grinned. "Yes, but I want to make some changes, so we don't have an out-and-out copy of the previous saloon."

Outside, the taxi she'd called waited at the curb. With a sigh and a shiver, Lucinda slid into the back seat and gave the driver her address. As they pulled into the street, she slipped her gloved hands into her sleeves for further warmth. The moonlight glinted off the fresh snow and reduced the normal darkness for the time of night.

Passing the driveway leading to the back of the studio, Lucinda peered out. Was that Arabella Weston in a taxi parked near the rear entrance? The woman certainly looked like Arabella, but why would she be waiting outside in this weather? Unable to see clearly enough to be sure, Lucinda slumped back in her seat but instantly sat upright and ordered the driver to slow down. Parked down the street from the studio was another vehicle, and this was one she recognized—Theodore Weston's Packard with the special gold trim. As her taxi crept past, she focused on the driver sitting hunched against the cold in the front seat.

Sean Rogan.

Why? Her mind sorted through possibilities until she remembered finding Matt and Arabella Weston in the conservatory at the reception. If her suspicions were right—and they always were—the woman in the taxi must be Arabella Weston. Sean must have followed her. And Matt was working late at the studio. How very very interesting.

32

The LaSalle Hotel waiter rolled a cart with sandwiches, coffee, and three bottles of whiskey into Chester's suite. Delia poured coffee into two cups while Chester fumbled in his pants pocket and pulled out a five dollar bill. He waved off the clerk's effusive gratitude, closed the door firmly, and locked it. Delia held out a cup of coffee. He ignored it, seizing instead one of the whiskey bottles.

Delia sipped her coffee, and watched him pour a full glass of the whiskey. She'd hoped he'd stay sober for their wedding night because he usually turned nasty with too much alcohol, and she had the bruises to prove it. Seeing him drink nearly half the glass quickly, she sensed the time had already passed for a serious conversation. She'd need to tread lightly if she wanted to get information from him.

"Don't drink too much," she said, putting a teasing note in her voice. "I'm looking forward to a romantic wedding night."

He blinked at her, narrowing his eyes. "I guess I can drink as much as I want in my own suite." He put his finger under her chin and tipped her face up to his. "A romantic wedding night? It's not as though I haven't had you already."

Delia ignored the taunt. In spite of his occasional slaps and drunken insults, Chester's desires and her ambitions blended very well. She studied her new husband, trying to judge whether she could get solid information out of him before he slipped into drunken rambling. "Have you talked to anyone about a job in California?"

He peered at his half-empty glass and refilled it. "Sure, I've talked to people. I'm holding out for a lot more money. Matt hasn't paid me what I'm worth." He lifted his glass in her direction, "Your big talent is taking off your clothes, but I'm an actor. I have awards. I should be paid plenty, and *Barriers* is making money, getting good reviews. California studios know how to treat actors properly."

"Who have you been talking to?" Delia put her coffee cup on the service cart and forced a smile. "The studios must be begging you to come to Los Angeles. You'll be a big star once we get out there."

"I'm a star in Chicago." He glowered at her.

"Of course you are. I meant you'll be an even bigger star in Los Angeles. The studios out there are getting bigger every day, and they know you're a great actor." How drunk was he? She pressed a little harder. "Who have you talked to?"

"People," he snapped. "I've talked to people. Don't know whether to trust them. Everybody lies about deals. Hard to tell what they're thinking." He put his glass down hard enough to splash the whiskey over the rim. Turning to her, he placed his hands on either side of her head, palms pressing on her temples, as if he were going to squash her head into pulp. "Can't stand liars," he mumbled. "Don't ever lie to me, Delia."

She went dry with fright. "I won't, Chester. I'd never lie to you. My sisters—we were raised to tell the truth."

He dropped his hands and cuffed her on the chin hard enough to send her staggering a few steps away from him. "Your sisters," he muttered. "You'd better not tell them we're planning to go to California. Rae—she's loyal to Matt. She'd go to him and tell him what she knows without a second thought for you or me."

"I won't tell anyone."

He coughed. "Lily—she's a wonder. Thinks she's above all of us. The Carletons showed her where she ranked. Matt keeps her on because she's pretty—doesn't have any more talent than you do."

She wouldn't argue with him. She wanted him happy and content. Now that she was his wife instead of merely a lover, she was more confident about her future. He'd take her with him. She'd dreamed the fantasy until it seemed inevitable—warm weather, swimming pools, palm trees, and gobs of money. "My sisters don't know anything," she assured him. "It's just you and me, Chester."

He eyed her. Flopping into an upholstered chair, he stretched his legs. "Time to start the honeymoon," he mumbled, unclasping his belt. "You know what I like."

33

Matt adjusted the pillow and sank back on the four-poster iron bed, the main prop in Billy's latest comedy *Ghostly Nights!* "Merry Christmas," he muttered.

Shivering, Arabella pulled a patchwork quilt over them. "That," she murmured, running her hand down Matt's chest, "was not entirely the act of a gentleman."

He kissed her shoulder. "I wasn't trying to be a gentleman just then. Are you complaining? I got the impression you rather liked it."

Her lashes veiled her eyes, but she smiled. "What made you think that?"

He slid his hand under the quilt. "Your moans and your little scream tipped me off."

She tilted her head back against the pillow and laughed. "All right, I confess—I did like it, but I like everything you do. I'm not much of a lady I suppose."

"Being a lady might be highly overrated," he murmured, stroking his hand across her stomach and down her thigh, enjoying the tremor following his touch. Whenever he was with her now, the present faded, and in his mind they were in her mother's gazebo where Arabella had gasped and clung to him while they made love.

"You've been in the company of movie actresses too long. Everyone knows they aren't ladies."

He propped himself up on one arm so he could watch her face while his hand under the quilt continued its exploration. "Some are," he said.

He'd seen Rae kiss Gil goodbye. She was on the verge of growing up. She'd never mentioned a birthday, so she might be fourteen by now. How long could she play Dora as a young girl? How long would she want to? Another worry he could add to his list.

Arabella frowned. "I suppose you've enjoyed the ones who aren't ladies."

"Let's not examine what we've done when we weren't together," he murmured, kissing her shoulder again. "Let's pretend it's summer, and I'm leaving for Harvard and we're in the gazebo, saying goodbye."

Arabella kissed his jaw and ran her fingers through his hair. "I was so desperate for you to touch me that night, I touched you first. So, I'm not a lady either." She paused. "If I were, I wouldn't be here."

"You're my love," he said, pressing a kiss on the curve at the base of her throat, "from the instant you gave me an extra piece of cake at your birthday party."

"My eighth birthday. I didn't want you to go home, so I used chocolate cake to hold you."

"I'm glad you're here tonight—an early Christmas present for me. How did you . . . where is . . ." He couldn't bring himself to utter the name.

"Theodore's in Detroit for some business. I don't ask why he's traveling because all I care about is that he's gone. He'll be back tomorrow. Tonight is our only chance to be together for a while. The holidays, you know. My mother has teas and parties planned."

"The holidays," he echoed. Her words dragged him away from his memories about the past to the present. "Ida talked me into giving everyone ten days off."

"Are you behind schedule?" She shifted closer to him.

"A little. I planned to work extra days on Chester's detective movie and finish before Christmas, but he got married today to Delia Kelly, so I don't think he'll be co-operative about doing more scenes right now."

"Married? Isn't she the one who takes off her clothes?"

"She's the one, but most of the scenes have been cut until now."

"Is the censor board making you take them out?" she asked.

"Not last week." He hesitated, not sure what she knew about Weston's connection to the censor board or about Lukas's visit to her husband. Whatever she knew, he didn't want to think about her husband or that she had one. "That censorship problem might be solved. Delia was practically naked in the bath last week, and the censors didn't notice it or didn't care."

"So the censor board isn't a problem. *Barriers Burned Away* got wonderful reviews in all the papers. People are rushing to the theaters to see it, and the Dora serial is selling lots of tickets. You'll be rich again very soon," she said, twisting to gaze up at him. "Promise me you'll be rich very soon. Then I can leave Theodore." She kissed his mouth lingeringly.

His eyes darkened. "What if I don't become rich very soon?"

"Oh, darling, you will! I have absolute faith in you."

"All right—I promise to become rich as King Midas."

"And soon." She reached under the quilt and directed his hand. "Please, please," she whispered, "tell me it will be soon."

Emeline Graham paced the dark hallway at the top of the stairs. She tightened the sash of her heavy cotton wrapper and pulled the collar up around her neck to keep out the chill. It was three o'clock in the morning, and her daughter was missing. Emeline wasn't worried. She was furious.

The front door creaked softly as it swung open on its hinges, and Emeline leaned over the railing, peering through the dark. The front hall was shadowy, but she had no trouble recognizing Arabella as she slipped through the door and closed it silently behind her. She waited in the darkness until Arabella came up the stairs on tiptoe and reached the landing.

"Where have you been?" Emeline's voice, low and harsh, broke the night stillness.

Arabella started, grabbing the banister for support. Looking up, she shook her head with a defiant air. "I don't have to tell you anything." She climbed the last flight of stairs and faced Emeline. "You know where I was—or if not, *where*, then you know *who* I was with."

Emeline winced. "You're mad," she whispered. "You'll destroy us."

"There's no need to whisper, Mother. The servants are at the other end of the house. Only the two of us know I was gone this evening."

"Don't be too sure," Emeline said, keeping her voice low. "Sean took the Packard out late tonight. He could have followed you—found you."

"I took a taxi," Arabella said. "The Packard was still here when I left. He couldn't have followed me."

"He wouldn't have to follow precisely," Emeline snapped. "It would be enough to ascertain where you'd gone."

"How could he *ascertain*, as you put it, if he couldn't follow me?"

"Heavens, Arabella, it wouldn't require Sherlock Holmes! Theodore probably told Sean to keep track of your activities when he's gone on business." Emeline paused as a shiver of terror went through her. "If Sean says you went to Matt's studio, Theodore could throw us out. We'll be back where we were before you married him—penniless."

"I won't give up Matt." Arabella's whisper matched her mother's. "I can't."

"You have to! You have to give him up before Theodore is certain enough to accuse you." Emeline twisted her hands. "I warned you over and over you needed a child for security."

"You convinced me to marry Theodore, but that's all I'm willing to do." A look of revulsion crossed Arabella's face. "You can't know . . . Theodore won't give me up. He won't accuse me."

A sympathetic light shone in Emeline's eyes. "I know he's visited your room more frequently these past weeks. A man can fool himself into thinking a woman young enough to be his daughter—or even granddaughter—wants to be in his bed. Men have enormous egos in these matters, but his ego will not let him live with betrayal, especially if rumors start."

"He won't give me up," Arabella repeated.

Emeline gripped Arabella's arm. "Scandal will wreck his standing in business and politics. He couldn't live with that." She released Arabella and made a helpless gesture. "If he doesn't abandon you, then he'll do something drastic to save his pride. Whatever he does, you and I will certainly suffer."

Arabella shrugged. "Don't worry, Mother. I know what I'm doing."

"You have to stop this madness!" Emeline reached for her again, but Arabella had already walked away.

34

Out and About with Lucinda Corday

I have exhilarating real-life romantic news from RidgeW Pictures! Chester Slater, the dynamic star of *Barriers Burned Away*, and Delia Kelly, who has been eye catching recently in certain risqué scenes, fell desperately in love while they worked on the mature dramas RidgeW is producing. After a whirlwind romance, the two lovebirds are beginning married life in Chicago as well as maintaining their careers at RidgeW. Friends tell me they are deliriously happy and look forward to working on more movies together.

Unfortunately, because *Barriers Burned Away* has been such a smashing success, RidgeW is losing Eve Darling. The popular actress is leaving Chicago to work at Keystone

Pictures Studio in California, where she will co-star in a series of charming comedies opposite rising actor Tommy Roland. My sources tell me Eve's salary is tripling at Keystone, and she's been promised a dressing room as lavish as Mary Pickford's.

Duty calls another RidgeW star away to join the war in Europe. Gil Owen, who has been starring in westerns and co-starring in the *Danger for Dora* serial has returned to his native Canada to join the forces being sent to support the British army in France. We certainly wish him well. It looks as though Matthew Ridgewood will have to restock his studio with more actors!

Finally, do look for the next month's issue of *Motion Picture Magazine* because I have an exclusive interview with Rae Kelly, the perky star of *Danger for Dora*. We discuss the future, and Rae confides her most private hopes and dreams to me. I'll be doing more special interviews for *Motion Picture Magazine* to bring you the latest and most intimate news about the actors in your favorite movies.

Until next time, dear readers.

35

Rae had always hated the days after Christmas. The drab period of winter seized the city while snow swirled through the streets and temperatures dipped into single digits.

Missing Gil, she told herself she understood the dark side of love now. Maybe love never worked out. Lily still suffered from Eddie's betrayal, but she'd moved from weeping to fury. Delia claimed to be happy, but Rae saw her bruises. Lily predicted Chester would never take Delia to California because men could not be trusted to live up to their promises. Delia had turned white at the mention of California and made them swear to keep Chester's plans secret, especially from Matt.

Rae had debated whether she should warn Matt about Chester, but she'd decided not to add to his troubles if Chester didn't have any offers yet. Matt had hired new actors for the westerns, but they didn't look right.

Even handlebar mustaches did nothing to cover their city looks, and the new westerns weren't as popular as the ones with Gil. Matt kept a smile on his face, but Rae suspected he was losing money in spite of her serial and Billy's comedies.

Rae balanced on a stool while Ida pinned her overalls. "Matt gave me a raise to fifty dollars a week. I feel guilty about taking it."

"Don't feel guilty. You have to look out for yourself."

Gus opened the door. "You got a letter," he said waving the envelope under Rae's nose. Fred told me to bring it as long as I was heading this way."

"Don't you know how to knock? Ladies are changing clothes in here." Ida put her hands on her hips and glared at Gus.

He turned dark red. "Sorry, didn't think."

"Well, next time think," Ida snapped.

Rae ignored both of them. "It's from Gil," she said, staring at the Canadian stamp.

Ida jabbed a pin in the bib of her apron. "Go ahead and read it. I can't pin you if you're fidgeting." She looked at Gus. "Why are you hanging around?"

"Ain't hanging around. I got business with Matt."

"Well, go do it then. You've got no business in my costume room." Ida twitched her skirt as if shooing him away.

"Saw Matt already, and I had some extra time. So I came to see you." He folded his arms and leaned against the door frame.

"I've got work to do."

"Sure, but I sorta wanted to see you." He didn't move.

Ida smoothed her hair. "With Rae busy reading her letter, I guess I could brew some coffee if you aren't going anywhere."

"I got time. Ain't going anywhere right now," Gus mumbled as he followed her out the door.

Rae tore open the envelope the instant they left.

> *Dear Rae,*
>
> *I have arrived home in Ottawa, and I am pleased to say that I have enlisted in the army. I don't know where I'll be sent next, but I suppose I'll go to France before long. I have made a good friend in Jack Sommers from Toronto. We hope to be in the same unit and do our fighting together. Most of the fellows think the war could be finished before we are needed. I miss you and everyone at the studio. Say hello for me. I will write again when I have time. Your friend, Gil.*

She and Lev poured over the newspapers every day, and she'd bought a map so they could find places with strange names like Ypres, Le Havre, and Neuve Chapelle. Hand-to-hand fighting—No-Man's Land—flame throwers—casualties. She'd pictured Gil in all those places and shuddered.

She read the letter again. If only he'd written *love* instead of *your friend*. People at the studio flung that word around all the time. He didn't have to mean it, not really, but it would have been nice to see it written. Slowly, she folded the letter and tucked it inside her camisole.

"Rae." Bud stopped in the doorway. "There's a fellow at the front. He asked for Delia, but she's not here. Then he asked for Lily or you."

"I'll go," she said.

The man had his back to her, but she knew who he was the instant she saw his dark brown hair curled over his ears and half-way down his neck. Tall and brawny, he filled his faded jacket so it stretched tight across his back and shoulders. When her shoes clicked on the smooth floor, he spun around and grinned. "Rae!"

"Hal," she answered, barely able to keep the shock out of her voice. Bud had disappeared, but she took Hal's arm and pulled him in the direction of the costume room. "Let's go somewhere private."

"Good to see you, Rae. I asked for Delia, but the fellow said she wasn't here."

"What are you doing in Chicago?" Rae said in a low tone as she closed the door behind them.

The cheerful look in his eyes faded, and his mouth tensed. "I came for my wife. I read in the newspaper she got married to some actor fellow. How could she do that, Rae? I'm her husband—she can't have two."

"Delia just does what she wants."

"I figured she'd visit you and Lily, have some city fun, and come back to me."

"She said she didn't like living on a farm. She wasn't cut out for it."

His big hands clenched together. "I saw one of those movies where she didn't have any clothes on."

Rae winced. "She had clothes on, just not enough of them. No one forced her. Delia volunteered." She didn't want him to blame Matt.

"I don't care what she's been doing." He shook his head. "I want her back."

"Delia's in sort of a complicated situation," Rae said.

Ida and Gus opened the door, both holding mugs of steaming coffee. Gus scowled. "Who are you? Rae, you all right?"

She put her hand on Hal's arm. "This is Hal Bauer, an old friend. He's visiting Chicago and stopped by to say hello." She mumbled introductions.

Gus eyed Hal's muscled arms and shoulders. "Staying in Chicago?"

"I might." Hal looked at Rae. "I got some things to work out."

"Got a job?" Gus asked.

"No, got to Chicago this afternoon."

"Ever do any boxing?"

"Not boxing official." Hal straightened. "I've been in some fights all right. I guess I handled them."

"If you're staying in town, my boss might have a job. He'd have to meet you. You could make some good money if he takes you on."

"That sounds fine to me," Hal said with a glance at Rae. "I think I'll be staying in town for a while."

Gus set his coffee mug on a table. "Come on then. I'll take you to meet the boss." He turned to Ida. "Be back tomorrow."

Ida sniffed. "I might be busy."

Gus shrugged. "Coffee don't take long."

Hal bent close to Rae's ear. "Tell Delia I'm here." He straightened and said in a louder tone. "Nice to see you, Rae."

She watched them go. What would Delia do when she found out husband number one was in town and wanted her back?

36

Lily spent her "kiss-off money," as Delia called it, in a frenzy of shopping. She wasn't brokenhearted anymore. Instead, anger sizzled whenever she let herself think about being cheated of everything Eddie had promised. Matt had taken her back at RidgeW, but he cut her salary, and although Rae had never said so, she suspected her little sister had begged Matt to give her another chance. Maybe Rae had even threatened to leave RidgeW. Lily didn't want to know the details. Being abandoned on her honeymoon was embarrassing enough.

In Marshall Field's "Stylish Young Women" department, she bought a black ponyskin coat lined in red with a matching muff and hat, white kid boots that buttoned past her ankles, patent leather pumps, leather handbags with silver trim, nightgowns trimmed with ribbons, silk crepe shirtwaists, a selection of satin petticoats, and a dozen lace-trimmed silk drawers that stopped at the knee—the latest style the clerk assured her. Except for the one hundred dollars she'd already deposited in the bank to placate Rae, the last of the Carleton payment for her short marriage was gone.

"Deliver all of it," Lily said. She ran her fingers over the black lace on the cream-colored silk drawers. "Wait, I'll take these with me." Seizing the paper bag from the clerk, Lily went to the elevator and then strolled through the first floor perfume section before she reached the outside doors and looked out at State Street in horror.

Sleet mixed with snow blew sideways, so thick she could barely see across the street. The February sun had been shining when she arrived at the store, but now the sky was a stormy dark gray. The icy mix on the sidewalk had already been churned by passing feet into dirty, slick ridges. She looked down at her black suede pumps with their two-inch Cuban heels. They'd be ruined. She had to get a taxi.

Sleet whipped into her face, stinging her cheeks and forcing her to squint into the blowing wind. Every step she took resulted in one of her shoes sliding over the icy sidewalk, and she struggled to maintain her balance against the gusts tearing at her. People wearing practical boots and overshoes passed her, but everyone lurched unevenly over the ice. Baby steps, she thought as she moved her feet an inch at a time. Baby steps.

Looking over her shoulder through the blowing snow, she saw the outline of a taxi and took a step closer to the street, waving, but it passed her without slowing. Her heels skidded on the ice, sending her wobbling dangerously close to the curb. There might be more taxis on Washington Street. She had to reach the corner. Her fingertips already were numb in her thin gloves, but she couldn't hurry. Every step she took felt treacherous. Keeping her eyes on her feet, she moved slowly through the freezing muck. Close to the corner, she slid again and staggered, gripping the paper bag now soggy from the sleet. Next to her, an auto horn blasted. She swayed, fighting for balance, but her shoe caught on an icy ridge at the edge of the sidewalk. With a scream, she fell backwards, landing in a mound of softer snow. Her ankle twisted with a sharp pull as she sprawled, the pain jolting up her leg.

Gasping, she lay on her side unable to get her legs in position to rise. Feet in rubber overshoes stepped close to her. Strong hands clutched her arms and pulled her to her feet. The hands shifted to her waist, steadying her in the blasting wind. Putting most of her weight on her good ankle as the snow swirled in her face, she blinked and looked into dark, familiar eyes.

"I'm sorry," Lukas said. "I didn't mean to frighten you. I wanted to catch your attention." He kept his hand under her elbow and motioned to the Pierce-Arrow at the curb. "Can you walk?"

"Yes, but I—" The paper bag sagged, opened, and her new silk drawers fell onto the snow. "My . . . I must get them." Her cheeks turned hot in spite of the cold.

Lukas bent, collected the silky garments, and jammed them under his arm before he steered her to the auto. "Get in."

She couldn't let him rescue her—a gangster—no matter that Rae always said they owed their jobs to him. "I'll get a taxi at the corner." The useless paper bag fluttered away as another blast of wind and sleet hit them.

"No, you won't. This storm came up fast. There isn't a taxi around. Get in." He half-lifted her onto the running board, pushed her onto the seat, and tossed her drawers into her lap.

The snow in the streets collected around the tires as traffic moved a foot at a time or not at all. Horns blared without effect. Snow flew into the open sides of the auto while Lily made an attempt to fold her wet drawers into one compressed pile, trying to conceal them in her lap.

Lukas, hunched over the steering wheel, peered into the street in front of them. "I've seen ladies drawers before," he said.

"Oh, I'm sure you have. At that . . . house of yours." She saw his jaw tighten. "I . . . I do appreciate your help. I'm lucky you were passing." She hadn't lost all her manners although she knew Rae wouldn't be satisfied with her stiff comment.

"I was at the LaSalle Hotel for a meeting. I doubled back to State because the traffic wasn't moving, and I saw you on the sidewalk." He leaned farther over the steering wheel. "It's getting worse. I'll turn and try to get to Clark."

Lily clutched the door handle as Lukas turned into Washington Street. The brakes failed to stop the tires as they slid over the rutted ice and snow, forward, then sideways, heading into the traffic stopped ahead of them. Lukas fought the wheel, straightened the tires, and managed to pull to a stop inches behind a trolley car. In another hundred feet, they slid again in a direct angle leading to a utility pole. Lukas flung his arm across Lily as she shrieked and seized his sleeve. The auto collided with the pole, tires sinking into deep snow at the curb. Her drawers spilled on the floor between her feet.

"Are you all right?"

"Yes." She couldn't bring herself to gather up her drawers while he watched.

Lukas spun the tires in the snow. No movement.

"Are we . . . stuck?" She brushed at the sleet collecting on her shoulders.

"Looks like it." He tried once more. Nothing. He stared out the windshield at the snow accumulating on the hood. "We can't stay here. The LaSalle isn't too far. We can walk."

She looked at her wet shoes just as her ankle sent a warning throb up her leg. Biting her lip, she smothered her urge to cry. Shopping had helped sooth her lingering disappointment about Eddie and the end of her hopes for high society, but now she was trapped in the middle of a storm, in an accident, and dependent on a completely inappropriate man. "How far?"

"Not far. When we get there, I'll call Gus and tell him to come with the truck," Lukas said as he opened his door and stepped into the snow.

Lily glanced at her new drawers crumpled and dirty on the floor. "I'll stay here and wait for you."

Lukas opened her door. "You'll freeze sitting here. We have to get to the hotel." He followed her gaze. "Leave them. I'll make sure you get them back." He grinned. "I'll have Gus pack them up for you."

Her feet slipped as she stepped off the running board, but he caught her while snow, sleet, and bitter wind sliced into them. Reaching the curb, she took three wobbly steps. Pain circled her ankle. She gasped. Lukas, a step ahead of her, turned.

"I can wait in the auto," she said, her voice shaking.

"No, you can't," he said. He bent, picked her up easily as if they weren't in a blinding storm, and took a minute to settle her in his arms.

She stiffened and curled her hands into fists, trying to remain disconnected, but the wind tore at her, stinging her cheeks. Softening, she sank against his chest, put her arms around him, and buried her face between his coat collar and his neck, breathing in his warmth. The faint citrus scent from his shaving soap was oddly comforting as he carried her.

At the hotel entrance, he moved to put her down, and for a second, she resisted leaving the safety of his arms, forgetting she didn't want to be seen with him. She had to lean heavily on him as they entered the luxurious main lobby—it was overflowing with people. Every green and gold upholstered chair was occupied. Businessmen, women, and restless children clustered along the walls, leaned against marble statues, surrounded decorated pillars, and blocked the registration desk. Lily couldn't suppress a faint moan. Her ankle pulsed as if answering.

"Over here," Lukas said. Keeping his hold on her, he pushed past two older men at the entrance to the hotel's Blue Fountain Room. The room was nearly full, but he steered her to a small table near the fountain spraying water lit by blue lights. "I'm going to find the telephone," he said. "If a waiter comes anywhere near, order something."

Lily tugged off her gloves and rubbed her fingers together to bring feeling to her skin. Her coat was stiff with frost, and when she took it off, chunks of ice and snow fell on the thick carpet. She didn't care. Let someone complain, she thought darkly. She'd tell them off, so they'd never complain to her again. Her hair pins had fallen out. Wet, loose locks hung around her face. She pushed at them. Seated, she worked her wet shoes off her feet, so the shoes dropped silently underneath the table. Drawing a long, exhausted breath, she glanced around the room. No waiter in sight. Then she saw him.

Eddie.

He sat at a table next to a ridiculously high statue of Venus at the other end of the room talking to a dark-haired young woman dressed in a smart green wool suit and a matching velour hat with a feather. A dark brown full-length fur coat was draped over the back of her chair. Everything about her said *debutante*. The young woman smiled, dipped her head, flirted, touched Eddie's hand to make a point. He laughed.

Fury boiled thick and suffocating as she watched them.

Without a plan, she rose, teetering slightly as she tested her ankle—painful but it held her. She hobbled in stocking feet across the room, heading straight for Eddie's table. When he looked up, he turned pale and rose to his feet.

"How . . . how nice to see you," he stammered.

Lily put her best movie smile on her lips. "What a surprise." She glanced at the young woman, who looked at her with a curious expression. "Everyone at RidgeW Pictures misses you. You used to visit us all the time." The surprise registering on the young woman's face encouraged her, and she plunged on. "Matt always said he might as well put you in his movies, you were at the studio so much. He thought you might be serious about becoming an actor."

The young woman made a faint gasping sound and put her hand on the velour-trimmed lapel of her suit—over her heart.

"You were always so much fun at our parties, Eddie." She deliberately used his first name, drawing another faint gasp from the debutante.

Eddie cleared his throat. "I've been tied up with the printing company. My father gave me new responsibilities." He glanced at his companion. "Matt Ridgewood's an old friend." He made a half-hearted start to an introduction, but Lily dismissed it with a wave of her hand.

"I don't want to interrupt. I can see you're fully engaged in whatever you think you're doing." She looked at the teapot on their table and the tiered desert tray. "How fortunate you found a waiter. I haven't seen one anywhere." She picked up the teapot with one hand and clasped the handle at the top of the tiered server with the other. "The storm has made me ravenous."

Carrying the teapot and server, she limped back to her table, heart pounding, electric with triumph and power. Eddie was nothing to her now. Her dreams about a life of luxury with him were dead. His wretched mother probably approved of that debutante. Maybe his mother had selected her from an appropriate family. Well, he could have her or a dozen other society girls if he wanted. Easing into her chair, she poured the tea into a cup and selected a tiny chocolate cake from the server. It was utterly delicious.

Lukas stood in the doorway holding an ice bag. To be honest, Lily looked somewhat bedraggled sitting where he'd left her. Her hair had fallen out of what had been a neat coil when he saw her on the street. A lock of blonde hair dangled across her eye, and he watched her push at it several times before she managed to tuck it behind one ear. Her clothes were wet enough to look ill-fitting and twisted, a sleeve drooping, a collar crumpled around her throat. One stocking had a hole in it. She was gorgeous. An urge to sweep her upstairs to one of the lavishly furnished rooms the hotel bragged about in its advertising took possession of him. He drew a long breath and walked slowly toward the table, hoping she'd smile when she saw him. She did not.

"I see you found a waiter," he said, glancing at the teapot.

"Not exactly. Did you call Gus?"

"He's coming but it will take a while. The streets are bad." Lukas held out the ice bag. "This is for your ankle." He moved an empty chair close to her. "Put your feet up."

She lifted both feet to rest on the chair and let him drape the ice bag over her ankle. His fingers lingered on her ankle bone as he adjusted the bag.

She didn't protest. Instead, she wiggled her toes and sighed. "That feels so much better. Have some tea."

"It's nearly cold," he said after taking a sip. "We should get the waiter back."

"I haven't seen a waiter," Lily said, reaching for a pecan tart.

He eyed her. "I met someone in the lobby just now as he was leaving. You know him too."

Lily nibbled at the tart. "He was in here. Eddie. I stole his tea and cakes."

He stared and then laughed. "I thought seeing him would upset you."

"I don't intend to be distressed about him ever again." Her blue eyes looked straight into his, her expression fierce. "My mistake was depending on Eddie. It's no secret. Everyone knows. I'll survive the embarrassment."

"I'm sure you will," he said. He glanced at the ice bag resting on her ankle. Her skirts were still damp and clung to her slim legs, outlining their shape. His imagination began to roll down her black stockings and push up her skirt. He was probably a fool for trying, but he'd felt her lips brush against his skin while he carried her. The temptation was too strong. He tapped his fingers on the linen tablecloth. "That chair doesn't look comfortable." He carefully put a teasing note in his voice. "The LaSalle advertises one thousand rooms. I'm sure we could get one. Gus might not get here for hours."

Lily stared at him, eyes wide, until her gaze turned frosty enough to chill him. "Mr. Krantz, I do appreciate your help in getting me to safety, but I am not at all interested in going to a hotel room with you. I will never be. You've behaved like a gentleman today, but you aren't respectable. If it weren't for RidgeW, we would never have met."

He rose immediately, humiliation burning. "I apologize for implying—anything. I'll wait for Gus in the lobby. If I find a waiter, I'll order more tea for you."

In the lobby, he had to restrain an urge to punch the wall. Anger and frustration mixed wildly in his thoughts. She was right—he wasn't suitable, but that truth made the frustration worse. He paced a few steps back and forth, dodging people and replaying her words in his head.

"Lukas!" Chester Slater beckoned to him from across the lobby. Delia was with him, her hand on his arm. "Couldn't stand the suite anymore," Chester said. "Felt trapped by the weather. Ran out of whiskey and came down for a substantial drink. Join us."

"Good idea," Lukas said. He looked at Delia. "Lily's alone in the Blue room."

"You two go ahead. I've been meaning to talk to Lily about something important." Delia hurried toward the open doors.

37

ily gently turned her foot back and forth, testing her ankle. It twinged when she moved a certain way, but the sharp pain had faded. A box with her drawers, laundered and carefully folded, had arrived two days after the storm. She'd given Rae a brief version of her encounter with Lukas, but she'd omitted her blunt and hostile exchange. Rae, for some reason, liked the man, probably because she was full of gratitude about ending up at RidgeW. Lukas and his insulting suggestion about a hotel room wasn't important. What Delia wanted from the two of them was.

In the living room, Sophie Tucker's low voice sang "Some of These Days" on Rae's Victrola. "Shut that off. We have to talk," Lily said. "When I saw Delia at the LaSalle, she asked me if she could meet Hal here."

Rae gaped. "Here?"

"Delia said you've been carrying messages back and forth."

"Yes, but I don't read them. She gives me one at RidgeW. Lev takes it to Hal and brings one back."

"Delia told me messages aren't enough. She says she has to see him personally to persuade him to go back to the farm. She says our place is the only safe way to meet."

Rae's face took on a horrified expression. "What about Chester?"

"Chester doesn't care if she visits us. It will only be this one time. Delia said she has to get rid of Hal."

"Chester's so unpredictable," Rae said.

"That's why Delia has to send Hal away. They're coming here tonight. I had to say yes. Delia begged me. She said sisters have to stick together."

When Hal knocked on the apartment door, Lily barely recognized the farmer she'd known. He wore a gray overcoat, navy wool suit, navy knit tie, and gray fedora. Thrusting a box of chocolates at her, he grinned. "Hi there, Lily."

She stared at the split in his bottom lip. A purple bruise underlined his left eye, and a jagged cut over the other eye was beginning to heal. "Were you in a fight?"

He slipped off his overcoat, folded it over a chair, and balanced his hat on top. "Three fights already." He noticed her puzzled look. "I'm boxing for Lukas Krantz. Didn't Rae tell you?"

"Rae doesn't always tell me everything," Lily said with a sharp look at her sister.

Hal leaned against the edge of the table. "Won the fights, and Lukas gave me a bonus to get some new clothes. Delia doesn't like me in overalls."

"Are you going to keep boxing?" Lily made no attempt to hold back the disapproval in her voice.

"Sure I am. He pays me good, and he pays the police so we don't get raided." Hal touched his chin tenderly. "Gus says I got to practice more, so I can dodge better."

Footsteps pounded up the stairs. Delia burst through the door—breathless. She ignored Lily and Rae. "Oh, Hal, why did you come to Chicago?" she wailed. Her muskrat fur coat slipped off her shoulders and dropped to the floor as she flung herself into Hal's arms. "Darling!" she murmured before he pulled her close and kissed her.

Lily looked at Rae. Rae raised her eyebrows.

"No, we can't." Delia pushed Hal away. "I'm married to Chester now." She sighed dramatically, unwrapped the long scarf tangled around her neck, and let it hang loose over her shoulders. "I don't know what to say to you." She put her hand on her forehead and gasped. "You've taken me by surprise. I'm overwhelmed."

Lily repressed a smile. Delia was repeating a scene Matt shot two days ago in *The Mysterious Mr. Jones,* Chester's latest movie.

"You married me first, so I'm the one who counts." Hal said. "I came to Chicago to claim you."

Delia put out a hand to hold him off although he hadn't moved toward her. "I can't return to that farm. I can't!"

Hal frowned. "You knew I was a farmer when we got married. You said it didn't matter."

"I was young—naïve. Your mother hates me. I can't live there. It's too hopelessly boring."

"I guess I knew you'd say that." He started to chew his lip and winced when his teeth touched the split. "I want you, Delia, so I've been thinking what we can do. If you won't come back to Wisconsin with me, I'll stay here. I've got a job—boxing for Lukas Krantz."

"Boxing?" Delia seemed to notice the others for the first time. "That's illegal. Rae, did you get Hal into boxing for Lukas?"

Hal cut her off. "I met his man, Gus, and he got me set up. Boxing is only a little illegal. The police don't care much about it."

Delia sighed. "Still, it's against the law, and Lukas isn't exactly—"

"Bigamy is illegal too," Lily snapped. "You ought to think about that."

Delia looked from Hal to Lily and back again. "I did what I had to do," she said with a flourish of the scarf.

Hal took a step toward her. "Delia, I want you back."

"We have to talk." Delia took his hand and pulled him toward her old bedroom. "We have to talk alone." She slammed the door behind them.

Lily hung Delia's coat behind the door while Rae collected her records and stacked them next to the Victrola. They pretended they weren't straining to hear the voices rising and falling in the bedroom.

"You neglected me for onions!"

"Delia, honey, the crops have to be . . . I thought about you all day long, every minute."

"Your mother thinks I'm . . ." Crying and gasping.

"Doesn't matter what she thinks. You're mine, and we're married."

"She was always listening to us when we . . ." More crying.

"We might've been a little noisy sometimes. I can't turn my mother out."

"Then the next morning, she looked at me like . . . I couldn't bear it."

"So you decided it was better to take off your clothes in the movies like you were working in the hootchy-kootchy shows at the carnival?"

"Matt's movies are artistic creations!" A wail. "I don't know what to do with you here."

"First thing is, you have to dump that actor fellow."

"He promised to take me to California!"

"All right! We won't go back to the farm. I can box in Chicago and make money. You belong with me."

Mumbles and murmurs.

A long sigh. "Boxing is so dangerous. You have a bruise under your chin."

"I can take it all right. Doesn't even hurt much."

"Your lip is cut too. Let me . . ."

Murmurs. A long silence. The bed springs squeaked.

"I knew it," Lily said.

More squeaks from the bed springs.

Lily snatched their coats. "Let's go. We'll find Lev and take him to eat."

While Rae and Lev stuffed themselves on lasagna at Gino's Trattoria, Lily poked at her food, worrying about Delia and Hal—and Chester. Maybe the Kelly girls were doomed to have ill-fated romantic lives. Her notions about Eddie had certainly been stupid.

The apartment was empty when they got back, but Delia's perfume and Hal's cigarette smoke lingered in the air. Lily checked Delia's old room. The bed covers were on the floor.

Rae peered over her shoulder. "Is she going back to Hal?"

"Who knows? Delia's gotten herself into a mess."

38

Rae stood on a chair while Ida repaired a rip in her costume and snapped at her to stop fidgeting. Climbing over rocks and up trees as the plucky kid saving the day in every western was hard on costumes. To avoid Ida's flashing needle, Rae froze in place, watching Matt out of the corner of her eye. He worried her. He'd been so happy at Christmas, but winter was almost over, and he looked glum most of the time these days, especially when he and Fred huddled over the budgets. She couldn't think how to help him. She'd kept quiet about Chester's plans to go west. No need to add to his worries. Besides, Delia said Chester wasn't getting any offers from the California studios. Lately, Chester had started drinking at lunch, so Matt usually didn't break until two o'clock. After lunch, Chester was useless.

"Letter, Rae." One of the crew handed her an envelope. Ida sighed, threw up her hands, and stepped back. Adrenaline spiked as Rae jumped off the chair and ripped open her letter.

> *Dear Rae,*
>> *I hope you are well. I had time to see one of your adventures last week. You did a good job. I am ready to sail for France. My friend Jack is in my unit, and we expect to be in action soon. Everyone tells us the war will be over quickly. Please send my good wishes to everyone at RidgeW. Your friend, Gil*

The letter was shorter than the last one and he didn't write anything private for her. He probably didn't even remember their kiss at the Christmas party.

Matt paused next to her. "Letter from Gil?"

Rae gave it to him. "He doesn't say much."

"We all miss him," he said after quickly reading the few sentences. "He was a good western actor." He patted her shoulder. "You probably miss him the most. I don't know what girls your age think about, but don't let yourself get heartbroken, Rae. You'll like quite a few young men before you grow up."

She flushed. "I'm not heartbroken. Just worried about him over there in the mud."

"Sure." Matt ruffled her hair. "We're all worried about that."

❦

Matt made everyone work late to finish the western and Billy's comedy, so Rae and Lily stopped at Ma Fischer's and bought chicken dinners to take home.

"Are Delia and Hal using our apartment again?" Lily asked as they walked. "They come almost every night. We should charge rent."

"Not tonight," Rae said. "Delia said Chester's been asking why she has to spend so much time with us after she sees us at the studio most days." She clutched the bag from Ma Fischer's close to her chest and inhaled the scent of the food. Her stomach rumbled. "I heard Hal say he wanted to have a baby."

"While she's married to two men? She'd be in a bigger mess than she is."

"How does Delia . . . keep from . . ." It was embarrassing not knowing these things. Maybe a thirteen year old wouldn't know, but her fake age felt more and more like a trap. She tripped on the uneven sidewalk and nearly dropped the food.

Lily stopped walking and looked at her. "Delia showed me. You're old enough to know. I'll explain when we get home."

Outside the apartment, Rae fumbled with the key while Lily sniffed the air. "Mr. Chemnitz must have been smoking out here."

Rae pushed open the door. Lights glowed in the living room.

"There's my little girls. Movie stars now!" Maxie sat in a chair, smoke curling up from the cigarette between his fingers. "Glad to see me?"

Rae backed up a step. "How did you get in?"

"Landlady let me in. Nice woman. A little old but well rounded." He pulled on the cigarette and sent a sharp glance at Rae. "What kind of welcome is that? I never told you I'd be gone forever."

"I thought you owed Lukas Krantz a lot of money. You said you had to stay out of town."

Maxie shrugged. "Lukas and I had a little misunderstanding."

"You owe him three thousand dollars," Rae said.

"How would you know about that, my girl?" Maxie's gaze drilled through her. "How would you come to know my business with Lukas?"

"I sold him something—that I found—and he told me you owed him money."

Maxie grinned. "Picking pockets were you?"

"You left us without a cent." Lily glared at him. "We had to make our way without any help from you."

"You got money now. I been seeing you in the movies. I was flabbergasted, I was, the first time I saw Lily in one of those funny stories. The next day I saw Rae climbing in and out of trees. My girls have done good for themselves."

"No thanks to you," Lily muttered.

Maxie crushed out his cigarette in Rae's new copper bowl. "Don't get sharp with me. Who kept this family together after your ma ran off with that limey? I got us a roof over our heads and food, didn't I? Delia too. Didn't send you three to an orphanage or to another place I could mention that takes young girls."

"Are you hungry?" Rae pointed to the bag in her arms. "We've got chicken."

"Don't mind if I do," Maxie said. "Got a beer?" he asked as Rae divided the food.

"We don't drink beer," Lily snapped.

"Still high-toned, aren't you? Now you've got plenty of money, I suppose you only drink champagne." He slid into a chair at the kitchen table and waited for Rae to put a plate in front of him.

They ate silently until Rae twirled her fork in her mashed potatoes and glanced up at him under her lashes. "Pa, what are you going to do about the money you owe Lukas? What if he finds out you're back in Chicago?"

He grunted, belched, and took out a cigarette. "Lukas won't be a problem for me. You can pay him off." He looked around the room. "Thought you'd be in a fancier place. I heard Mary Pickford makes a thousand dollars a week."

"Nobody here is Mary Pickford." Lily said. "We don't have the money to pay your debts. I get paid twenty a week, and Rae . . . Rae gets the same."

"Sorry to hear that." Another deep, rumbling belch came from Maxie, and he patted his stomach. "What about Delia? I read she married a stage actor. I guess she left that farmer boy. What about this actor? Fellow like that must get paid plenty."

"We all work at the same place," Lily said. "No one's rich enough to pay your debts."

Conflicts raged in Rae's mind. She'd never thought she'd have to tell Lukas Pa was back. He said it right—some fathers wouldn't have stayed with three young girls after their mother deserted them, but Pa had kept them together. Of course, she owed Lukas too, but she couldn't betray Pa no matter what she'd promised. A headache began to throb in her temples.

"Lukas is a busy man." Maxie lit another cigarette. "He won't look for me. That bedroom," he motioned to the one Delia used, "will do fine for me. I'll stay low while you girls figure out how to pay him off. I'll need some spending money too."

"We can't pay your debt," Lily said in a flat tone.

"I admit it doesn't sound like you can—not right away." Maxie exhaled smoke. "I figured you girls were rolling in money. Sorry to hear the opposite, but you can save up and get it together. In the meantime, I'll stay away from Lukas. Once he's paid, we can find a bigger place to live. I like being back with my girls. Proud of you making money in the movies."

"You can't stay here," Lily said. "We couldn't hide you. The landlady would know. People would talk. Lukas would find out."

"Lukas owns most of RidgeW Pictures," Rae added. "In a way, we work for him."

Lily shot a warning glance at Rae. "I've got some money put away. A hundred dollars. You can take that and get out of town. It'll last you a while—until you find a job somewhere."

White smoke from his cigarette curled into the air. "I can use a hundred, that's for sure. I owe a few people, and I need some spending money." He looked at his shoes. "Maybe new clothes and shoes too. I want to look snappy for my girls. No need for me to get a job if you two can make a fortune in the movies. Maybe you ain't rich yet, but no reason to think you can't move into the bigger bucks like Mary Pickford. I got to clear myself with Lukas. You girls have to come up with the money I owe him. In the meantime—"

"In the meantime," Lily interrupted, "you can't live here. I'll get you a room somewhere, pay for it, and you can have the rest of the money."

He scratched his chin. "You might be right. Put me up in a boarding house with some decent food, I'll stay away from Lukas until you come up with the money he wants." He grinned. "Nobody needs to know I'm back in town. It'll be our secret."

39

"What do you mean Schroeder won't pay?" Weston pushed back from his desk and glared at Sean Rogan.

"Schroeder said business at the shop wasn't good. He'll pay next month."

"I put his street on the top of the list for repaving just to accommodate him. Now he says he can't pay?" Weston squashed his cigar into a tangle of tobacco bits in his new ashtray. The bronze plate on the side of the granite square proclaimed Weston the "City Council Member of the Year—1914."

"Said the war was bad for business."

Weston looked at the clock. Three in the afternoon. Too early for a drink. He stood, went to the side table, and poured one anyway. The sharp taste slid down his throat, relaxing him. "The war has nothing to do with us.

Skipping payments has been happening too much lately. I can't do favors for nothing. I have expenses too."

"Yeah. Do you think Krantz put out the word not to pay you? Maybe he gave that paper to the police commissioner."

Weston sank into the chair behind his desk and took another swallow from his glass. "I'd know if anyone got that paper. Everything would explode. I'd . . . we'd be up the creek."

"You mean down the river to Joliet Prison."

"Something like that," Weston drained his whiskey. "What about that other matter?"

"I followed her every time you were out of town. It's always the studio. She doesn't go anywhere else at night."

"So . . . how long?"

"The actors and the crew finish for the day about seven. The costume lady is usually the last to leave. Then Ridgewood locks up and leaves—except when he doesn't leave. If he stays, her taxi comes about nine. A taxi comes back for her about three—brings her straight here." Sean stared at his shoes.

"I need Ridgewood to disappear," Weston muttered. "I want him gone."

"I don't do stuff like that."

"Ask around," Weston said. He exhaled and waved a hand in the air. "I'm not serious, of course. But it would be interesting to know—what's the price for an accident?" He turned his gaze on Sean again. "Ask around."

Weston found Emeline reading in the music room. She looked up as he came in and smiled. "Hello, Theodore, I didn't see you this morning."

"Had an early meeting." He sat on the settee next to her and glanced at her book. "*Daddy-Long-Legs,*" he read. "Why are you reading about a spider?"

Emeline laughed. "It's not about a spider. It's a charming story about a young girl who falls in love with her older guardian although she doesn't realize he's her guardian. I haven't finished, but I assume it ends well."

"We all want things to end well, don't we, Emeline?" Weston shifted to look directly at her. "You know, I've been thinking how much I've enjoyed your company over the years. When I married Arabella, I insisted you live with us. Do you recall, Emeline?"

Her smile froze, and she carefully placed a bookmark in the novel, putting it on the settee between them. "You have always been very generous, Theodore."

"I try to be. Duty's very important to me. I try to do my duty." He gazed over her head for a moment at the high windows behind her. "I can't help being disappointed when others fail. My boy, Simon, for instance, has never lived up to my expectations. He's tried several businesses in Boston, but he can't seem to keep steady. He's easily distracted." He sighed heavily. "I'd hoped when I married Arabella, there would be more children. She's young and healthy."

"I'm certain Arabella has been disappointed too."

"Has she?" He let surprise linger on his face. "I can't tell. She's always been rather closed about her hopes for the future."

"She's often preoccupied with her charity work," Emeline offered. "She's the chairwoman of the committee for the Hull House Benefit next month, and this evening she's at a meeting with Mrs. Blake about raising money for the children's summer camp."

Weston stood and straightened his tie. "I'm going out myself—a council dinner. I've enjoyed our little visit, Emeline. I would hate to lose your company for any reason." He sent a half-bow in her direction and left the room.

Fingers shaking, face pale, Emeline reached for her book but let it slip out of her hand back onto the settee.

40

Lukas looked up from the newspapers on his desk as Gus walked into the office. "Where have you been? There was a fight across the street. I had to go over there myself and settle it."

He was in his shirtsleeves, cuffs rolled up, a dark smear of grease streaking across his white shirt. His suit coat hung on the back of a chair where he'd flung it while he was ripping off his shirt collar, now crushed and abandoned on top of the desk. Reddened splotches on the knuckles of his left hand were darkening into bruises, and his hair flopped in disorderly waves around his ears. Tipping his chair back, he glared at Gus. "Well?"

Gus shuffled his feet. "Sorry, Boss. I guess I stayed too long at RidgeW."

"You mean you stayed too long visiting Ida. You can't spend all your time hanging around there. I need you here. Take Ida out for a meal instead of drinking Matt's coffee. That's my coffee as a matter of fact."

"Sure, sure." Gus coughed. "I brought someone who wants to see you. Miss Lily Rose."

Hot and cold ran through Lukas simultaneously. She'd come to her senses. Almost violently, he pushed his chair back and rose to his feet. "Where is she?"

Gus made a gesture indicating the front of the shop and left to get her. Lukas took a step toward his crumpled suit coat, stopped, and turned toward the wrinkled shirt collar on his desk. He cursed silently but fiercely. Useless to try to straighten his appearance into something dignified now. He looked like a thug who'd been in a fight. He had time only to run his fingers through his hair before Gus reappeared, escorting Lily into the room.

One dark look from Lukas and Gus disappeared, closing the door behind him. Lily glanced uncertainly around the room.

"I apologize for my appearance. I've been . . ." Lukas trailed off, not wanting to mention where he'd been. He gestured to the chair in front of his desk. "Please sit down."

"No, thank you. I . . ." Her fingers tightened around the metal frame of her gray leather bag. "I have something to discuss. Of interest to us both," she added.

Lukas's jaw clenched as he gazed into her blue eyes. Matt's movies didn't do her justice. On the screen, she was gorgeous but remote in flickering black and white. In person, her skin was soft, luminous, her blonde hair flecked with gold lights beckoning a man's fingers, her mouth full and pink promising kisses.

He gestured to the chair again, but she didn't move. If she wouldn't sit down, he couldn't. He waited, fighting his urge to cross the room and sweep her into his arms, so they wouldn't have to talk at all. A slight nervous tremble went through his fingers, and he shoved his hands in his pockets. "What did you want to see me about?" A pulse beat rapidly in his neck where the abandoned collar would have concealed it. In spite of his impatience to hear her say what he'd wanted to hear for months, he kept his voice calm.

Lily drew in a long nervous breath. "It's my father. He's back in Chicago."

"Maxie?" Lukas slowly took his hands out of his pockets. A faint stirring of disappointment raced through his mind while he took in her news. "He's back?"

"He was in St. Louis and saw Rae and me in Matt's movies. He's back in Chicago because he thinks we're rich now."

"I thought he'd see you in those movies some day," Lukas said. "How long has he been in town?"

"Over a month." She gripped her bag so tightly her fingertips turned white. "Rae told me she promised she'd tell you if he ever came back, but she can't bring herself to do it. She feels guilty, but she says she can't be disloyal to her father—our father."

"It was a joke," Lukas said. "I never expected her to tell me if Maxie came back to town. For a kid, she has a huge protective streak in her."

"Rae couldn't tell, so I came to do it."

Bleak understanding rippled through him. She hadn't come for him after all. "If Rae wouldn't tell me Maxie's back, why would you?" He kept a flat business tone in his voice.

"He's taking all our money. We can barely make ends meet these days, and he wants us to pay off the money he owes you," Lily said, her tone as impersonal as his. "We're paying for his room at a boarding house and giving him money. It would take us years to save enough to pay you what you say he owes you."

"If he's in Chicago now, he must know you two aren't rich."

"We've told him over and over how much money we make at RidgeW, but he doesn't believe us—or he says we'll be rich soon."

"Is Delia paying him too?"

"It's only Rae and me. Delia's married to Chester. She can't get involved."

"You mean Chester wouldn't like having an ex-boxer who needs money as a father-in-law."

"Delia's married. She isn't giving him money." Lily hesitated but kept her eyes locked on his. "Rae and I— we—could save money to pay you if we weren't paying his expenses every day." She nervously pushed a loose strand of hair back from her forehead. "We could save the money to pay you faster if he was gone. It would be best if he went away forever. You could make him disappear."

Lukas stared at her for a long moment until he realized he was holding his breath and inhaled sharply. "You want me to kill him?" he asked.

Lily gasped, shock in her eyes. "No!"

He took a step closer. "Whatever you think of me, Lily, I don't kill people as a regular thing."

"We want him to leave town so we don't have to pay his board and give him money every few days. If he were gone, we could start to pay the money he owes you."

"You want me to persuade him to leave?" He made it a question, knowing the answer, but he wanted to hear her say it, to ask him for something, to need him for anything.

"Yes. Once he's out of town, Rae and I can start to pay you."

"I get rid of Maxie, and you and Rae will pay me what he owes," Lukas rephrased her statement again.

"We'll have to pay in installments," Lily amended. Her voice had become breathless as if she'd been running.

He'd thought so many times about the ways he could make her breathless, hearing her ragged breathing now flooded his mind with old fantasies. He pushed them away. This was territory he knew well. She was here to make a deal, and he made deals all the time. Deals that favored him. His mind cleared.

"I can take care of Maxie," he said. "I won't hurt him, but he'll know he has to leave Chicago and stop hounding you and Rae for money." He hesitated, but it was too late to pull back. She'd come to him for a deal, and he was ready to make one. "I don't want your money, Lily," he said. "I want you. In my bed."

His pulse raced while he focused on her face. Shock. Confusion. But no disgust, no horror, no terror. He let his breath out slowly.

She gasped and touched shaking fingers to her lips, her eyes fixed on him. "I could not possibly—"

"Yes, you could. You've been married. Eddie Carleton had you. You aren't an untouched flower any more. You understand what I want." A sense of calm took him. His muscles relaxed. He was, after all, only making another deal.

Lily paled. "No gentleman—"

"You never thought I was a gentleman," he interrupted. "So let's be honest—and practical. We each have something the other wants. We can trade."

Lily pressed her gray bag close to her chest. "Rae and I can save the money and pay you. We'll sign an IOU."

"Weekly payments for years," Lukas said. "You don't want that. Come to me, and I'll cancel his debt completely." He watched her look around the room, eyes darting aimlessly.

"No." She lifted her chin. "We'll pay you the money somehow." Turning, she wrenched open the door, and left.

He stared at the open doorway, clenching his jaw so tightly a pain shot up the side of his face. Failure. He was surprised to realize he wasn't sorry. A clean defeat was better than endless frustration. Walking behind his desk, he glanced down at the newspapers and forced himself to focus on the headlines.

German Subs Prowl the Atlantic
Merchant Ships are Target for German Subs

His father would be upset over this, he thought. The old man was proud of his life in Chicago, but he loved Germany too, and he wouldn't like the death, the turmoil.

A rustle in the doorway made him look up.

"All right," Lily said in a low voice. "I agree."

Adrenaline jarred his pulse into a staccato rhythm. "You understand what I want?"

"Yes." She took a few steps into the room. "You cancel the debt and get my father out of Chicago, and I'll come to you." A dark flush stained her throat. "I promise. If you do your part, I'll do mine."

"You're certain?" Damned if he'd let her claim later she hadn't known what she was agreeing to.

"I'm certain." She swallowed hard but looked at him steadily.

"Where's Maxie?" He scribbled the address she gave him on the edge of a newspaper.

"When will you—how will I . . . ?"

"You'll know when I finish with Maxie. For the other, I'll arrange a time and place. Gus will come for you."

Lily bit her lip. "All right. Should we shake hands?"

"I trust you, Lily. We have a deal."

41

"Pull over here," Lukas said.

Gus frowned. "It's a couple doors down. Don't you want me closer?"

Lukas stepped on the curb. "You're close enough if Maxie gives me trouble. But he won't. Our little talk shouldn't take more than ten minutes."

He slammed the door behind him and walked the few feet to the front of Maxie's boarding house—a middle-class Victorian, painted white with green shutters. Well-kept bushes framed the steps leading to a porch that covered the front of the house. A swing moved gently in the evening breeze. The air was warm enough to allow half-open windows, and the faint, sweet aroma of apple pie reached Lukas. The place was a notch upscale for Maxie, he thought.

Once Lukas was inside the foyer, a boarder directed him to the third floor. When Maxie opened the door,

Lukas put his hand on the center of his chest, pushed him off his feet, and sent him staggering backward into the room until he hit the edge of a table and caught his balance. Lukas shut the door behind him.

"How'd you know I was back?" Maxie asked. He straightened his belt buckle and slowly curled his hands into fists at his side.

"I hear things," Lukas answered.

He surveyed the room. Two obviously new pairs of shoes jutted halfway out from under the bed. In the open closet, new shirts hung next to a light wool gray overcoat and a dark brown khaki suit with the tags still on it. A dark brown fedora sat on the shelf above the hangers. On a small table under the window, four empty beer bottles lay at angles along with two decks of cards and several copies of the *Daily Racing Form*.

"You betting on the horses, Maxie?" Lukas asked, as he turned over a couple of pages of one issue.

Maxie ran his tongue over his bottom lip and attempted a smile. "Not much, but we're getting to Kentucky Derby time, and I wanted to check out the contenders, you know."

"Since you're back in town, I suppose you have the money you owe me from your last fight. I had to pay off all the bets when you made a mess of it."

"Haven't got it yet." Maxie swallowed hard and ran his tongue over his lip again. "Not all of it, but I'm getting it, Lukas. My girls are making money now, and they'll be putting it together for you. Should be any time now. A couple of days. Maybe a couple of weeks."

"Rae and Lily are going to pay me?"

"They're doing good—in the movies."

"I own most of RidgeW Pictures. I know what they're making." Lukas stepped closer to Maxie. He was taller than the older man and loomed over him. "They don't make enough money to pay me off in a month. Not in a couple of months. Not in a year."

"I forgot. They told me they were working for you," Maxie said. His voice cracked, and a line of sweat glistened at his hair line. "I swear Lukas, my girls will get the money real soon."

Lukas strolled around the room and came back to Maxie. "You're a lucky man," he said. "I have a deal for you."

Maxie blinked rapidly as if clearing his vision. "A deal?"

"I'll forgive the money—wipe it out—you won't owe it anymore."

"I won't?" Maxie swallowed hard. "What's the rest?"

Lukas pulled a business card out of his pocket. "Mainline Pittsburgh Gym," he read before handing the card to Maxie. "You're going there—on the first train tomorrow. Ask for Carlo. He has a job for you. I'll throw in twenty-five dollars for your expenses."

Maxie read the card. "Why?" he whispered when he looked back at Lukas.

"You don't need to know why," Lukas said. "Your side of the deal is you never come back to Chicago, and you never ask your girls for money again." He reached for his wallet. "Understand the arrangement?"

"I can't just go off and leave my girls," Maxie said. "They need me."

Lukas raised an eyebrow. "You had no trouble leaving them when you thought I was coming after you. That was almost a year ago. They're all grown up. Delia's a wife. Lily," he paused, "she was almost a wife too. Rae's doing fine."

"Girls always need their father. You saying they don't?"

Lukas opened his wallet and began pulling out bills. "I'm offering you a very good opportunity, Maxie. You leave Chicago—never come back—and I'll cancel your debt." He finished counting out twenty-five dollars. "You don't have choices. If you don't agree . . ." He paused for emphasis. "I can't see my way clear to letting you run around town. There'd have to be consequences if you refuse." He held out the money. "Don't think you can gamble this away tonight."

Maxie put the business card in his pants pocket and snatched the money. He started to count, but then caught Lukas's eye and stuffed the bills into his other pocket. "As you say, my girls are pretty well grown." He shifted awkwardly on his feet. "Keep an eye on Rae. She's the baby."

"I'll keep an eye on all of them," Lukas said. "I take care of my interests."

Maxie shifted his feet again. "Sure. They work for you."

"Gus will have your ticket and take you to the station to catch the train in the morning. He'll be here at six o'clock. Be ready for him, or you'll have to abandon all those nice new clothes in the closet." Lukas lowered his voice. "With or without a suitcase, you'll be on that train."

Maxie nodded. He was still nodding when Lukas closed the door behind him.

42

Chicago Dispatch, **April 20, 2015**

Out and About with Lucinda Corday

C hicago will be sorry to learn that Billy Tucker, the comic star at RidgeW Pictures, is leaving us for the sunny climes of California. Although Billy's contract with RidgeW is not over for several months, he has already departed for Universal Studios. Universal has been expanding rapidly during the last three years. On March 15, the company opened a 230-acre production area, and Universal is luring talented actors and directors with big salaries and attractive movie choices. Billy was a popular visitor at our local nightspots, and our Chicago young ladies will miss him.

Matthew Ridgewood tells me he has two more Billy Tucker comedies to release, but he has no comic actor to replace Billy at the moment. With giant California production centers raiding our local studios, can it be long before a movie boss turns his eyes on our darling Dora? We hope RidgeW keeps her in Chicago for a long time.

The war in Europe touches our lives in strange ways. Last week, RidgeW was shooting a scene with Lily Rose and Chester Slater in front of Krauss's German Bakery when an anti-German crowd gathered and disrupted the businesses on the street. The RidgeW crew had to pack their equipment and retreat to the studio, leaving the police to handle the crowd.

Until next time, dear readers.

43

Alone in the apartment, Lily slipped into her plain black poplin coat. The end of April was too warm for her luxurious pony skin coat, and even if it were colder, she'd never wear her prized fashion to a sordid meeting with a man no better than a gangster. She buttoned the coat and pulled on soft kid gloves. Stepping in front of the full-length mirror Rae had purchased at an auction, she tilted the hand-carved redwood frame in its stand to check her appearance. She'd twisted her long hair into a severe coil at the back of her head, and only a few shorter strands had escaped to curl along her temples. Her cheeks were pale, but she was relieved to see a calm, determined expression on her face. She didn't want Lukas to think she was afraid of him. For a moment, she closed her eyes to ward off tears of frustration. She wouldn't have to give Lukas anything if Eddie hadn't deserted her. She opened her eyes and pressed her lips together. She didn't need Eddie. She could handle Lukas Krantz.

She'd told Rae Lukas only wanted an evening out with her in exchange for erasing the debt, but Rae had snapped at her. "I'm not a kid in spite of playing Dora. I know what Lukas wants."

"It's not really so difficult," she'd told Rae. "The whole thing only takes a few minutes. Eddie always went to sleep right after, and when Lukas does, I'll slip out and come home. I swear, Rae. It will be all right. Don't be angry."

Rae had groaned. "I should have told Lukas. I was the one who promised."

It was better this way, Lily thought. When she walked out of the apartment, Gus waited for her at the curb. He swung open the door to the Pierce-Arrow and tipped his cap. "Evening, Miss Lily."

She nodded at him and settled into the seat, folding her gloved hands in her lap. Her mouth was dry, and her heart thumped faster than it should, but she didn't regret her decision. Lukas wanted what all men wanted, and he'd paid three thousand dollars for it. During her week-long marriage, Eddie was quickly excited and quickly finished, and after the first time, it didn't hurt, so she could manage. She'd made a business deal, and she intended to keep it.

Gus made no attempt at conversation as they drove through the twilight. When he eased the auto to a stop, she blinked, confused. She'd expected Gus to take her to an out-of-the-way hotel, probably a garish, tasteless place, and she'd even feared they might go to that vile, disreputable house Lukas owned. Instead, they'd parked on a quiet street in front of a Tudor-style brick and stone house.

"Where are we?"

"The boss's house, Miss Lily." Gus hopped out, came around to her door, and opened it. "Otto will let you in."

Stepping on the curb, she murmured a polite thank-you. As she opened the gate in the cast-iron fence, the wooden door at the top of the front steps swung wide for her. Walking up the short flight to the entrance where Otto waited, Lily kept her eyes straight ahead and moved with deliberate slowness. She imagined she was playing a part for Matt's camera, so she could ignore her certainty Gus and Otto knew why she was here. As she entered, Otto silently pointed to sliding doors at the end of the hallway.

The corridor was bare of furniture except for a marble-topped table against one wall. A dark, leafy pattern in the wallpaper matched the shadows cast by the electric lights in the obviously new chandelier overhead. Curious, in spite of her nerves, she paused. He needed brighter, more welcoming wallpaper, and the table needed a vase or one of those Oriental lacquered figurines. Her heels clacked on the polished parquet floor. And carpet. Lukas should put down an Oriental carpet to match the figurine. The house had an unfinished air as if the decorator had been delayed.

She paused in front of the sliding doors. Did one knock and wait for an answer when one had appointments like this? She drew several long breaths to quiet her pulse thumping a fast rhythm. Formality didn't seem necessary. She hadn't come for a tea party.

Lukas rose from a chair as she slid open one door. In the glow from the two lamps in the corners, he was a dark figure, black hair falling over his forehead. He'd taken off his jacket, and his white shirt gleamed in the dim light. Lily's breathing quickened. His presence filled every empty space, making her feel crowded although he wasn't close to her and the room was sparsely furnished.

"I wasn't certain you would . . ."

He was nervous too. She heard the slightest tremor in his voice, usually so casual and firm. "You did what you promised, so I'm here," she said, careful to keep her tone businesslike.

"Would you like to see the rest of the house?"

She shook her head as she unbuttoned her coat and put it with her gloves over a chair near the door. A fluttery feeling had taken over her insides, and she clutched her hands together for an instant, suppressing an overwhelming urge to run away. Desperate for a distraction, she glanced around the room and noticed a chess set with large wooden pieces on a small table. She picked up an intricately carved piece resembling a tower with tiny indentations to allow defenders to shoot at attackers. "A little castle," she said, holding it up to the light.

"It's called a rook," he said. "I carved the set for my father."

"You?" She didn't try to conceal her surprise.

"When I was young, I carved things for my parents—bowls and kitchen things for my mother and three chess sets for my father. This one was his favorite, and I managed to keep it after . . . they died." He touched the top of the piece, brushing his finger over hers. "I haven't done anything like this in a long time."

She returned the chess piece to its place on the board. "The pieces are beautiful."

"Do you play chess?"

She shook her head.

"I'll teach you."

"No need to do that." She wanted to add they'd never talk after this night, but surely he understood that quite clearly.

He gestured toward the sideboard and a tray of delicate sandwiches and small cakes. "Something to eat?"

"No, nothing. I'd like Gus to wait for me and take me home."

"Wait for you?"

"Yes, there's no need for him to rush away for this short while, and it's often hard to get a taxi at this time of night because of the restaurants and clubs."

He stared at her. A half-smile crossed his lips. "This time of night," he repeated as if she'd said something highly amusing. He walked to the sideboard and poured wine into two glasses. "Gus will be close by," he said, holding out a glass. "You should have wine, Lily."

The wine slid down her throat, sending a trail of warmth through her body. Nerves rattling, in spite of her resolutions to be calm, she drained the glass too quickly, and the wine rushed to her head, making her dizzy.

Lukas drank only a sip from his own glass before he set it back on the sideboard and took her empty glass from her hand. Stepping close to her, he tipped her face up to him and brushed his lips lightly over hers. He took her into the kiss slowly until his mouth pressed hard against hers, sending tremors through her body.

When he released her and stroked his thumb over her bottom lip, she swayed, her legs wobbly. I'm dizzy from the wine, she thought, and put her hand on his shoulder to steady herself.

"So soft," he murmured against her ear. "The first time I saw you—when Rae said *this is my sister*—I knew you'd feel like this." He kissed her again.

She'd expected Lukas's kiss to be different from Eddie's. Eddie's kisses were pleasant and fun, but Lukas's mouth hot against hers made her pulse flutter so erratically she could hardly catch her breath.

He flicked at the pins in her hair, and long, wavy strands fell across her shoulders, curling around his fingers. The lamplight created a soft halo around her hair. "Beautiful." he whispered. He brushed her hair away from her face and kissed below her ear, his hand on the nape of her neck holding her in place.

Opening the collar of her shirtwaist, he caressed her throat, lingering where her pulse throbbed. He kissed the underside of her jaw while he unbuttoned her shirtwaist, slowly moving the back of his hand over her skin along her collarbone. Separating the silk edges of the shirtwaist as if unwrapping a package, he stroked lower to the top of her chemise. Heat raced along her nerves. She struggled to keep her breathing steady, but it sounded ragged in her ears. Eddie had moved so quickly she'd been naked in an instant, but Lukas moved slowly, burning where he touched.

She fought to keep her mind locked on the bargain they'd made—a perfectly sensible business arrangement, but when he dropped kisses along her collarbone and nuzzled the soft skin in the curve of her shoulder, she lost her concentration on anything but the sensations rippling through her body.

Pushing the shirtwaist off her shoulders, he pulled the cuffs past her wrists and sent the silky garment to the floor. His hands stilled on her hips. Their eyes met. Embarrassed, she closed her eyes. Pushing aside the wide, pink-ribboned strap of her chemise, he bent his head to kiss her shoulder, then her throat, then her mouth, his arms going around her, holding her tight against him. Her bones felt soft and weak. She opened her eyes, hoping he hadn't felt her tremble, but his smile said he had.

"So many buttons," he murmured, as he shifted his attention to her skirt. The buttons fastening her skirt went from her waist to her ankles, and he carefully slipped enough buttons free so the skirt slid over her hips to the floor. "Thank god, you aren't wearing a corset."

He hooked his thumbs in the waist of her narrow petticoat and pushed the silk off her hips, leaving her in only her chemise, drawers, and stockings. Kneeling, he lifted her leg so he could slip off her shoe. She had to rest her fingertips on his shoulder for balance. He moved to her other shoe, slipped it off, tossed it after its mate, and kissed her ankle through the thin silk stocking. With one movement, he scooped her into his arms.

"The others?" A faint whisper.

"No one else is in the house. We're alone."

Carrying her, he headed for the stairs in the hallway. She put her hand against his chest, meaning to keep some distance, but instead she clutched his shirt and rested her head against his shoulder. He took the stairs two at a time and turned into a bedroom. Pausing, he shifted her in his arms, so she could see the wide bed at the other end of the room. She lifted her head and met his eyes. He kicked the door closed.

He watched her sleep—lashes dark against her cheeks, blonde hair spilled across the pillows, lips rosy and swollen from kissing. A stray curl fell across her cheek. He looped it around his finger and moved it to join the others. He'd never be tired of looking at her.

He hadn't been nervous with women since he was fifteen, but he'd been nervous tonight, afraid he might not please her. When she'd turned breathless, melting against him, he knew she was his. She'd taken over his thoughts permanently the first time he saw her, and he could never give her up now.

44

Rae nibbled at her chicken while Lev ate as if he hadn't had a bite since the last time they were at Gino's Trattoria. He'd turned thirteen—bigger hands and feet and wider shoulders. Two orders of spaghetti and meatballs followed by chocolate torte. She watched him eat, listened to his chatter, and worried about Lily.

She should have told Lukas when Pa came back. Instead, she'd wavered back and forth between her promise to Lukas and her loyalty to Pa. Lily had sacrificed herself because Rae lost her nerve.

Lev licked the chocolate from his fork.

"More?" Rae asked.

He stifled a burp and shook his head. "Can't get any more in." He smothered another burp. "I only got one more day on your movie. Pretending to be the farm boy while you're acting Dora is okay, but I like the other stuff better. Would Matt hire me to help George? George said he'd teach me to run the projector in the negative room, or maybe I could help build sets."

"Ask Matt tomorrow," Rae said. "George is always complaining he needs help."

"I'd do it for free," Lev said.

"No." Rae cut him off. "Ida told me when I started— *never work for free*. Ask for what you're getting now." Her conscience stabbed her. To help Matt, she'd told him Lev only wanted three dollars for two days of playing Dora's friend, and she'd told Lev that was the regular wage. "After a couple of weeks, ask for a raise," she added.

The apartment was quiet when she unlocked the door. She'd hoped Lily would be home. Settling on the sofa to wait, Rae slid down until her head rested on the armrest. Trying not to think about how Lily must be paying Lukas for cancelling Pa's debt, she concentrated on planning the action for one of Dora's scenes. Run in. Take the pitchfork and stab at the hay stack. Run out. She closed her eyes to visualize the scene.

When she opened her eyes, birds chirped in the trees outside, and first light shone through the windows. She groaned. Her neck had a crick in it, and her arm, twisted under her, was numb. She wiggled her fingers while she checked the bedrooms. Lily wasn't home.

Should she call someone? Who? An image of Lily pale and hurt flashed in her mind and stuck there. Maybe she'd been wrong about Lukas being safe. Too tense for breakfast, she decided to go to the studio early. Matt or Ida would know what to do.

At the studio, Ida put her hands on her hips and laughed. "I wouldn't be home early either if I had an evening with Lukas Krantz." She poked her finger at Rae's shoulder. "You get in these overalls and stop worrying."

"I know what you mean, Ida, but Lily doesn't like Lukas. She only went with him because Lukas did us a favor, so Lily said he could take her to a restaurant. Lily told me she'd be back by nine o'clock last night."

Ida exhaled another short laugh. "It's long past nine, isn't it?" She held the overalls as Rae stepped in and jerked the shoulder straps into place. "Sometimes a young lady doesn't know what or who she likes right away. She has to discover it—realize what she's been thinking is wrong. That whole business with Eddie Carleton—Lily had a lot of nonsense in her head about a fancy society life. She found out quick enough it wasn't going to happen, and Eddie wasn't the man she thought he was. Now she's a grass widow."

"It was an annulment. An annulment means it didn't happen."

Ida tightened the shoulder straps on the overalls. "Well, it did happen, and Lily isn't the girl she was. Maybe she's discovering other things she likes." Stuffing the ends of Rae's gingham shirt into the pants, she stepped back to survey the costume and frowned. "You've got a lot more figure than Dora's supposed to have."

Rae looked down at the bib on the overalls. It should have been flatter, but the material curved over her breasts. "Ida, we have to do something."

"I'm thinking," Ida snapped. She grabbed a long scarf and tied it around Rae's neck, leaving the ends dangling. "That's worse." She tore it off. Roaming the room, she poked through racks of costumes, and finally pulled a man's vest off one of the racks. "Let's try this." She sighed. "It's too big, but it covers what it should. It'll have to do. Go on now. Fred's waiting, and Dora's adventures are bringing in most of the money these days."

The day didn't go well. When Rae opened the door to the sheriff's office, the door stuck, and everyone waited while the crew oiled the hinge. The next three times she opened the door, the wall fell over, narrowly missing the actor playing the sheriff. George cursed loudly. Fred yelled at the crew. Rae slumped in a chair and wondered where Lily was.

It was late afternoon before she got back to Ida. "A letter came for you." Ida pointed to a crumpled envelope on the shelf.

Rae stared at the writing. Her name and RidgeW's address were scrawled crookedly on the dirty envelope. She ripped it open and pulled out a single tattered sheet marked with a oily smear.

> *Dear Miss Raeanne Kelly,*
>
> *You do not know me, but my friend Gil talked of you, and I promised I would write to you if it were needed. Our unit near Ypres was attacked in our trenches one morning by German troops, and we held pretty well.*

When we tried to attack their trenches in turn, we were beaten back. The German fire was plenty hot, but Gil went over the top again to pull one of our wounded boys back to our trench. The smoke was so thick we could see nothing beyond a foot. I am sorry to say Gil was shot and died before he could reach our trench. He was a good friend and a brave soldier. I am yours most sincerely, Jack Sommers.

"Ida!"

Ida seized the letter and glanced quickly down the page. Her breath caught, making a strangling noise in her throat. She wrapped her arms around Rae, and they clung to each other, tears slipping down their cheeks, crying together for the boy they'd loved.

45

While Rae alternated between stoicism and tears, Lily reverted to mothering her the way she had when they were young. An atmosphere of gloom hung over RidgeW. Lucinda wrote a full column for the *Chicago Dispatch* about Gil's talent and virtues, listed all his movies at RidgeW, and finished with tributes from Matt and other studio owners in Chicago. Lily hugged Rae while they read the column over and over.

As much as she felt Rae's grief, Lily couldn't stifle a selfish throb of relief at not having to explain her evening with Lukas. Rae seemed to have forgotten it. To keep her busy, Lily sent her out to eat every night with Lev, hoping his chatter would distract her.

Alone, Lily had time to dwell on Lukas. She'd spent the first week after being with him anticipating a phone call, flowers, or jewels, which she intended to thoroughly reject now that the debt had been paid. It was mortifying to remember the way she'd reached for him during that long night. She wanted to harshly reject him again and prove she'd not felt anything—not really—even though she'd been unable to stop herself from gasping and arching against him when he'd touched her in those scandalous, delicious ways. None of that mattered of course. She'd simply been taken by surprise.

But days passed without a sign from him. She was puzzled, then felt abandoned, and then grew furious at being used. She had to lecture herself. They'd both understood the bargain. He was a gangster—not a man she should give another thought to.

At the studio, she paid more attention to her acting with the new comedian, concentrating on the advice Billy had given her about how to move and react in comic moments. Matt was pleased with her efforts. She decided to focus on her career the way Rae did and stop thinking her future was in any way connected with a husband. Her experience with Eddie certainly had shown her how inconsistent men could be.

Another week passed before she answered a knock on the door to find Gus standing on the outside step. Behind him, the Pierce-Arrow sat at the curb, a street light gleaming off the windshield while rain spattered the glass. Gus held an open umbrella, bobbed his head in an awkward bow, and announced he'd come to drive her to Lukas's house.

"Does he think he can summon me whenever he wants?" Lily put her hands on her hips and glared at Gus.

Her pent up anger at Lukas boiled immediately, but having only Gus to snap at wasn't satisfying. She needed to demolish Lukas with a clever but cutting statement he would never forget. She had to show him he was nothing to her. Less than nothing. Gus stood awkwardly at her door. He closed the umbrella under the shelter of the overhang, pulled off his cap, shoved it in his pocket, then took it out again, and nervously twisted it in his battered hands. Gus was not the person she wanted to spurn. She bit her lip and beat down her irritation. "We don't have an appointment," she added in a calmer voice.

"Don't know about appointments and such," Gus mumbled. "Boss said to fetch you. For a supper, I guess," he added diplomatically, avoiding her gaze.

"*Fetch?*" Lily's voice rose again. "Tell Mr. Krantz we've settled our business, and I didn't agree to be *fetched* any time he gets a whim."

He groaned. "Oh, Miss Lily, I can't tell the boss you wouldn't come with me. He'll think I made you mad or didn't treat you right. When he tells me to do something, he expects me to do it."

"I don't work for Lukas Krantz," she said.

The lines around Gus's eyes deepened as his face contorted into a sheet of wrinkles from forehead to chin. "Please, Miss Lily. You have to come with me." He fumbled with his cap before his eyes brightened. "You come with me and tell the boss you won't stay. Then I'll drive you back here."

His suggestion was tempting. She'd be able to reject Lukas in person, show him how little she thought of him, how meaningless his attentions had been. While Gus drove her to the house, she'd invent several devastating remarks to fling at Lukas when she saw him.

"All right," she said. "Wait for me. I need to change."

In her bedroom, she hurriedly stripped off her dress and cotton underclothes. She wanted to look forbidding and serious. She searched her closet and rejected several possibilities—too dark, too light, too warm for May, scratchy material, too fancy, not her best color, too plain, not serious enough.

Finally, she slipped on black hose and slid thin pink garters through the loops at the top. Next, she put on her ivory silk drawers, edged with black lace that matched the lace along the bodice of her silk chemise. Her ruffled petticoat was too bulky. She selected a narrow, black crepe skirt and a white silk shirtwaist, tied at the low collar with a braided cord. Gazing in the mirror, she decided she looked forbidding with a no-nonsense air—a secretary perhaps or a librarian. Pleased with the effect, she twisted her hair into a tight coil at the top of her head. She checked the mirror again. Her face was flushed. Her heart pounded inside her chest, and she couldn't pull in a long breath. Her mind filled with fragments of sentences and shaky protests at being summoned, but a coherent—biting—sentence that would stun Lukas did not form in her brain.

During the drive, she gave up trying to think of a sharp, crushing remark and, instead, stared blankly out the front window as Gus bent over the wheel, peering intently through the scattered rain drops splashing on the windshield. Her pulse thumped so heavily she could feel it in her head. Through force of will, she slowed her breathing and stopped her hands from shaking. In front of the stone house, she waited for Gus to hold the umbrella over her as they walked up the steps.

"I'll wait at the curb," Gus said as he opened the door for her.

At the end of the hallway, she paused in front of the sliding doors and made a last attempt to form a stinging rejection. Nothing came to her. Her brain was useless—turned to mush. When she entered the room, Lukas turned from the window. She almost felt his hands on her again, the way they'd moved that night, warming her skin. Dragging in a long, uneven breath, she took a step backward. She shouldn't have come in person. No matter what Gus suggested, she should have sent him back to Lukas with a note. Now she was here, and she couldn't retreat. Her heart pounded with apprehension at the same time tense awareness of Lukas clouded her thoughts.

He smiled. "I'm sorry you had to wait," he said before she could speak. "I had problems—the boxing—and other business matters. I had to go out of town. I wanted—"

"I wasn't anticipating I'd hear from you," she burst out. "We concluded our business. I only came tonight to tell you not to expect me here again."

"I shouldn't expect you?"

"No, you shouldn't." She struggled to slow her wildly thumping pulse. "We agreed I would come only one time. That one time would repay you for canceling the debt."

"I never agreed to one time," he said. His voice was low and dangerously calm.

She gasped. "Of course, you did."

"I did not agree to one time, and you don't remember me saying it."

She struggled to recall their conversation and failed to summon a clear memory of either of them saying the bargain was for only one meeting. "I'm sure . . ."

"You aren't sure at all."

A shiver went up her spine. "Nevertheless, I believed that was the arrangement. One time. You have no proof to the contrary."

"You could have told Gus you wouldn't come or given him a note."

"Gus didn't want to carry a message." He was too close to her now—she felt his heat. "I decided . . . I thought I should tell you in person."

He lifted a loose strand of her hair and let it run through his fingers, dipped his head, and put his lips against her ear. "You liked everything we did that night," he whispered.

Her thoughts became a disordered jumble. Sharp memories of how she'd behaved while he made love to her turned her cheeks red. She crossed her arms over her chest, not knowing how to form a denial he would believe. "We made a bargain. Our business is settled."

He straightened and gazed at her. "Did you tell Gus to wait for you?" At her nod, he picked his suit coat off a chair. "Come with me."

The rain turned into a fine mist as they hurried down the steps. At the curb, Lukas dismissed Gus. "You can go home. We're taking a drive."

Lily pressed against the passenger door as he drove. She hadn't agreed to come with him. He'd simply swept her out of the house and into the auto. She seemed unable to summon steady resistance when he was with her. Threading her fingers together, she stared into the night while he talked about his parents and how they'd immigrated from Germany in time for him to be born in Chicago. His father had been a printer in Munich and quickly got a job with Carleton Printing, a new Chicago company then. His mother had baked pastries and breads and sold them to local bakeries.

"I can still taste her rye bread," he said. "Nobody ever made a better rye bread."

His voice was casual, friendly. She knew he was trying to soften her, but every moment with Lukas was a mistake. He wasn't respectable. Confusion took over. She found herself offering bits of her childhood in return for his stories. Her memories were darker than his—battles between her mother and father over money, her mother demanding changes and her father refusing whatever the demands were. Finally, Maxie took up boxing to make money, but her mother left them anyway.

Lukas pulled to the curb on a quiet street lined with nearly identical one-story wooden houses. The front porches held swings or chairs, and flowers grew alongside the four or five steps leading to the porches. The motor still running, Lukas turned to face her. "She left three girls without a word?"

Lily nodded. "She . . . wanted to escape."

"Lots of people want to escape, but children usually keep women home. Do you know where she is?"

"No, she disappeared. There was another man. But our father stayed with us—until he had to leave town."

"I suppose you blame me for that."

"He was afraid you'd hurt him—maybe kill him."

"Maxie might have had the right idea at the time. I was damn mad over the money."

"You gave up the money."

"I wanted you more," he answered. He lightly traced her jaw with his finger, stopping before she could form a protest. "That house," he pointed, "was ours until my father was killed."

Lily stared at the white shutters reflecting light from the street lamp. "We never lived in our own house," she said. "There wasn't enough money." She turned to Lukas. "How did you manage after your parents died?"

He frowned. "I found a way. Sometimes honest, some-times not."

"I suppose it was difficult. That's why you helped Rae when she came to you."

"Picking pockets isn't a good line of work for a young girl." He touched her shoulder, again so briefly she couldn't protest. "Are you hungry?"

The restaurant was tiny, only eight tables in the room, each with a long tapered candle flickering in a glass vase. A stout, middle-aged woman directed them to the empty table next to the only window. She offered a paper menu, but Lukas waved it away and ordered chicken soup with dumplings and stuffed cabbage rolls.

When the woman left, he leaned back. "She'll bring rye bread with the soup. Almost as good as my mother's."

Her resistance seemed to amuse him. He clearly didn't believe she could say no to him. She no longer knew if she could.

"Tell me the first thing you remember," he said after a silence.

The soup came, and Lily told him how she and Rae played together, how they shared a doll, how they'd take turns jumping rope with one end tied to a tree and one of them turning the other end. Delia was older and didn't want to play with them. When the cabbage rolls arrived, she told him how Rae learned to pick pockets from a neighborhood girl and sometimes lifted wallets from un-suspecting men four or five days in a row when they were desperate for money even though they knew it was wrong. She rushed on, telling him about working in shops and living in dingy apartments—details she'd never shared with Eddie. Sorting through her memories calmed her lingering nerves, and she laughed, describing games they played. He listened attentively to her trivia, laughing with her in the right places, offering his own childhood memories occasionally. She resisted a shocking impulse to touch him.

In the dark parking lot after the meal, Lukas took her hand and kissed her palm. He stroked her wrist where her pulse thudded unevenly. "Come back to the house with me. "

She steeled herself and pulled back her hand. "No." She was afraid to look into his eyes. She couldn't let herself weaken—not after all her protests.

"I think you want to." He recaptured her hand and traced the lines in her palm. "I did odd jobs for a Chinese gambler once. He told me the life line shows energy and joy. Your life line is very strong."

"You're making that up." She struggled to keep her voice steady. "Please stop." But she didn't pull away.

He kissed her palm again, moving his lips softly over her fingers and her wrist, until her breathing grew uneven. Then he released her hand and turned to the steering wheel.

When they reached her apartment, she was relieved to see a light in the window. He wouldn't be able to follow her inside. "Rae must be home," she murmured.

Lukas put his hand on the nape of her neck and turned her face toward him. He kissed her lips softly then harder. She should stop him—she would—in another minute or two. Her hands fluttered ineffectively against his coat until they settled on his lapels and tightened, pulling him closer. Suddenly lightheaded, she kissed him as deeply as he kissed her.

He pulled away abruptly, leaving her breathless. Victory glinted in his dark eyes. Grinning, he reached across her to open the door. "Good night, Lily."

46

Arabella Weston brushed her teeth for the third time since she'd awakened an hour before. She'd vomited twice quickly and then once more although she no longer had anything in her stomach this early in the morning. Her free hand clung to the edge of the bathroom sink as a wave of nausea gripped her. Staring at herself in the mirror, she willed her body into a semblance of normalcy. She wasn't confused. She didn't need to look at a calendar. She'd been dreading this morning for over two weeks. As she slid her toothbrush back in its ceramic holder, her mother opened the door.

"I heard you," Emeline said in a low voice.

Arabella swished her dressing gown as she left the bathroom, padding noiselessly on bare feet back to her room. Emeline trailed behind her. When the door closed, Arabella tightened her sash. "The fish last night must have disagreed with me."

Emeline sighed. "I'm not an idiot, Arabella. I feared this would happen. I assumed—god knows, I hoped—you were taking care to avoid this eventuality."

"I did." Arabella abruptly pressed her hand on her stomach and sank into a chair, her face pale. "I did everything I've always done. The instant I came back here, I used vinegar. I did it twice every time. It's always worked with Theodore."

"I've observed over the years," Emeline said, "quicker is always better. You spent as little time as possible with your husband, and you were close to your own bathroom. With Matt," she made a helpless gesture, "you spent hours with Matt."

Arabella put her fingers on her temples and closed her eyes.

"Does Matt know?"

Arabella shook her head. "I wanted to be sure."

"Listen to me." Emeline bent over her daughter. "You have to tell Theodore he's the father. He'll be thrilled. He wants another son."

"Why would he believe me?"

"He's been with you recently, hasn't he?"

"Yes." Arabella grimaced. "He . . . from time to time."

"That's close enough," Emeline said. "He'll believe you because he wants to."

"He won't. I don't want him to. Matt promised me the studio will make him rich any time now, and we can go away together."

"Read the newspapers more often. When Matt lost Billy Tucker, he lost his main attraction. That stage actor,

Chester whatshisname, hasn't had a success since that fire movie. Matt's westerns aren't as popular as the ones the Broncho Billy actor makes for Essanay. RidgeW's only success is that serial with the young girl." Emeline took Arabella's hand. "I'm not dead to your feelings. I know it's romantic to think of being with Matt, but you've lived in luxury for a long time. You can't give up what you have—and neither can I."

Arabella's gaze sharpened. "This is about you."

Emeline pursed her lips. "Do you remember what our lives were like after your father died in disgrace and debt? We lived on credit, month to month. I won't deny I'm quite apprehensive about what my life would be if you left Theodore. I couldn't stay in this house, and we'd both be immersed in a scandal. You'd lose your reputation entirely, and I . . . we'd be penniless."

A shaft of morning sunlight came through the window. Arabella groaned and shaded her eyes.

Emeline halted her lecture and drew the drapes, keeping the room in shadows. "Women have to put feelings aside and think of the future. We don't have many choices. If you have a Weston heir, even a daughter, you'll always have a claim on Theodore's money." She paused. "He's considerably older. In time, perhaps not too much time, you might be a widow. You could make another fortunate marriage. If there's a scandal, you'll never have another chance at a marriage with a man of substance."

Arabella rose to her feet and swayed slightly. "I have to see Matt."

Emeline blanched. "You can't tell Matt." She grasped Arabella's arms and shook her. "Think! Once Matt knows, you'll have no control over the situation. Consider the child—the life he could have if you use some sense. After all, you can't be certain Theodore isn't the father." Her fingers dug into Arabella's flesh. "I'm begging you, Arabella, don't be a fool."

Arabella wrenched away. "Let me go. I have to talk to Matt."

The taxi stopped in front of RidgeW Studios in the fading light. Arabella put her bronze kid boots firmly on the running board and stepped out of the taxi. Her stomach had settled, but she'd eaten little all day other than some toast and tea. Her nerves were frayed. It was after eight. Surely, the crew and actors were gone by now. The front door was unlocked, and she waved away the taxi driver before going into the studio.

Voices sounded dimly in the back of the building, and she followed the sounds down the long hallway, around a bend, then down stairs leading to the basement. At the bottom, she paused. The girl from the serial—Rae something—and a boy were struggling to help Matt raise a large, canvas tent. Grunting, the boy pushed the central pole into place. Matt followed with another pole, and they both whooped with success.

Glancing over his shoulder, Matt saw her, took a step in her direction, but halted. "Mrs. Weston. How nice of you to drop in. Can I help you?" His shirt sleeves were rolled up, his arms streaked with dust and dirt.

"I wanted to talk to you, Mr. Ridgewood." Arabella glanced at Rae who was staring at her, suspicion in her eyes. "A possible funding idea," Arabella added.

"Rae, you and Lev can go home," Matt said instantly. "We'll put out the cushions and rugs tomorrow." He waited, his eyes on Arabella, until he heard the distant slam of the front doors. Then he smiled. "I didn't expect you." He reached for her, but she backed away.

"Don't you have a crew to set up these things?"

"I had to let a couple fellows go, so Lev and Rae usually help me set up some props the night before we need them."

The stark basement walls depressed her. "Let's go upstairs," she murmured.

Waiting in the office while he went to clean up, she looked at the schedule on the wall, the piles of screenplays, the messy stack of bills on the desk. Nothing had changed since the first time she'd been here. The signs of wealth and success she'd been expecting for months were absent. Her mother's cautionary words repeated in her head.

When Matt returned, she moved into his arms and kissed him. "You work too hard," she said. "I thought by now you'd have more help."

"It's been a little rough lately. The comedies aren't as popular without Billy." He wrapped his arms around her and pulled her tight against him. "What did you want to talk to me about?"

"Nothing really." She rested her head on his shoulder. "I just wanted to see you."

He kissed her cheek. "I missed you too."

"So much," she murmured and guided his hand to the buttons on her suit jacket. "So much."

47

"We should have stayed," Rae grumbled. "Another half hour and we'd have finished." Thunder rumbled in the west as they walked.

Lev sniggered. "Maybe Matt couldn't wait a half hour. Mrs. Weston is a good-looker."

"Mrs. Weston helps Matt raise money."

"Rae, sometimes I think you don't notice nothing. That lady was all fluttery when she looked at Matt."

"How would you know when a woman is fluttery?"

"I get around," Lev said. "I know what's what, and both of them were plenty keyed up the minute she walked in. Matt couldn't wait to get rid of us."

Rae punched him lightly. "Don't go spreading stories like that. Lucinda could put it in her column."

Laughing, he returned her punch. "I asked George about working on the cameras and projectors, and he said

I could. Hope RidgeW doesn't go bust before I get the hang of it."

"RidgeW won't go under," Rae said. "Matt's had some bad luck, but RidgeW will be all right."

Rain began as they separated, and Rae sprinted the rest of the way to the apartment. She'd pretended she hadn't noticed how Matt had looked at Arabella Weston, but his expression had stirred an uneasy mix of irritation and possessiveness in her. It wasn't her business, but Matt deserved better than a married woman, who, according to Ida, had already abandoned him once before. Matt deserved the best.

Reaching the apartment, she paused on the front landing. A vase of flowers sat near the door, a white card tucked between the green leaves. Lukas sent flowers almost every day except when he sent jewelry or gloves or something else to thrill Lily. Rae hefted the vase in one arm, unlocked the door, and pushed inside. Delia sat on a kitchen chair, her wrist in a splint.

"What happened?" Rae put the flowers next to the vase holding yesterday's delivery. The apartment smelled like a florist shop.

Delia stroked her free hand protectively over the splint. "It's not broken, just a sprain. I didn't answer the door all afternoon. I was afraid Chester would barge in."

"Will he? Barge in?"

"I don't know. He said I was nagging him about California, and he lost his temper and twisted my wrist." Lightning cracked overhead followed by a roll of thunder. Delia half jumped out of the chair. "He hasn't gotten any offers from other studios, and he's in a foul mood most of the time. I told him I was staying with you for a few days until he calmed down." She sighed. "Hal's boxing tonight and can't see me."

"Maybe that's best," Rae said. She filled the tea kettle and turned up the flame on the stove. "What if Chester did barge in and found you with Hal?" Opening the cupboard, she took out a tin of Oreo biscuits and shook a pile of them onto a plate. "What are you going to do if Chester goes to California?"

"I can't go back to that farm. Hal's mother's on a rampage. She knows about Chester, and Hal said she's begging him to abandon me and come back to the farm." Delia raised her gaze to the ceiling. "It's so complicated, Rae. You're too young to understand. You've never been in love. You don't know what it's like."

Rae remembered Gil. She knew something about love. "You have to straighten this out. Do you want Chester or Hal?" She put two tea cups on the table and poured hot water into the tea pot.

"Hal makes me . . ."

"Quiver?"

"Exactly." Delia eyed her. "Have you gotten a call from a studio in California?"

"Why does everyone think I'm going to get a call from California?"

"Because your serial is so popular."

Rae poured the tea, and they sipped in comfortable silence—broken when Lily rushed through the door. Rain dripped off her shoulders and streaked down her skirt. Her long hair glistened with rain drops, and she shook it like a dog shedding water.

Delia squealed as the drops sprayed through the air. "Be careful! Where have you been?"

Lily sank into a chair at the table while Rae poured another cup of tea. "Lukas took me to a new restaurant tonight."

Delia's smile took on a wicked cast. "Lukas Krantz? How interesting. When did you stop moaning and groaning over Eddie?"

Rae caught Lily's warning glance. They'd never told Delia about Pa's debt or how Lily had paid for it. "Eddie who?" Rae answered Delia. "We've forgotten all about anyone named Eddie."

Delia glanced around the room at the vases of flowers. "Are all these from Lukas? And he takes you to a restaurant every night because he's a generous fellow?"

"I have to eat," Lily said, lowering her gaze to her tea cup.

"Why are your lips so puffy? Maybe you have an allergy. Have you been touching anything you shouldn't?" Delia winked at Rae.

Lily turned bright red and made a threatening gesture. Delia pretended to duck. They giggled and had a battle over the last Oreo. Rae twisted it apart, giving one half to Lily and one half to Delia but only after she'd scraped off some of the cream filling for herself.

48

Theodore Weston poured a cup of coffee from the side table in the breakfast room and glanced out the window facing the garden while he tested the strong brew. A flock of small brown birds clustered around the edges of the carved stone bird bath Emeline had installed in the center of the lawn.

They were sparrows, he supposed, watching them maneuver for the best positions near the water. He didn't care much for wildlife, but Emeline had insisted every well-appointed house needed a bird bath in the garden. He added a splash of cream to his coffee, selected two pieces of toast, and carried his breakfast to the table. Petra had placed the three morning papers he read every day next to his usual seat. He stared at the headlines.

British Passenger Ship Sunk by German Submarine
Lusitania Torpedoed off Irish Coast! 1200 Lost
Lusitania Sinks in Minutes with Americans
Aboard

He opened one of the papers to an inside page. The damn European war was encroaching on business interests. There were plenty of German businessmen in Chicago, some of whom paid him regularly for special considerations. He couldn't imagine what would happen if the United States got sucked into the war. Surely President Wilson could be relied upon to maintain neutrality. He spread a dab of strawberry jam on a piece of toast and raised it to his mouth.

"Theodore! We must speak to you." Emeline walked into the room, clinging to Arabella's hand. Emeline's smile was so intense and wide the muscles in her cheeks pulsed. Arabella's face was ashen with dark circles under her eyes.

"What is it?" Vaguely irritated, he rose to his feet. He hated being interrupted at his morning breakfast. Arabella and Emeline rarely awakened early enough for breakfast, and he enjoyed planning his day in silence.

Emeline glanced at Arabella, but Arabella seemed frozen. Emeline plunged on. "Such wonderful news, Theodore. You're going to be a father."

He stared at the two of them. "What?" His gaze drilled into Arabella. She looked back at him, her expression blank, her lips white and trembling.

"I know you're surprised." Emeline's tone shifted from exciting to entreating. "Of course, a wife wants to tell her husband before anyone else, but I discovered the happy news quite by accident when I found Arabella ill several mornings in a row."

"I've been too sick to talk to you the past few days," Arabella whispered.

He made a quick calculation in his head. The child could be his although he doubted it. If Emeline hadn't been in the room, he'd have shaken the truth out of his wife. As it was, he felt entitled to express astonishment. "I'm stunned," he said, letting his caustic tone hang in the air. "After all this time, it's amazing. I'd given up all hope of this happy event."

He noticed Emeline's delighted expression falter for an instant before she reinstated it. For a fleeting moment, he contemplated the inevitable scandal if he didn't accept this absurd announcement. Scandal interfered with business prospects and tainted everyone involved. People took sides. You could never predict the results of a public disgrace.

"We're going to see Dr. Bradshaw this afternoon," Emeline said.

He nodded. "We'll want the best of care." If they were going to convince people the child was his, he'd have to participate. He stepped to Arabella's side and put his arm around her shoulders. "Don't strain yourself, my dear. Follow Dr. Bradshaw's instructions completely. This is wonderful news." His hand tightened on her shoulder, fingers digging into her flesh. "I do hope the child looks like you—a little girl with dark eyes and hair who looks like her mother."

Arabella's lips trembled. "Perhaps we'll have a boy."

"Another son for me. Then we'll want the boy to look like you with dark hair and eyes," he answered. "It's always best when a child looks like his mother." He smiled at Emeline and was gratified to see her go pale as well. "Don't you think so, Emeline?"

He had to listen to Emeline's prattling about setting up a nursery for another fifteen minutes before the two women left him. His zest for breakfast had vanished. The coffee was cold, the toast was soggy from the jam, and his thoughts focused on what needed to be done next. He headed downstairs to his library office.

Sean leaped from his chair when Weston walked into the room. "Did you see the papers? The Germans blew that ship out of the water, women and children and all."

"I saw the headlines," Weston answered. He sat behind his desk and twirled a letter opener in his hand.

"The Germans in town might have some trouble over this."

"The war is in Europe."

"People get excited," Sean said. "Americans were on board. Could be somebody's relatives."

Weston looked at him. "Do you remember when I told you to ask around for a man who might cause an accident?"

Sean licked his lips. "I didn't think you—"

"Get on it." Weston slapped the letter opener on the desk blotter. "I'm going to need a special job handled. Find me someone."

49

Lily pushed open the RidgeW front doors, walked outside, and stopped. The Pierce-Arrow waited at the curb. Fury bubbled. He'd disappeared again for over a week without a word and now was here just as though he hadn't neglected her. She contemplated walking past him and heading for a taxi, but when she reached the curb, she opened the door and climbed inside. Competing emotions churned in her brain. She should make him suffer, but she'd been slowly losing their unspoken battle for control. He knew it every time he kissed her goodnight, sliding his hands over her shoulders and along her hips until she clung to him and kissed him as wildly as he kissed her. Then he'd smile and put her out of the auto. It was infuriating.

She slammed the door and settled into the seat next to him, gazing out the windshield, lips tight, but her pulse thumping in the familiar irregular beat he caused whenever he was near.

Lukas grinned at her. "Miss me?"

"I haven't seen you for days," she said. "You didn't tell me you were going out of town, and Gus claimed he didn't know where you were."

"You asked Gus where I was?" He sounded surprised, but she heard the amusement in his voice.

She smoothed her skirt, striving for a semblance of indifference. "I was curious." She'd waited three days before questioning Gus, knowing perfectly well he'd tell Lukas she'd asked. She hadn't been able to stop herself.

"You missed me."

Lily kept her gaze straight ahead. "Not at all." She sighed. "Oh, all right. Yes, I missed you." She turned her head to look at him. Strong jaw, angular cheekbones—not at all the smooth boyish looks she'd liked in Eddie. She wanted him to kiss her, but the late afternoon sunlight was still bright. Anyone walking down the street could see them. She looked at his hands, sliding up and down the steering wheel while the auto idled at the curb. An ache of longing consumed her.

"Do you want to take a drive in the country before we find a restaurant?"

"No. I want to go to your house." Surprise flashed in his eyes. Had she been too bold? She rushed on. "You offered to show it to me once. Now I want to see it."

His hands tightened on the steering wheel. "If you're sure . . ."

"I'm sure." Lily settled back on the seat and waited for him to pull away from the curb. Her heart pounded with a sense of power. She'd startled him. She'd taken charge and decided what would happen next. Sensual anticipation flowed through her.

At the house, Lukas parked, opened her door, and slipped her arm through his as they walked up the steps to the front doors. "No one's here, and I don't think I have anything to eat," he said as he unlocked the door.

"I'm not hungry," Lily said. Memories of the first time she'd been in this house whispered through her mind—fiery kisses—shocking caresses—her astonishment at how different the night had been from what she'd expected.

Inside the shadowy hallway, he moved to switch on the overhead lights. Lily followed him, erasing the distance between them. When he turned, she stood on tiptoe and put her arms around his neck. Even on her toes, she could only reach the edge of his chin with her lips. She kissed his jaw and then his throat above his shirt collar.

"Come down here," she ordered.

He bent his head and lightly kissed her cheek, her chin, her lips.

His tenderness made her bolder. She unbuttoned his suit jacket and ran her hands across his white shirt, enjoying the sensation of hard muscles under her fingers. He stood motionless, keeping his hands at his sides while she caressed him, dark eyes watching her, his mouth curving in a smile. Confidence—energy—took hold of her. He made no move to stop her when she pushed his jacket off his shoulders and let it drop to the floor. She smiled up at him. "Are you shocked?"

"Not shocked," he said. "Amazed."

She slipped her arms around his neck again. "Did you stay away so I would miss you desperately? You did, didn't you? Did you miss me, too? Did you dream about me? I dreamed about you." She tugged at his shoulders to force him to dip his head again, so she could reach his mouth and drop kisses along his lips. "Show me upstairs first," she whispered.

As he lifted her in his arms and turned toward the stairway, one of her shiny patent shoes slipped off, and the other quickly followed. She rested her head in the curve of his shoulder as he carried her. Running her hand across his chest, she fumbled with a shirt button and smiled when she heard his sharp intake of breath.

A light May evening breeze drifted through the window as they lay entangled on the bed, moonlight casting shadows through the trees over their naked bodies. Crickets hummed outside, noisy in the quiet, and the faint sweet smell from the lilac bushes below came through the partially opened window. Lily slept, but he didn't. He stared into the darkness, his thoughts fixed on the still astounding fact that Lily had come to him—her desire so intense, so remarkable, he couldn't allow himself to sleep.

She stirred, lashes fluttering. Lukas kissed her forehead.

"Did I fall asleep?" she asked in a dreamy, soft voice, a half-smile on her lips.

"For a minute or two," he answered.

She pressed close against his body. "My clothes are in the hallway," she whispered and kissed his shoulder.

"We'll collect them." He caressed her bare hip. Contentment blunted his usual caution with her. "Stay with me," he said.

She brushed his hair back from his forehead. "I'll stay, but you have to take me home in the morning. I don't want Gus to know I spent the night here."

"I mean I want you to stay with me for good."

"I don't want to be a mistress." She stroked his chest. "I want this—I want you. But I still don't know you, not really."

"You didn't know Eddie Carleton either." He regretted those words immediately. "Never mind." he said quickly. "I didn't mean it."

"You're right," Lily said. "I didn't know Eddie, and I made mistakes."

"Eddie doesn't matter anymore." He drew her into his arms. "I don't want a mistress. I want you. I wanted you the instant Rae dragged you across the room to meet me." He kissed her. "Let's get married right away."

She pulled away and lay back, gazing at the ceiling. "Married?"

He braced himself on one arm so he could look down at her and gestured at the rumpled bedclothes. "It's what people do." Her face was blank, giving him no clue as what she was thinking. He inhaled slowly. Ease off. Don't push too fast. "We don't have to get married tomorrow. You probably want Rae and Delia to be there. Now that I think about it, women always need to shop for new dresses when they get married." He forced a smile.

"I haven't thought about marriage."

He stroked her arm. "We fit together, Lily. We'd be happy."

"I trusted Eddie, and he made a fool of me—abandoned me—didn't tell me the truth about his parents," she said. "Where were you last week?"

He recognized the test and flopped on his back. How stupid to bring up Eddie Carleton. He didn't want her thinking about Eddie now—or ever again. "I went to Missouri. The war in Europe is getting hotter, and the armies need mules, I can buy and ship hundreds of mules to Europe. That business will be legal."

"Which army?"

Although he'd missed being born in Germany by two months, he was an American, and he'd known and liked Gil. "I talked to a British officer in Kansas City. I have a deal with him."

"RidgeW is legal," she said, "so when will you give up the illegal businesses? That awful house . . ."

He couldn't tell her RidgeW was probably on its last legs. She'd feel compelled to tell her sisters, and bad news always managed to travel into the wrong circles. Matt was making a desperate effort, but he'd gone over Matt's books with him, and they'd concluded RidgeW had to have a big success with Chester Slater's next movie or the studio would be broke. No studio could stay in business with one successful serial and nothing else.

"I've been talking to dealers about buying scrap iron. I can sell it at a profit," he said.

"Scrap iron would be legal," she murmured.

He turned on his side and kissed her temple. "Before long, everything I do will be legal," he said. "Marry me."

Her blue eyes reflected uncertainty. "I don't think I want to be married. Eddie wasn't . . . I have to think."

He lifted a lock of her hair and curled the end around his finger. "Eddie's gone. He isn't important now." He took her lips in a lingering kiss. "I'll make you happy, Lily. I promise."

She ran her fingers through his hair while he trailed kisses along her collarbone. "Don't disappear again." She shifted closer to him. "I miss you too much." Her fingers tightened in his hair.

He'd give up anything to keep her. Those mules—the scrap iron—had to pay off. He kissed her gently, then fiercely, to block everything but him out of her mind.

50

Chicago Dispatch, **June 4, 1915**

Out and About with Lucinda Corday

I am still trembling as I write this column, dear readers. Danger surrounded me yesterday afternoon because I had the ill fortune to be swept up in the riot at the Carleton Printing Company. As you will read in other pages of this newspaper, an angry crowd, enraged by the barbaric attack on the *Lusitania,* gathered outside this company long known for hiring immigrant Germans. My taxi turned the corner and was suddenly surrounded by the angry mob. In spite of my driver's best efforts, we were unable to go forward or to retreat. Consequently, I was forced to witness the horrific events that ensued.

Profane shouts and appalling threats, which I cannot repeat, filled the air as the rioters, armed with clubs, attacked the company entrance. In spite of the attempt by Carleton workers to hold the doors closed, the mob broke through. The hooligans pulled the German immigrants out of the printing shop and beat them as they called for help in broken English. After what seemed like hours, but was only a few minutes, the police arrived to disperse the crowd and make arrests. I was quite overcome with the horror of the situation and can hardly believe that in our city three people were killed and sixteen suffered serious injuries because of the events in a war so far from our shores.

Chicago society is in mourning today. Mr. Edmund Carleton, the owner and founder of Carleton Printing, was one of the fatalities. Before my very eyes, Mr. Carleton tried valiantly to protect a worker, only to be confronted by a ruffian wielding a brick. The brute attacked Mr. Carleton and pounded him into unconsciousness.

His son Edmund Carleton III was at his father's side in the hospital when the elder Mr. Carleton succumbed to his injuries. Mrs. Carleton is, of course, prostrate with grief. I can only offer my heartfelt condolences and assure the Carleton family their loved one died a hero.

This tragic event has shaken Chicago's social leaders. Mrs. Theodore Weston and her mother have departed for an extended visit to Charleston. Mrs. Albert Gregory has cancelled the reception she had planned as a return to society after a long winter stay in Savannah with her daughter Marigold. No doubt, the social scene will remain unsettled for a time.

Until next time, dear readers.

51

ily stirred milk into her tea and glanced out the window of the small café facing Michigan Avenue. In late afternoon, the street was crowded with horse-drawn carriages and wagons negotiating for space among Model T Fords and streetcars. The noise from the street became a muted buzz within the walls of the partially filled café. On the opposite side of the room, two women leaned across their table to gossip over sandwiches and tea. At another table a middle-aged man sat alone with coffee, pastry, and a newspaper.

She hardly knew why she was here. She hadn't told Delia and Rae about his pleading note because they'd have been opposed to her meeting him at all. She closed her eyes for an instant to blot out the list of people who wouldn't approve. When she opened her eyes, she saw him crossing the street, dodging the horses and streetcars, jumping over a steaming pile of horse droppings as he headed toward the café.

He nodded at other pedestrians as he walked with the jaunty stride of a rich, confident young man—his usual manner except for the day he'd left her in the Palmer House and crushed all her dreams. Pushing through the café door, his smile widened, and he doffed his summer straw hat with a slight bow.

"I'm glad you came," Eddie said, sinking into the chair opposite her. "I was afraid you might not." He shook his head. "Never mind. I'm just happy to see you." He reached for her hand over the table, but she moved it away. A faint twitch of his brows nearly turned into a frown, but instead he smiled again. Signaling the waitress for a cup of tea, he leaned back in the chair and gazed at her. "I've missed you, Lily. I thought about you every night since we've been apart. Looking at you now, I can't think at all."

Lily glanced at the women at the other table, but they showed no signs of having overheard him. She was grateful for the waitress's arrival with the tea. "I'm sorry about your father," she said. "The newspaper description—it was terrible."

Eddie's smile faded. "I appreciated your letter, especially since you couldn't have had warm feelings toward my father after his interference." He looked away for a moment, gazing out the window. "He thought he was doing the right thing I suppose."

"It hardly matters now," she answered in a flat tone.

He looked at her, leaned closer, and lowered his voice. "You're right—that's all over. When we saw each other at the LaSalle, I was too surprised to respond properly. That young lady was just an acquaintance. My mother suggested . . . never mind. I've been miserable without you. I've seen every movie—your beautiful face—please tell me there's a chance for us again. I've thought about you constantly."

She stiffened. "Eddie, don't say things like that." Flustered, she lifted her cup and took a sip. Her eyes met his. "You left me, remember? Your father made the decision for you, and you left me."

His ears turned red and he flinched. "I—it seemed to me I had no choice. My father was adamant. I know you have reason to hate me, but I'm hoping you don't." He seized her hand, crushing her fingers. "Please, Lily, we can be happy now."

"That's a ridiculous idea. Everything between us ended months ago." She made an attempt to reclaim her hand, but he kept it firmly grasped in his.

"My father was a rigid man, but he was successful and respected in Chicago. The mayor gave the eulogy at his funeral. I respected my father too." A pleading expression settled on his face. "His death was horrible, but it does free us. I've inherited everything, and no one can stop us from being together." He pressed a kiss on her fingers before she could snatch her hand away.

Her memories were suddenly sharp and painful—his helplessness in the face of his parents' displeasure—his feeble attempt to convince her the annulment was for her benefit—his suggestion that he'd continue to make love to her after they separated. "Your mother," she said making it a statement rather than a question.

"I'm responsible for Mother of course. She's inconsolable right now, and after the funeral, she went to Saratoga to visit her sister. I imagine she'll be gone for several months." He leaned forward again. "We could be married before she returns."

"Do you mean you wouldn't tell her you were marrying me?"

He shifted awkwardly in his chair. "I just mean I wouldn't tell her immediately. She's grieving, so there's no need to add to her . . ." He paused, obviously searching for a suitable word.

She almost laughed at the idea of standing at the door of the Carleton mansion as Eddie's wife and greeting his mother when she returned to Chicago. Curiosity made her pretend to consider his proposal. "She'll return to Chicago sometime. What will you do then? Where will she live?"

He stared blankly at her. Frowning, he inhaled slowly and blew out his breath. Then he brightened. "I'll get her another house. She'll want a smaller house in any case with my father gone."

"Don't be too sure."

"Then I'll get a big house for her. The point is I'm rich and I'm in control. My mother can't stop us. She may decide to stay with her sister for years."

"You aren't thinking, Eddie. Your mother won't accept me—ever. Have you forgotten her reaction the last time you told her we were married?"

"It'll be different this time." He hitched his chair closer to the table, his gaze intense. "I know I hurt you. I wasn't strong enough at the time to defy my parents, and I'm sorry for that. You have to admit, my father's threats were serious. We'd have dropped into poverty with no hope of avoiding it."

"You were being practical. I don't hate you anymore."

Eddie relaxed. "We can be together now, and everything will be wonderful this time. We'll give fabulous parties. You'll be the most beautiful hostess in Chicago—your picture in the society pages. Every man in town will envy me."

She wavered. She let him take her hand again and kiss her fingers. She let him murmur how much he loved her, how beautiful she was, and how wonderful their life could be now that he controlled the Carleton fortune.

"I want to make love to you again," he whispered.

Her mind whirled as if she'd had wine instead of tea. A succession of shocking comparisons between Eddie and Lukas filled her head. Embarrassing and exhilarating.

"Tell me you'll come back to me."

She jerked her hand away and caught her breath. "I have to think."

"I knew you'd say that." He reddened. "I'm sorry for the past. You can trust me this time."

"Can I?"

"There's nothing standing in our way now. You see that, don't you?"

"Yes, I see that."

He took his hat and rose from the table. "I know you need some time." He grinned. "Not too much time. I want you back."

The café door closed behind him, and she watched him cross the street, dodging the traffic, until he disappeared from sight. The waitress brought her fresh tea. She added milk but didn't lift the cup to her lips. She contemplated life in Eddie's mansion, parties with Eddie's friends, dresses from French designers. Only a year ago, all she wanted was someone like Eddie to propose, but now every thought of Eddie was overtaken by one of Lukas—his smile, his touch, his lips against her skin as he whispered to her.

To accept Eddie's offer of luxury, she had to give up Lukas.

52

Delia smelled the liquor the instant she opened the door. An empty whiskey bottle lay on its side on a table cluttered with newspapers and coffee cups. Another bottle on the table stood open. She'd planned to take a bath before Chester got to the hotel—she needed to wash Hal off her skin and push him out of her mind, so she could concentrate on handling Chester's increasingly bad moods. Now she had to hope he was too drunk to sense what she'd been doing all afternoon.

He sat in a chair across the room, a tumbler of whiskey clutched in one beefy hand. He grinned oafishly as she walked into the room, but his eyes were narrow slits, reddened and hot with suspicion. The windows were closed, and the room was stuffy with the June heat and stale aromas of smoke and liquor. A line of sweat rimmed his forehead.

"Where you been?"

Delia pulled off her soft, wide-brimmed hat, a red satin ribbon decorating the crown, and shook out her short dark hair. She forced a smile, her heart thumping in her chest. "Darling, I didn't think you'd be back yet. Didn't you have some scenes with Rae today?"

He took a swallow from the tumbler and coughed. "Matt decided to do the scenes she has with other characters. He said I wasn't up to it today—told me not to drink tonight." He held up his glass and grinned crookedly. "Still afternoon, isn't it?" His face darkened. "He's never respected my talent—spent more time on Rae's stuff than he has on mine, and I told him I didn't care for it. I'm not about to let a girl who jumps out of trees in her movies outshine me in a real drama. Made Matt promise I'd get the most close-ups. *Back to Our Home* is my picture after all." He rubbed his eyes and coughed again. "This movie should get me some offers from California—pay me what I'm worth."

"I should think so," she said in a soothing tone. "You're the real actor."

He grunted agreement. "Where you been?"

She studied him for a moment. He was close to being thoroughly drunk but not enough to be pliable and easily distracted. Walking with a stiff gait, she went to the table and poured some coffee from the carafe into a cup. Her mind raced over possible answers. "I went shopping." She crossed her arms over her chest and held the cup so tightly her fingertips turned white. "It's getting so hot, Chester, I needed new dresses in summer material." She smiled so widely her cheeks hurt. "I wish I'd known you finished early at RidgeW. We could have had lunch together."

He leaned forward, elbows resting on his knees, and tilted his head while his narrow gaze moved up and down along her body.

She couldn't control a shiver, but she kept her smile tight on her lips. "Why don't we go out to eat? I'm starving." She made a show of glancing around the room. "Nothing here looks like food. I'll change my clothes, and we can go to the Palmer House or that Italian restaurant you like."

"You've been shopping all day?" He lurched to his feet, swaying slightly, but carefully holding his glass so it wouldn't tip.

Delia took a step back. "You know how women are. We have to try everything on, and it takes hours to find the right fit. The packages are being delivered tomorrow," she added quickly.

He drained his glass and blinked at her. "I got a letter at the studio from a woman in Wisconsin." He pulled a crumpled blue paper from his shirt pocket and waved it in the air.

Her adrenaline spiked. "A fan letter?" Her mouth turned dry, and she had to muster enough saliva to keep her voice clear. "Aren't they silly? They say the most out-landish things. I got one myself yesterday. A man went on and on about my breasts and how much he wanted to touch them." Her knees were shaky. She wanted to sit, but she had to stay on her feet, had to be mobile. "We should ignore these letters," she added. "The things they make up—outrageous stories. Last week a woman wrote to me and said I'd ruined her marriage because those sheer veils I wore in *My Arabian Sheik* drove her husband mad. She claimed he left her because I was so enticing." She forced a thin laugh.

Swaying slightly, Chester hiccupped and sank back into the chair. "You visit your sisters nearly every day. Why?"

"I'm the oldest one. I have to look out for them. Rae is only a baby really, and we've always been so close." She considered trying to snatch the blue paper out of his closed fist but knew it was impossible. She'd never manage to get her hands on it before he slapped her across the room.

He snorted. "Look out for them—you? Rae's the sensible one." He raised his fist in front of his face and stared at the blue paper. "This letter." He squinted up at her. "Says you have a husband in Wisconsin."

"How silly." Her laugh sounded hollow even to herself. "People see movies and get so involved they think the stories are real. Remember that western where I was married to the sheriff? The woman must have seen that one. We really can't spend our time on these stupid letters from people who don't know us." She fumbled in her bag and took out a folded envelope that held a bill from a milliner. She crushed the envelope into a tight ball. "I got this letter from a fan yesterday, and I'm throwing it away right now. Crazy people write to actors," she said. "Full of nonsense. Let's burn that letter of yours."

53

Tears streamed down Rae's face in her last scene with the actor playing the druggist, as she begged him to stop selling morphine to her father. Nearly every scene in the movie called for her to cry, and she'd discovered she could bring up tears whenever Matt needed them. He said crying on command was a special skill only a few actresses could manage. Playing Dora involved a lot climbing and jumping, but this movie made her consider emotions and how to react to the other characters. Thinking that way about acting was new, but she liked planning how she'd feel in certain scenes.

"Cut! That was great, Rae," Matt said. "You always give me what I need." He motioned to the crew. "Leave the set as is tonight. We'll do Chester's drugstore scenes in the morning." He put his hand on Rae's shoulder as they walked down the hall to Ida's wardrobe room. "If Chester gives a great performance in this story, we could be all right."

"Chester will do it," Rae said, looking at the dark circles under Matt's eyes and wishing she could muster more conviction. "Lucinda said the new Dora serial is getting good crowds."

Matt paused outside the wardrobe room. "I'll tell you the truth, Rae. Your serial is the only sure thing I've got right now. Losing Billy was tough, and if Chester doesn't bring in a giant hit, Lukas isn't sure how much more money he wants to put into RidgeW." He ran his fingers through his hair. "Without a big success soon, RidgeW's going to lose out to mules and scrap metal. Chester's unpredictable. You're the only one I can rely on."

Her throat tightened. She almost blurted out the truth—he couldn't trust her either. Guilt washed over her as she changed the subject. "Lily and I are making stew tonight. We'll have plenty. Do you want to come home with me?"

"Maybe next time. I'm going to work on the books tonight."

In the wardrobe room, Ida unbuttoned the red and white checked little girl dress that helped Rae look twelve years old. "What are you upset about?"

"Matt's worried about money." Rae peeled off the rest of her costume—thick white stockings and a tight cotton camisole. She drew in a gulp of air as she tossed the camisole on a chair.

Ida shook the dress and hung it on the rack. "I know. I've been thinking what I'll do if RidgeW closes. I might get on at Selig or Essanay. They wouldn't put me in charge of anything. I'd be sewing all day."

"What about Gus? Selig wouldn't let him hang around the studio every day."

"Gus! That man takes two steps back for every one forward. I'll be in my grave before he gets serious. Don't know why I put up with him."

Rae laughed. "He's shy. You'll have to urge him along."

Ida gave a harrumph. "He's an irritation." She put her hand on her chest. "I admit he does set off palpitations in my interior." She fixed a sharp look on Rae. "What will you do if RidgeW closes?"

"Haven't thought about it," Rae mumbled as she folded the camisole and stockings.

Rain, heavy enough to create puddles along the curb, had darkened the skies by the time she got home. Standing at the kitchen counter, she cut the chuck roast into small stew pieces while Lily peeled potatoes next to her and reviewed, for the one millionth time, her feelings about Lukas and Eddie.

"Which one makes you quiver?"

Lily turned red and bent over the potato. "That's so silly, Rae."

"No it isn't," Rae answered. Gil's kiss had sent a quiver through her she still remembered. "Never mind," she said. "I know it's Lukas."

"With Eddie, I could be the center of everything in Chicago society. Lukas can't give me that," Lily murmured, scraping hard at the little potato eyes. "Don't forget some of his businesses are illegal—especially that house." She made a vicious jab at the potato, digging out an eye with a twist of the paring knife. "When I told Lukas about Eddie's proposal, he turned cold and told me to make up my mind."

Rae glanced sideways at Lily. "Ida says you might have found something you want more than being in high society. Ida says when a girl discovers—"

"Never mind what Ida says," Lily snapped, cheeks still pink.

"Whatever you decide, I guess you'll be marrying one of them and leaving me and RidgeW." Rae put down the knife, thoughts about Matt and his problems jumbling together with her news. "Lily, a fellow from Universal stopped me outside RidgeW last week. He offered me a job in California making movies there."

"What did you tell him?"

"I told him I'd think about it."

"What did he say exactly."

"He said I'd make adventure movies and maybe a new serial for Universal. He gave me his card and offered me two hundred dollars a week."

Lily screamed and jumped out of her chair, the potato and paring knife rolling across the counter. "That's unbelievable!"

"It's sure hard for me to imagine," Rae said.

"Why didn't you say yes right away?"

"I don't want to leave Matt. He took a chance on us when we didn't know anything about movies." She blinked away threatening tears. "Matt makes me feel safe, and he needs me to play Dora in the serial."

"You have to think of yourself—"

The front door rattled in its frame. "Let me in," Delia shouted, pounding on the door. "Let me in!"

She raced inside, terror on her face. "Lock it," she shrieked. "Chester knows about Hal. He's furious." She was wet from the rain. Her cheek was swollen and marked with a dark red streak from her eye to her chin. Red bruises the size of fingertips circled her throat. One of the buttons at the front of her dress was missing, and lace on a sleeve dangled half torn.

"How did he find out about Hal?" Rae locked the door.

"Hal's mother wrote to him. That witch. She's always hated me." Delia gulped for air and paced the room. "I knew right away he believed the letter. I could see it in his eyes." She leaned against the wall and gasped. "He was suspicious anyway because of all the times I told him I was visiting you two."

Lily frowned. "Did he hit you?"

"Oh course, he hit me!" Delia shouted. She paced again, looking around the room as if she expected Chester to leap out from behind a chair. "I tried to persuade him to ignore the letter. I told him she was a fan who was crazy, but he didn't believe it." She squeezed her eyes shut and wrapped her arms around her middle, hugging herself. "I swore none of it was true. He was drunk and crazy. He blamed me for not getting an offer from California—claimed I poisoned his performances."

"Maybe he'll calm down," Rae said.

Delia ignored her. Panting, she paced the room again. "Where's Hal?" she asked, looking at Lily. "He's boxing tonight. Where did Lukas put the match?"

"I haven't seen Lukas for over a week," Lily said. "Eddie proposed to me again, and I have to decide—"

"Oh, for heaven's sake!" Delia shifted her gaze to Rae. "Do you know anything?"

"I think the boxing is in Waukegan," Rae said. "Gus let it slip when he visited Ida yesterday. He said Otto was handling it."

Delia chewed at her lip. "That means I can't reach Hal until he gets back and that could be tomorrow."

A horn blared in the street. A door slammed. Lily looked out the window, inhaled sharply, and turned back to her sisters. "It's Chester."

54

The front door rattled in its frame. "I know you're in there, you lying bitch."

Rae moved closer to Lily. Delia's breath rasped in her throat. In seconds, Chester's pounding splintered the wood around the doorknob, and he pushed into the apartment, leaving a chunk of the door frame hanging from the lock. A thick whiskey smell floated off him, filling Rae's nostrils.

Chester wobbled on his feet, until he planted his legs wide to hold himself in one place. Blinking, he peered at them, eyes moving back and forth as if he didn't recognize them, until he focused on Delia.

"You!" He fumbled in his coat pocket and pulled out the crumpled letter, waving it in the air. "I've had this for a week. Couldn't believe it at first. Got a lawyer to check it out." He lowered his head like a bull about to charge. "He told me I've been taken advantage of by a cheap trick who takes her clothes off for a camera as easy as she tells lies." He shoved the letter in his pocket, clenched his fists, and swayed toward Delia.

She squealed, raising her hands protectively. "Chester, I swear, I meant to tell you about Hal, but it didn't seem important after I left him! You know I fell in love with you that first day. I wanted you! Only you." Backing away, she hit a chair and halted.

He faltered, his face twisting into a scowl. "Can't believe a thing you say," he mumbled, fists still clenched.

Rae retreated a step toward the kitchen. Delia's frantic pleading with Chester resurrected memories of drunken fights between her parents while she hid in the bedroom. Delia was crazy to put up with Chester no matter how much she wanted to go to California. Lily's terrified expression said she thought the same thing. Rae backed up another step.

"I didn't take advantage of you. We were both having a good time, weren't we?" Delia gasped for air in a series of little pants. "No harm done."

"She's right, Chester." Lily's voice crackled with fear, but she moved protectively to Delia's side. "She didn't mean any harm. You're free—no obligations now that you know about Delia's other marriage."

He wagged his head from side to side and suddenly lurched toward Delia, seizing her arm before she could move. He shook her. "Told you never to lie to me. Warned you." Pulling her arm to bring her closer, he slapped her hard with his other hand. She screamed and tried to wrench away, but he kept his hold on her and slapped her again.

"Stop it," Lily cried. "Let her go."

Still gripping Delia, Chester shifted his attention to Lily and Rae. "You two—just like her—covering up for her. You all deserve what you're going to get from me." He shook Delia again. "I'll make sure none of you look good enough to work in the movies." Bracing his legs for balance, twisting Delia's arm to keep her close, he focused his bleary gaze on Rae. "Matt's little pet. He says you bring in most of the money. Don't think audiences will want to watch our darling Dora when she doesn't have a nose."

His big hand wrapped around Delia's arm like a vise while his body blocked the door behind him. Moaning, Delia continued to swear she loved only him, she'd never leave him, they'd always be happy together. Lily added to Delia's frantic promises. Chester cursed. Voices rose.

Desperate, Rae backed into the kitchen and searched for an escape, but there was none. She'd never wiggle through the tiny window over the sink. Yelling into the alley wouldn't bring any help. In the other room, the three were shouting at each other.

Fighting panic, Rae spun from sink to counter to table looking for anything she could use as a club. The rain had stopped, and a faint glimmer of fading evening light came through the window. It glinted on the butcher knife she'd used to cut the beef for stew. She stared at it. She could threaten him. If she held the knife steady and sounded calm, he'd probably leave without arguing. In the morning, he'd be sober, ready to give up Delia. Heart pounding, she curled her fingers around the knife handle.

When she got back to the living room, Delia and Lily were tangled with Chester, struggling—to escape or to hold on—she couldn't tell from the swinging arms and kicking legs. Delia stomped on Chester's foot, and bellowing his rage, he slapped her before gripping her throat with both hands. Lily shrieked as she pulled on his arm. With a violent jerk of his shoulders, he shook her off. He tightened his fingers on Delia's throat. She tugged at his hands, weakened, gasped for air, a strangling sound coming from her lips. Her breath rattled hoarsely in her chest—her hands slipped away—her eyes closed. Chester tightened his grip.

"Chester," Rae called from only a few inches behind him, "Chester, stop!" She clutched the knife close to her waist, blade pointing toward him.

He ignored her. Grunting, he pressed his thumbs into Delia's throat.

"Chester, stop! The police are here!"

He turned, his hands loosening on Delia, who slumped to the ground. "What?" He peered at Rae, eyes narrowed, weaving unsteadily on his feet. Then he lurched toward her. His hands touched her throat, sliding over her skin.

She shoved the knife deep into his stomach, twisted, and pulled it out.

Chester panted, surprise, shock, and pain flashing across his face. He took a stumbling step, spun in a half circle, and fell backward to the floor. Choking, he pressed his hands against the wound. A horrible gurgle came out of his mouth as he tried to talk. Rae's hand went numb. The knife slipped out of her fingers and skittered across the floor until it hit the base of the wall and rested there.

Faint, bubbling noises came from Chester's throat—blood seeped across his stomach, soaked his shirt, and dribbled onto the floor. He shuddered, legs twitched, chest heaved. Faint breaths. Then inhaling a long, ragged choking gasp, he slumped boneless, his open eyes staring at Rae.

"Is he dead? What are we going to do?" Lily's voice was weak.

"He looks dead." Shivers raced along Rae's body.

Still limp on the floor, Delia groaned, gasping for breath. Lily helped her sit up. "Stay calm," she whispered to Delia. "We have to think." She turned to Rae and put her arms around her. "It wasn't your fault. He was crazy and drunk. He might have killed all of us. You saved us." She tightened her grip and turned Rae to face her. Are you listening to me?"

Blood slowly pooled under Chester's body, a steady drip continuing from the knife wound, adding to the first violent red gush. Delia slowly got to her feet, holding her throat where reddened blotches showed on her skin. She stared at Chester's body. "I'm glad," she said hoarsely. "He was a bastard. Did you do it, Rae?"

Lily snatched towels, dropped them around Chester, and patted them into the blood. Silently, Rae put a towel over his face. She couldn't bear to close his eyes or touch him. The towels absorbed some blood, but a sticky smear covered the floor, seeping into the cracks in the wood and between the floorboards.

"We'll scrub the floor." Lily said. Her hands were bloody from the towels.

"I have to call the police." Rae looked at her sisters, her face white. "I'll probably be arrested."

"We can't call the police," Delia snapped, some of her vigor returning. "We have to handle this problem ourselves. You could go to jail—I suppose we could all go to jail."

Lily sank into a chair. "Rae was defending us. No one would put her in jail." Tears sparkled along her eyelids.

"Are you crazy? Think of the newspapers— *Movie Girls Murder Popular Actor.*" Delia swallowed painfully and touched her throat again. "We have to think of a way to make him disappear. We have to get him out of here— away from us."

"We can't bury him." Lily squeezed her eyes shut for an instant. "We can't take him anywhere."

Delia paced. Lily cried. Rae stared at Chester. Shuddering, Rae leaned against the wall for support. An icy tremor started in her legs, traveled up her spine, and bit into her shoulders. She pressed her body against the wall and spread her arms flat against the surface to keep from falling. She swallowed hard, beating down the urge to be sick.

Delia stopped pacing. "We need help. Hal isn't in town tonight. We need someone we can trust. Matt. He could help us lift—"

"No." Rae shook her head violently and crossed her arms over her body, fighting her churning stomach. "Not Matt! He can't be involved in—murder."

Lily wiped her eyes on her sleeve and rose to her feet. "We need Lukas."

55

Lukas pointed to the broken door frame. "See if you can get that in shape, so we can lock the door," he said to Gus.

While Gus tinkered with the door, Lukas stepped into the apartment. Rae leaned against the wall, her face blank, her body trembling in a long unending shiver. Lily, eyes damp, clung to Rae, giving support or seeking it. Lukas couldn't tell. When she'd called him, her voice sounded in control. Now she looked fully panicked, shaking nearly as much as Rae. He hadn't seen her since she'd told him about Eddie's proposal. The terror on her face chilled him, but he resisted his impulse to take her in his arms and calm her. They had no time for that even if she'd let him hold her. Delia stood next to Chester's body in the center of the room, her hands clasped, shoulders stiff. All three had blood on their clothes and hands. Bloody towels surrounded Chester's body on the floor.

Regardless of what Lily described when she called him, he had to be sure. He knelt on one knee, removed the towel draped over Chester's face, and felt for a pulse in his throat. Nothing. Chester was already cool to the touch. "Have you heard anything from the neighbors?" he asked, rising to his feet. "Anyone come over here to see what was going on?"

"No." Delia shook her head. "We . . . there was screaming, but no one came to check."

"Mrs. Romano lives next to us, but she works until eight," Lily said. "She's not home yet."

Gus pulled the door shut. A hole where the wood had been ripped out kept the lock from catching. "It closes, but the lock won't hold," he said.

"We'll fix something up later to keep it bolted," Lukas answered. He turned back to Delia. "Who knows he came here?"

"I . . . I don't think anyone knows. We were fighting, yelling, at the hotel. He hit me." She pointed toward her bruises. "He was drunk. I ran out, found a taxi, and came here. He followed in the Stutz. It happened so fast." She squeezed her eyes shut. "It's all my fault."

Rae made a whimpering sound. "We have to tell the police."

"We don't need the police," he said softly. "That's why I'm here."

"His Stutz is outside," Gus said. "Neighbors might have noticed—might remember it." He scratched his chin. "Rain's heavy again. Kinda dark all afternoon, so maybe nobody noticed."

Lukas glanced out the window. "We have to wait for middle-of-the-night dark." He picked the knife off the floor. "Scrub this blood off," he said to Gus. "Put the knife in a drawer. We need to clean things up here." With Gus in the kitchen, the three sisters fixed their eyes on him, a mix of panic and hope in all of them. "You need to wash— get the blood off," he told them. "Change your clothes. We'll burn what you're wearing."

"What about him?" Lily gestured in the direction of Chester's body.

"Later," Lukas answered. "We can't do anything outside until it's pitch dark." He glanced out the window again. "If we're lucky, there'll be heavy clouds tonight."

The sisters retreated to the bathroom while he surveyed the room, stepping around Chester's body. Running water and splashes coming from the bathroom muffled the voices, so he couldn't distinguish words, but he recognized Lily's distressed tone. Delia's voice rose. Rae was probably still talking about the police.

Gus cut the bloody towels into pieces and slowly fed them into the wood-burning kitchen stove. When Delia opened the bathroom door and tossed out shirtwaists and skirts, Gus cut those into pieces and continued feeding the stove. Delia, wearing only her drawers and chemise, walked into the bedrooms, emerged after a few minutes with fresh clothing over her arm, and returned to the bathroom.

Lukas paid no attention to her. His mind roamed through possibilities while he stared at Chester's body. If

Chester just disappeared, the police would launch a search for a well-known actor, and he didn't dare try to bribe the entire police force much less the newspapers. Reporters would feast on the story of a missing movie actor. They'd want interviews with the bereaved wife Delia, and the case could drag on for months if not years—plenty of time for mistakes. Vanishing wouldn't do. Chester and his clothes still smelled like a tavern, and most likely the hotel staff would confirm Delia's report that he was drunk when he left his rooms.

By the time the sisters emerged from the bathroom in clean clothes, he'd made up his mind. The last of their bloody clothing smoldered in the stove, and the heat made the apartment uncomfortable on a June evening, but he didn't let them open a window.

"Sit down," he said. "We have to talk about what's going to happen." He folded his arms and looked at them, sitting in a row on the sofa, faces solemn. "Why were you fighting?" he asked Delia.

Delia wiggled on the sofa, avoiding his eyes. "Chester was drunk. He's always drunk if he's not working. When he's drunk, we fight."

"Tell him," Lily hissed at her. "Tell him."

"He found out I was already married to Hal, so I wasn't really married to him. He accused me of being unfaithful."

"Our Hal? Our boxer?" Gus asked.

Delia nodded.

"I suppose Chester was right, and you were unfaithful," Lukas said. "Where did you meet Hal? Who knew?"

"No one knew. We met here." Delia glanced at her sisters. "Lily and Rae knew. Hal's mother knew about Chester from the newspapers. She wrote to him. Chester blew up." She caught her breath. "He has her letter."

Lukas motioned to Gus, who knelt next to the body and went through Chester's pockets until he found the crumpled letter. "Burn it now," Lukas said.

"Gus and I are going to take Chester away once it's late enough," he said. "Delia needs to leave now. Go to your hotel. Talk to the desk clerk, talk to a maid, ask if Chester's back yet. Be casual and don't act as if you're worried about him. At some point later tonight or tomorrow morning, the police will come and tell you about an accident. Be as surprised and horrified as you can be. If you're very upset, they won't ask you too many questions."

"What kind of accident?" Delia asked.

"It's better if you don't know ahead of time. Your shock will be more realistic."

"I'm an actress! I can be realistic."

Gus snorted. Lukas kept his face blank. "I'm counting on you. Make sure you act frightened and brokenhearted." He turned to Lily. "If the police say someone saw him here, tell them he came looking for Delia but she left before he got here. Even if a neighbor claims to remember seeing the Stutz parked outside for hours, stick to your story. Delia left before Chester, and he left after a few minutes. People get confused about times. Remember to say he was drunk."

Lily nodded. She gripped Rae's hand. Rae, looking dazed, said nothing. Lukas hoped she'd hold herself together. He glanced at the bloody smear, still sticky, on the floor around Chester. "After we take him away, mop this floor and get a rug in here." Lukas eyed Chester's bloodied shirt and pants. "Do you have any clothes we could put on him to help cover him?"

Rae stirred. "Pa left a few clothes here when he came back."

He and Gus peered into the closet. One shirt with worn cuffs, a torn undershirt, a baggy pair of pants, and one threadbare overcoat, once black but faded to a uneven gray. "Would a fellow like Chester Slater wear a coat like this?" Gus asked.

Lukas took it off the hanger. "It won't matter—in the end."

They waited until ten-thirty when it was fully dark. The rain had stopped, and thick clouds obscured the moon and stars. In the darkness, Gus stumbled on the steps as he and Lukas fought to hold Chester's dead weight upright between them.

"Getting stiff," Gus remarked as they dragged Chester along.

The neighbor wasn't home yet, and Lukas was both relieved she wasn't next door only one wall away and afraid she'd appear on the street at any minute. He and Gus had bundled Chester into Maxie's old coat. Chester was bigger than Maxie, so the coat didn't button, but it covered enough, especially in the dark. Lukas had sprinkled some of Lily's wine over Chester's clothes, so the reek of alcohol was strong enough to travel across the street.

They opened the door of the Stutz and shoved Chester onto the wet passenger seat. Gus tucked his legs inside, stepped back, closed the door, and Chester rolled sideways, his head falling into the driver's seat.

A door slammed. Footsteps sounded. Gus lunged for Chester and pulled him upright just as a man neared them and slowed his pace. Lukas hiccupped and slapped Gus on the shoulder. "He can't sit up—he's had too much. Can't handle his liquor like I can."

The man veered away, crossed the street, heading toward an alley that led to a busy avenue. Gus watched him disappear into the alley. "Think he'll remember?"

"Might not," Lukas answered. "He'll probably be getting drunk himself tonight, and the police might never ask if Chester came here."

They tied Chester upright in the seat with his own belt. Gus drove the Stutz, and Lukas followed in the Pierce-Arrow. They took quiet side streets leading to the south side of the city, far from any of Chester's usual stops. Winding through back streets among dark industrial sites, over railroad tracks, they headed for a gorge south of the city. Gus parked the Stutz at the top of the gorge and unhooked Chester's belt. Both of them dragged Chester into the driver's seat. Gus linked the free end of Chester's belt to the seat, keeping him steady. Next, Gus shredded the overcoat into long strips. He hooked Chester's arms through the steering wheel, tied his hands together with the cloth, and then tied his feet to the gear shift. Sending the Stutz careening down the hillside into the gorge was the easy part. The auto flipped over twice as it crashed to the bottom and then wobbled violently before it rolled upside down. The slight pause before the fuel caught fire sent Lukas's nerves buzzing, but then flames erupted, and Chester's official fiery end took place.

A strong odor of ammonia hit Lukas when Lily opened the apartment door. "It's done," he said, looking from Lily to Rae standing behind her. "Remember what I told you to say."

Rae nodded. "Thank you," she said in a dull tone as she walked away.

"She's not likely to sleep much," he said to Lily. "Better stay with her tonight."

"I will," Lily whispered. "Please don't leave yet. Will you come inside for a minute?"

He should have said no, but he stepped inside and closed the door behind him. He'd promised himself he wouldn't touch her, but she was so pale and looked so frightened, he instinctively reached for her. She sank against him, pressing her forehead against his shoulder, hands clinging to his jacket, and dragging in long, sobbing breaths.

"I didn't know what to do," she whispered.

"Don't think about anything but what you have to tell the police. Try to believe it."

"I knew you'd help us," Lily murmured.

He brushed his fingers in a soothing movement along her cheek while bitter understanding tugged at him. Of course, she'd rely on him to clean up a murder. She could hardly have called Eddie Carleton—that pillar of society. Maybe she'd already accepted Carleton's proposal. Already let him make love to her. Damned if he'd ask.

He put his hands on her shoulders and pushed her gently away. "I should go. We don't want anyone to see me here." He opened the door and turned back. "If you need me . . ." He shrugged and walked down the steps where Gus waited at the curb.

56

Chicago Dispatch, **June 18, 1915**

Out and About with Lucinda Corday

C hicago's entertainment community has been devastated by the shocking death in a motor accident of beloved actor Chester Slater. I joined the mourners gathered at the Faith Lutheran Church yesterday to bid farewell to this great thespian and to acknowledge the tragic end of the legendary love he shared with his actress wife, Delia Kelly.

Dressed in dramatic black silk crepe, Miss Kelly gasped and fainted when Pastor Renner promised she and Mr. Slater would be reunited in heaven. Her sisters, actresses Lily Rose and Rae Kelly, were at her side, looking completely stricken themselves. It was not possible to have an open casket as Mr. Slater was burned beyond recognition, and only his mangled Stutz Bearcat confirmed his identity.

The scene at the graveside was particularly heartbreaking. The grieving widow nearly fainted again but managed to remain standing as she leaned on the arm of a sturdy young man who, I learned, is a distant cousin from Wisconsin. Many notables from our thriving movie industry attended the services, and all expressed deep distress over the loss of this fine actor.

Alas for audiences, Mr. Slater's latest movie, *Back to Our Home,* cannot be completed because most of the actor's scenes in this dramatic story were not finished. I talked to Matthew Ridgewood of RidgeW Pictures after the services, and he told me he had only a few scenes with young Rae Kelly, and he had no way to conclude the movie without Mr. Slater. Mr. Ridgewood acknowledged a deep gap in his release schedule with the loss of *Back to Our Home.* Mr. Slater had been a central figure at the studio and certainly could not be replaced. We will have to wait to see how RidgeW copes with this terrible loss.

Until next time, dear readers.

57

S ean Rogan pulled his cap over his red hair and
   sauntered into Mama Rossi's Tap near the Union
   Stockyard as if he were a regular. Sliding onto a stool
near the end of the bar closest to the back entrance, he
motioned for a beer. The tavern doors didn't shut out the
pungent neighborhood odor of cattle and their droppings.
That stench mingled with the stale odor of spilled beer,
smoke, and working-class sweat in the tavern. The result
nearly gagged him. He breathed through his mouth for
a few minutes, until he had to give up and adjust to the
noxious fumes. The thickset bartender with a "Cuba, 1898"
tattoo on one arm slapped a mug of beer in front of him.
Foam spilled down one side, making a puddle on the bar.

He was early for the meeting with two men Sadie had
recommended, and he seethed with resentment at having
to be here at all. Yesterday, he'd spent fifteen minutes arguing with Weston about arranging this accident. It wasn't

needed. RidgeW was going under. Even that idiot gossip columnist in the *Dispatch* had said as much.

He gulped a mouthful of beer and resolved for the tenth time if Sadie's contacts looked even more unreliable than they probably were, he'd cancel the job and try again to talk Weston out of his crazy idea. Gloomy thoughts about serving time in Joliet Prison occupied his mind. Anything could go wrong. Collecting bribes for Weston didn't cause a stir. The merchants didn't like paying, but the public didn't know or care. What Weston wanted was the kind of crime everyone noticed. Citizens got worked up over public danger, and when citizens got agitated, police were forced to take action.

At least he'd been able to convince Weston he needed enough money for five visits to Sadie, so he could pay for names of men willing to do the job, which was somewhat true, although providing names was not the essential service Sadie performed for him. He took another swig of beer. Maybe he could see Sadie later, but Fridays were busy at Madame Yvonne's, and she didn't allow the girls to reserve time for favorites. He didn't like to wait in the parlor—the delay always shattered his conviction Sadie was especially fond of him.

The door to the tavern swung open, and two men entered, dressed in work clothes. One wore the red scarf Sadie said would be the sign he needed. Sean groaned inwardly. Standing there, casting searching glances around the room, they already looked guilty of something. He caught the eye of one and nodded to a stool next to him.

"You Rogan?" The shorter, older fellow put his hand on the bar and tapped tobacco-stained fingers on the surface. His greasy black hair and bushy mustache were streaked with gray, but his arms were heavily muscled, fingers thick, his body compact and tense. He looked ready for a street fight.

Sean glanced cautiously at the bartender who was at the other end of the bar. "That's right," he muttered. "Which one of you is Fritz?"

"Me," the older fellow answered. He tipped his head toward his younger, wiry companion. "He's Al. What's the job exactly?"

Sean shook his head in a warning and motioned to the bartender for two more beers. When they came, the men took their mugs to a table in the corner. Sean waited until both men had taken healthy swallows. "Listen," he said in a low voice, leaning over the table toward them. "This situation calls for absolute discretion and anonymity." The men stared at him, faces blank. Sean licked his lips. "I mean, you can never talk about what you did, what you got paid, or how you met me. No one can know about this job."

Fritz nodded. "We know how deals work." He looked at Al. "Hear him? No talking."

Al leaned back in his chair. "Yeah, we never talk."

Sean checked again to be sure no one was nearby and explained what the men had to do.

"That's it?" Fritz asked. "We thought maybe we had to kill somebody."

"No one should get hurt," Sean emphasized. "No violence. Just complete destruction. Wait until after nine o'clock—no one will be there. Then do it."

"You ain't the boss, I'm guessing." Fritz gulped his beer, belched, and wiped his mouth on his sleeve.

"You don't need to know about the boss," Sean answered. "I'm just a messenger," he added. "The boss—the real boss—stays anonymous—secret." Damned if he was going to take the responsibility off Weston's shoulders.

A few more questions—an envelope across the table with the first payment—arrangements for the rest of the money after everything was over—a deadline—a suggestion about leaving Chicago for a couple of weeks. Fritz and Al drained their beers and left after assuring him they could handle the job.

Sean wiped a film of sweat off his lip and stared at the half-finished beer in front of him. He didn't relish describing the thugs to Weston. If anything went wrong with this stupid plan, Weston would blame him. Tension settled in his shoulders, making his neck stiff, and he twisted his head from side to side to loosen his muscles. Maybe he'd stop by Madame Yvonne's after all. He could be lucky. Sadie might be available.

58

S team from the Atchison, Topeka, and Santa Fe passenger train coiled around Lily's feet as she stood on the platform in Dearborn Station and hugged Delia. Several reporters lingered nearby after listening to Delia's rehearsed answers about moving to California for her career.

"Be careful," Lily said. "You and Hal need to avoid publicity."

"Believe me," Delia said, "the last thing I want to do is give one more interview about my tragic love for Chester. I never imagined I'd go to Los Angeles with *my cousin Hal*. We're broke. Chester spent every dime, never got a studio offer, and the Stutz was a wreck, so I got nothing out of that so-called marriage." Her mouth twitched in a smile as she glanced at Hal helping a porter with the luggage. "Hal has to win a lot of matches for Lukas's boxing connection out there."

"I already miss you." Lily sighed.

"I wish Rae had come to see me off," Delia said. "I know she's feeling guilty about what happened, but Chester was going to kill me. The brute deserved what he got."

"I've told her a hundred times she did the right thing. She feels guilty about Chester, but I think she's more guilty about ruining Matt's last chance to keep RidgeW going. I asked her to come today, but she's climbing a tree or doing some stunt."

"What are you going to do about Eddie?"

"I asked him if he'd come with us to Chester's funeral, but he said he didn't want reporters to notice him. Didn't want newspaper stories connecting him with movie people." Lily sidestepped another burst of steam from under the passenger car.

"Eddie's useless—you know it," Delia said.

" I know. I was stupid to spend a minute thinking about his proposal when I knew I couldn't give up Lukas—I can't." She blushed. "He's—I can't imagine being away from him."

"The one who makes you happy is the one to keep."

The conductor shouted a boarding notice, and Delia yelped. "It's time!" She flung her arms around Lily again, and the two gripped each other for a long moment. "I hate sentimental goodbyes," Delia announced. "Give Rae one more hug for me. I'll write to you. I love you!" She ran to join Hal waiting at the steps leading up to the railway car. At the top, she turned, waved again, and disappeared.

Lily waited on the platform until the train pulled out of the station. She took a taxi back to the apartment and made herself a cup of tea before she sat at the kitchen table, a fresh piece of ivory stationery in front of her. She chewed her lip, remembering the fluttery excitement washing through her the day she married Eddie. Her dreams about living in a mansion, giving teas for society women, and going to fabulous parties seemed so distant, so foolish—all shriveled into nothing.

And she didn't care.

She wrote carefully, thanking him for his proposal but explaining she knew her feelings for him could never rise to the level appropriate for marriage. She did not think they would be happy even if they both tried very sincerely. She hesitated over how to sign the letter. Finally, she settled on "Yours most cordially" and wrote her name in a flourish of sweeping loops. Folding the paper, sliding it in the envelope, licking the flap, and pressing it shut made her a little giddy. Gazing at George Washington on the two cents stamp, she drew a long satisfied breath and carefully addressed the envelope. The nearest post office was three blocks away, and she walked at a slow pace, holding the envelope stiffly in one hand. When she dropped it into the mail slot, relief overwhelmed her. She would never have to think about Eddie Carleton again.

She took a taxi to Lukas's house, confident he'd be there because she needed him to be there. When she opened the sliding doors, he was sitting at the table with the chess board.

"Otto let me in," she said. "I told him to go home, so we could be alone."

"Why?" He rose to his feet.

"I want to be with you, just you," Lily in a soft voice.

"Is it gratitude? Because if it is—"

"I am grateful." Lily took a step toward him. "Horrible things would have happened to Rae, and I knew I could rely on you, but that's not why I'm here. I came because I realized I love you although you've never . . . you've never said you love me."

Astonishment crossed his face. "I thought women always knew that sort of thing without being told."

"Don't be ridiculous," Lily answered.

He frowned. "I'm sorry. I spent so many months trying to get close enough to touch you, I forgot to say what I should have. I love you, Lily—from the minute I saw you. I want you to stay with me—the rest of my life."

She drew in a breath. "Well, then."

They reached each other midway in the room. Lukas leaned down to kiss her as she went on her toes to reach his lips and wrapped her arms around his neck. Swinging her into his arms, he carried her to the sofa and held her on his lap while he kissed her throat where the collar of her shirtwaist gaped.

Lily sighed, letting her head fall back, giving him more of her throat to kiss, sinking into the pleasure, snuggling closer. A nagging thought cut though her dazed euphoria, and she threaded her fingers through his hair and tugged until he raised his head. "I can live with the rest, but you have to get rid of that house," she said, her blue eyes locked on his dark ones.

"I'm shipping five hundred mules from Missouri to Britain next week," he said. "I'm going to be a major supplier as long as this war drags on, and after that, I'll supply something else to somebody else. Entirely legal." He kissed her cheek. "You'll be the most beautiful bride Chicago has ever seen."

"Not yet." She stiffened slightly. "I've been married, and I'm not going to do it again—not for a while."

He groaned. "How long a time is *a while*?"

"I don't know. I don't have a mother nagging me to get married, and we aren't going to be in high society. You're a gangster more or less. I'm a movie girl. No one will care what we do. I want to be happy—no complications."

"Since when is marriage a complication?"

She stroked his cheek. "Indulge me."

"I must be old fashioned." He kissed her again. "I'll wait for you—as long as I have to."

She pressed her palms against his chest, holding off his kisses. "But that house."

He pulled her closer to him, while he played at the buttons on her shirtwaist, slowly opening one by one. "If it matters . . ."

"It matters," she breathed, keeping her serious tone although he'd opened three buttons, and his lips on her collarbone were sending familiar delicious shivers through her.

He raised his head and took in her solemn expression. "Since it matters to you, I'll sell the house." He hooked his fingers through the gap in her shirtwaist and slipped two more buttons open. "Will that do?"

She sighed a long hiss of relief. "Yes, that will do—for now," she whispered, softening against him. "Take me upstairs. Hurry."

59

Rae finished the final episode of *Dora and the Mystery at Lake Troy* on RidgeW's last day. Matt had given everyone a small portion of a week's salary, saying it was all he could do. The studio had an atmosphere of doom. People hurried away in the evening as if deserting a sinking ship, mumbling goodbyes, wishing each other luck. Ida, usually the last to leave, hugged Rae and rushed out with the others. Rae couldn't bring herself to abandon Matt. She found him packing equipment and props into crates in the basement.

"You don't have to stay and help me," Matt said, as he folded curtains and dropped them into boxes.

"I want to." She blinked rapidly to keep the tears away. RidgeW Pictures had failed, and it was her fault. Whenever she thought about the horrible moment she'd plunged the knife into Chester's belly, her insides churned. Maybe Delia was right and Chester deserved what he got, but Matt didn't deserve to be ruined. She gazed at him across the basement studio, seeing the worry lines on his face. If only she could cry on his shoulder and ask him for forgiveness. But if she did that, she'd have to confess, and too many people were relying on her to keep silent.

"Keep all these together," Matt said, passing her an armful of flags.

She lowered them into a box. "Should we label the boxes?"

"Don't need to. Lukas owns it all, and he's going to sell everything in one lot—props, cameras, projectors—to one of the other studios. He's selling the building too." A bitter smile curved his mouth. "RidgeW will disappear from memory."

A wave of self-hatred flashed through her. This disaster was her fault. "Maybe Mrs. Weston could help."

His smile faded. "Mrs. Weston is gone. She won't be back."

Relief flooded her. "She wasn't much help anyway," Rae mumbled. "She wasn't the right person for . . . us."

He stopped packing and looked at her. "You're way too observant for your age. But you're right . . . about everything," he added. They packed silently for a few minutes. He handed her a blanket and watched while she tucked it in a box and smoothed down the edges. "RidgeW's collapse is my fault. Relying on Chester when I knew he was a drunk was a fool's bet. I'm worried about you. Have you heard anything from another studio?"

"The Universal fellow offered me a contract. Lily said I had to take it."

"Lily's right. Billy's doing very well at Universal. You can too."

"What will you do?"

"I might get some work as a director at Selig or Essanay. Our movies got good reviews, so that might be enough to get me a job." He stiffened, inhaled deeply, and turned toward the stairs.

Rae smelled it at the same time. Faint, white wisps of acrid smoke floated down the stairway.

Matt grabbed her arm. "We have to get out of here—now!"

At the top of the steps, he hesitated. "Keep your head down," he said over his shoulder. Grasping her arm, he pulled her behind him as they headed for the front of the building.

Smoke swirled in thin ribbons around them. Rae took shallow breaths, but her throat stung, and her chest seemed to close up. She cupped her hand over her nose and mouth and stumbled after Matt, but when they reached the front of the building, he jerked to a stop. The entrance was on fire, bright yellow-orange streaks shooting up along the walls. The metal doors glowed from the heat.

"The back doors," Matt said, tightening his grip on Rae and yanking her toward the center hallway leading to the back of the building.

Crouching low, coughing, they ran along the hallway to the back entrance. Too late. They didn't have to get all the way to see the doors were completely aflame—worse than the front entrance. Fire streaked along the back wall, reached for the ceiling, and surrounded the high windows.

Matt pulled her to the floor where the smoke was thinner. "We have get out a window. Too late for these, but we can crawl back to the costume room and get out the window there."

Rae breathed in a lungful of smoke and choked. Her throat burned. Matt, coughing, tugged her forward. They crawled, sometimes sideways, sometimes going ahead, aiming toward the costume room. Her eyes stung and watered from the smoke. Snaking across the floor, Matt had to drop his hold on her, but he paused every few feet to see if she was still behind him. Following his shoes down the hallway through the smoke, Rae smothered the temptation to calculate how far they had to go—one foot at a time, one foot, and then another. When Matt stopped moving, she looked up. They were in front of the door to the costume room. He touched a finger to the door knob and nodded at Rae. Coughing spasms overtook her.

"Come on." Matt dragged her into the costume room, kicking the door shut behind them. The air inside was clearer, but trails of smoke drifted under the door. "We'll go out the window. Once the fire gets here, these clothes will go up fast."

The window was at least twelve feet above them. "It's too high," Rae said in a hoarse croak.

Matt ignored her. Pushing Ida's heavy sewing table directly under the window, he motioned. "This will do, but I have to break out the window. Get the hat rack," he said as he climbed on the table.

Rae maneuvered the heavy hat rack across the room, rolling the round metal base one way and then the other while smoke seeped under the door. "The window's too high. How can we jump out?"

He hoisted the hat rack onto the table. "Stand back."

He smashed the metal base into the window, shattering it on the second try. Glass and window frame splintered, flying outward. Battering the base against the edges of the window to clear the remaining glass pieces, he dropped the hat rack to the floor and reached for Rae, lifting her onto the table. For a minute, they wobbled on the narrow top, hanging onto each other. The cool night air rushed through the broken window, and they gulped deep breaths while they balanced on the table.

Rae eyed the open window. "How will we—"

"Listen to me." Matt turned her away from him and put his hands on her waist. "I'm six feet, and if I hang out of the window, that's another maybe two feet closer to the ground, so we'll have to drop only about four or five feet once I let go, and it's grassy out there."

"I'm not six feet tall."

"You'll hang on my back, so we'll go out together." He tightened his grasp on her waist. "I'll boost you to the window sill. Keep one leg inside and wait for me."

His confidence tamped down some of her fear. She trusted him. He lifted her close to the wall, so she could reach the edge of the window sill. Hooking an arm over the opening, she dangled for an instant and pulled herself up after Matt grabbed her ankles and pushed her higher. Settling on the edge, one leg in and one leg out, Rae waited for him. He had to jump twice before he was able to grab the window ledge, pull himself up, and straddle it, his back to Rae.

"Look!" Rae pointed. Flames crept under the door, crawled up a wooden rack of costumes, and licked across the clothes until the entire rack turned into bright flames.

"Don't think about it. Scoot closer to me now. Put your arms around my neck and your legs around my waist."

Rae scooted. Her arms around his neck, she linked her fingers together, praying she could hold on. As she hooked her legs around Matt's waist, she took another look into the costume room. All the clothing racks were on fire—flames streaked across the floor. The only escape now was the window.

"Hang on," Matt said.

He inched backward and twisted until Rae hung entirely out the window. Putting both legs out the window, he slid down the outside wall, still clinging to the sill. Rae clamped her lips tight against a scream as they swung into the open. Her legs scraped the side of the building, and she lost her grip on his waist. They bumped the wall as they both dangled in the air.

"Look for the grass," Matt grunted.

"It's Ida's flower bed."

"Drop off."

Rae let go, falling into the purple asters. She landed hard but managed to roll away before Matt came down in the same spot. For a minute, they lay there, gulping for air until Matt groaned, got to his feet and pulled Rae up.

"Can you walk?"

"Yes." Rae clutched his hand but yelped when she took a step. A knifelike pain shot through her foot. She gritted her teeth and clung to Matt as they hobbled away from the building.

Neighbors from nearby houses were already in the street. A man in shirtsleeves hurried toward them. "My boy ran to the alarm box," he said. "You hurt?"

Rae winced. "Just my foot—twisted it."

"You're a lucky pair. Anyone else in there?"

"No. We were working late." Matt gazed at the flames. "Strange fire to start on all sides at the same time."

The man grunted agreement. "Went up fast."

By the time one of Chicago's new fire trucks arrived, RidgeW Pictures was engulfed in flames. People gathered to watch as the firemen struggled to salvage the building, but it was useless. Matt put his arm around Rae, and she leaned against his shoulder as they watched it burn to the ground.

Rae's throat was raw. Scratched and bruised, she limped and wheezed great lung-clearing coughs for a week. Lily fussed over her, but Rae shook off all attempts at comfort.

She deserved the pain—her punishment for ruining Matt. She had to fix it somehow.

At the Western Union office, she slapped a bill on the counter. "I want to send a telegram."

The clerk eyed her bruises as he slid a form and pen across the counter. "Print carefully."

For days she'd thought about how she could make amends, how she could save Matt. She bent over the form and printed in capital letters—BILLY TUCKER, UNIVERSAL FILM MANUFACTURING COMPANY, LOS ANGELES, CALIFORNIA.

60

Lukas pounded his fist on the desk. "Every penny I put in RidgeW is gone." He looked at Gus sprawled in a chair. "What did you find out?"

"One of the cops told me it was probably arson—too many fires popping out around the building all at once for it to be an accident." Gus scratched his chin. "But they ain't doing any investigation. Said there wasn't enough evidence."

Lukas's mouth twisted into a grim slash. "No evidence. I can imagine who decided that. This fire had to be Weston's doing. Nobody else had any reason to destroy everything. RidgeW was going out of business anyway."

"Peculiar I'd say, if Mr. Weston was interested in RidgeW enough to burn it down. He ain't in the movie business—no money in the game." Gus cleared his throat. "Heard some talk Mrs. Weston visited the studio, so I guess she was interested in making movies."

"Too interested," Lukas muttered. "Weston wanted Matt out of town—as far away as possible."

Gus leaned forward, hands on his knees. "I got a little information from a fellow who goes to Madame's on a regular basis. He knows Sean Rogan. Says he saw him talking to some rough fellows in a tavern close to the stockyards a couple of weeks ago."

"Not surprising. Weston wouldn't arrange it himself."

"We could . . . you know . . . get some fellows ourselves."

"I'd like to," Lukas said. "I'd like to do it myself and watch Weston bleed, but I promised Lily I'd be legal from now on."

Gus chuckled. "Sounds like Miss Lily has you tied up."

"She does, and she won't marry me until I get legal in everything." Lukas tapped his fingers on the desk. "What's your friend Ida doing?"

"She got on at Selig, and they took that kid Lev as an apprentice in the camera room. The kid's excited, but Ida ain't too happy. She's sewing on a machine all day."

"Put a ring on her," Lukas said. "Get out of that boarding house you live in and buy a bungalow."

Gus turned red and stared at him. "Never heard you talk like that before. Don't think I'd know what to say to Ida. She's . . . I don't know." His neck got redder. "I ain't so good with decent women."

Lukas grinned. "You do all right. She wouldn't have tolerated you hanging around if she wasn't interested. This deal with the mules in Missouri and the scrap metal is going to be big, Gus. We'll make more money with less trouble before too long, and we won't have to pay off the police and politicians. You can settle down."

Still red, Gus straightened in his chair. "Now that you mention it, maybe I'll ask Ida something." He studied his thick fingers. "Are we all finished with RidgeW?"

"The money's gone. The studio's gone. The fire took out the building and the last episode of *Danger for Dora*. Weston needs to pay for this mess." Lukas unlocked his desk drawer and held up the red leather wallet. "I still have this."

"Will it send him to jail?"

"Rich men in politics don't go to jail," Lukas said. He opened the wallet and stared at the paper with its lists of numbers. "They can, however, lose their money and their prestige and be ruined." He put the paper back in the wallet. "If Weston is publicly shamed, his life will change forever. No more fancy parties and society dinners. No more political clout. Might have to sell that mansion." He stroked the leather. "I'd like to watch him go down."

"Will the cops investigate? They shrugged off the fire easy enough." Gus twisted in his chair. "Weston could buy them off."

Lukas opened a drawer and took out a large brown envelope. "Too much corruption at City Hall. They won't crack down on Weston. The *Chicago Tribune*, however, loves to expose shady politicians—the more important the person, the better." He scrawled a name on the envelope, wrote a note on a piece of paper, and put the wallet with the note in the envelope. He licked the flap, pressed it down, and handed the envelope to Gus. "Make sure this package is at the *Tribune* editor's office tomorrow morning when he gets to work."

Gus stared at the name. "You sure he'll investigate?"

Lukas grinned. "I'm sure, and when he has enough dirt on Weston, the *Tribune* headlines will put Mr. Weston in the gutter. Once people read the worst accusations, that's all they'll remember. He'll be more down and out than Matt is."

61

Out and About with Lucinda Corday

The tragic fire that destroyed RidgeW Pictures has left a chasm in Chicago's thriving movie business. Everyone is devastated by the loss of the talented people at RidgeW and the thrilling movies they regularly produced. Matthew Ridgewood, director and former owner, is heading to Universal Film Company in Los Angeles. It seems that comic actor Billy Tucker, who left earlier this year for the California studio, has insisted on Mr. Ridgewood as his director for his new comedy *The Mail Order Groom.* Billy is such a big star, his bosses at Universal Film Company want to keep him happy.

The adorable Rae Kelly, star of the *Danger for Dora* serial, also has been snapped up by Universal, and she will leave for Los Angeles shortly. She is bound to become a major star, and we can only hope she brings us another exciting serial adventure.

The young actress will not be alone in Los Angeles. Her sister and fellow actress, Delia Kelly, the grief-stricken widow of actor Chester Slater, has been staying with a distant cousin in the city. She is appearing frequently in movie parts very similar to those she played at RidgeW. I know she will be a welcome guardian for her little sister.

It thrills me to assure my faithful readers I will continue to report on these wonderful entertainers and their projects because I have just signed an exclusive contract with Apex World newspapers to interview rising movie players at all the California studios and report on their exciting personal lives. The *Dispatch* will carry my columns, so my Chicago readers will know the latest movie news.

Until next time, dear readers.

62

Travelers filled Dearborn Station, saying goodbye, saying hello, pushing into lines boarding trains, pushing through crowds to get out of the station. Rae could hardly draw a breath while Lily hugged her. Her heart pounded so fast from nerves and excitement she felt dizzy. She'd packed only one suitcase because she'd left behind all her too-young-clothes. She didn't think she'd ever feel young again. Her new dress—navy blue with white polka dots on the skirt and a silk belt wrapped tight around her waist—revealed her figure. Lace inserts along the sleeves and a lace collar made it the fanciest dress she'd ever had—and the most grownup. For the first time since she'd started at RidgeW, she looked entirely different from *Dora*. She wished Ida could see her.

"You look so pretty, Rae," Lily whispered. "I'm glad Matt's traveling with you, but I'll worry until I hear you've arrived safely." She looked weepy. "Los Angeles is so far away. Lukas promised we can visit soon, but I'll miss you so much."

"I'll miss you too." Rae was as weepy as Lily, and they clung to each other.

Lukas tapped Rae's shoulder. "Time to get on board," he said. "Matt seems to be late." He caught Lily's gasp and added quickly. "He's got some time."

Lily glanced at the clock above the wide entrance from the station to the train platforms. "He's got ten minutes."

Lukas shrugged. "Time enough." He made a awkward movement toward Rae, and she made an awkward movement back, and somehow they hugged. "Take it easy," he mumbled.

"Take care of Lily," Rae said.

"I won't let her out of my sight."

Lily clutched Rae again. "You and Delia have to come back to visit."

Rae promised, hugged Lily, and promised again. Climbing the steps to the train, she paused at the top and glanced along the platform. The big clock had moved three minutes closer to train time. When she got to her seat, she stood at the window and waved to Lily and Lukas on the platform.

Then she saw him. He ran along the platform, a suitcase in one hand and a newspaper in the other. He barreled past Lily and Lukas with a brief salute and dashed up the steps. Reaching Rae as the train lurched into motion, he slung his suitcase into the rack above and flopped into a seat.

He grinned. "That was close. Did you think I wouldn't make the train?"

"I wasn't worried. I knew you'd get here." Rae sat on the edge of her seat, watching Lily get smaller and farther away while the train moved slowly out of the station. Once in the open, the train gathered speed, heading into the countryside.

Matt took off his jacket and opened his collar. "It's amazing," he said, relaxing against the seat. "Billy's call came at exactly the right time. I asked him if he knew RidgeW had burned down, but he said he didn't. He's the last person I'd have expected to get me a job directing at Universal. What a coincidence." He touched the newspaper on his lap but didn't make an effort to open it. "Good day for travel," he remarked with a lazy smile.

"I'm glad you're with me," Rae said. "Not that I was nervous, but it's nice to know someone on the train."

"It's an adventure, Rae. We're going on a new adventure."

The train raced though the open country, and the sunlight coming through the window glinted on Matt's blond hair. He looked the way he'd looked the first time she saw him—happy, excited, golden.

The pounding wheels sounded like a drum beat in her head, and the faster the train went, the faster her heart thumped. She stood and gazed out the window while the sunlight glowed around her, warming her. When she turned back to Matt, his eyes were fixed on her, a puzzled expression on his face.

"You look different." His gaze traveled down to her toes and up again. "How old are you? Exactly?"

She tried to think ahead like she usually did, but she couldn't decide what her answer should be.

"How old do you want me to be?"

THE END

Thank you for reading CHICAGO MOVIE GIRLS. If you enjoyed it, please consider telling your friends or posting a short review. Word of mouth is very much appreciated by authors.

HISTORY NOTE

The characters in this novel are fictional, but movie making in Chicago was a bustling business at the beginning of the 20th century. Two studios mentioned here were highly successful pioneer movie makers.

Selig Polyscope Company was founded in 1896 in Chicago. Selig began producing short films, and in 1913, produced *The Adventures of Kathlyn*, generally regarded as the first serial adventure with cliff-hanger endings. **Essanay Film Manufacturing Company**, founded in 1907, was also a major studio in Chicago during the pre-World War I years. It's best known now for 1915 Charlie Chaplin comedies and Broncho Billy Anderson westerns, but the studio also gave an early start to Gloria Swanson, Ben Turpin, and Wallace Beery—all future Hollywood stars. Louella Parsons, who became a legendary Hollywood columnist, worked at Essanay as a screenwriter.

On the south side of Chicago during the same period, African-American filmmakers produced films about African-American daily life and historical events. Noted filmmaker **Oscar Micheaux** was one of these Chicago movie pioneers. By the end of the decade, most movie production had shifted to the Los Angeles area. The weather in California allowed filming year-round, and inexpensive land made possible huge studio back lots.

Early movies contained salacious plots, plentiful nudity, and shocking violence. The only restrictions on moviemakers came from city censorship boards that demanded cuts in the movies before allowing distribution. Vigorous public and Catholic Church protests over the morals, or lack of them, in movies increased at the same time attendance began to decline after the stock market crash of 1929. Because movies were an entertainment viewed by all ages, all social classes, and all religions, public pressure for reform increased. In 1930, in an attempt to forestall government censorship, studios owners agreed to a Production Code with specific restrictions concerning stories and scenes. Producers, however, continued to make pictures that violated the Code, and city censorship boards remained powerful. Finally in 1934, producers gave in to pressure and conformed to the Code restrictions, including the ban on nudity.

Also available in print and ebook
KISS'D
By D. C. Reep and E. A. Allen

Kissed by a ghost—Sixteen-year-old Jenny Tyler doesn't believe in ghosts, but her recent concussion gives her strange visions. After one of her aunt's séances, a ghost soldier asks for help and, with a kiss, takes Jenny to 1914 Belgium during the German invasion at the start of World War I. Hurtled through time, Jenny finds Jack, a Canadian in the British army trapped behind enemy lines and recognizes her ghost soldier. Amid danger and growing love, Jenny realizes she is reliving an adventure and romance from a past life.

> "gripping right from the earliest pages"—
> Historical Novel Society
> "tension levels high . . . through perilous
> encounters"—*Publishers Weekly*

THE DANGEROUS SUMMER OF JESSE TURNER
By D. C. Reep and E. A. Allen

When sixteen-year-old Jesse Turner lies about his age and joins Colonel Theodore Roosevelt's Rough Riders to fight the Spanish in Cuba in 1898, he expects to prove himself in battle. What he doesn't expect is a fellow volunteer who is determined to kill him for something his outlaw father did in the past. Jesse and his new friends, New Yorker Will and Ben, a Comanche from the Indian Territories, share the frustrations and hazards of a volunteer military force unprepared for war and the reality of deadly combat. Facing dangers from all sides, the three teens depend on friendship, courage, and integrity to get them through the bloody battles of the Spanish-American War.

> "Jesse's easygoing first-person narrative keeps the tone light, yet the authors don't avoid gritty details of the Rough Riders' experiences, including lice infestations, spoiled meat, and crabs swarming over fallen soldiers in the jungles of Cuba. Readers drawn toward war stories will find characters worth investing in with this vivid historical outing." *Publishers Weekly*.

ABOUT THE AUTHORS

D. C. Reep—Making up horror stories for classmates in elementary school was the beginning of a varied writing career. A former English professor, Reep taught American literature, film studies, the King Arthur Legend, and technical writing while publishing textbooks and literary articles. No longer grading papers, Reep now writes historical fiction set at the beginning of the twentieth century. A member of the Authors Guild, Historical Novel Society, Romance Writers of America, and the Society of Children's Book Writers and Illustrators, Reep lives in the Midwest and hopes every fall that the coming winter will be mild.

E. A. Allen—A former middle school and high school teacher, Allen enjoys digging into historical moments and finding exciting details. With an intense interest in interior design, and as a regular visitor to antique stores, Allen collects art deco vases, Federalist period mirrors, and long-forgotten sports trophies. A lover of all things Italian, including Italy's food and Cinque Terre, Allen likes country life in the Midwest during the warm months but flees to the Southwest when winter strikes.

CPSIA information can be obtained
at www.ICGtesting.com
Printed in the USA
LVHW05s2322160818
587184LV00009B/574/P